Witch Way Home?

Book 1 of The Witch, the Dragon and the Angel Trilogy

Titles available in The Witch, the Dragon and the Angel Trilogy (in reading order):

Witch Way Home?
Witch Armageddon?
Witch Schism and Chaos?

*Related books
(Later in the same Multiverse)*
Hubble Bubble
Toil
Trouble

Witch Way Home?

Book 1 of The Witch, the Dragon and the Angel Trilogy

Paul R. Goddard

© Paul Goddard 2014

The right of Paul R Goddard to be identified as the author of this work has been asserted by him in accordance with the Copyright, Designs and Patents Act 1988

All rights reserved. No part of this publication may be reproduced, stored in a retrieval system, or transmitted in any form or by any means , electronic, mechanical, photocopying, recording or otherwise, without prior permission of the copyright owner

All characters in this publication are fictitious and any resemblance to real persons , living or dead, is purely coincidental.

First published in the UK 2014

ISBN 978-1-85457-054-3

Published by: Clinical Press Ltd. Redland Green Farm, Redland, Bristol, BS6 7HF, UK.

Innumerable thanks are due to Jem, Allan and Lois who acted as my Alpha readers, correcting my mistakes and making very valuable suggestions.
Thank you!
Also to all our neighbours and friends on the beautiful Isle of Skye "Tapadh leibh."

- Chapter 1 -

My mother-in-law is a witch. Not always a bad witch but certainly a witch. I knew this from the moment I first met her but she certainly would not have acknowledged it until after the hurricane. She would liked to have thought of herself as a Duchess or perhaps as a grand Dame. Her husband, my father-in-law, was a doctor who had worked himself into an early grave.

My wife, to whom I have been married for ten years, is certainly not in the least witch-like. Sienna is petite, slim, dark-haired and beautiful. She does get angry sometimes if she sees an injustice but she works hard at seeing the best in people.

We have two children, Joshua twelve (yes, I know, I lived with Sienna 'in sin' for five years before we got hitched...no big deal) and Sam, aged six.

It was late March and an early Easter. We had decided to go to our holiday cottage on the Isle of Skye and we were taking the mother-in-law, Mary Atwell, the witch.

The trip from our home in Bristol to Lancashire had been fine. Sam had been particularly excited, asking where we would go and what we should do in Skye when we got there.

'Can we go to Dunvegan Castle?' he asked as soon as we got into the car.

'I expect so,' was my noncommittal reply.

'I want to see the fairy flag that they're supposed to wave when the MacLeods are in trouble,' Sam had said.

'It's just an old piece of cloth,' his brother had replied dismissively. 'You saw it last year.'

'There's the armour too and a lock of Bonny Prince Charlie's hair. That's real!'

2

'Well I want to go fishing,' Josh had replied loudly.

'Now don't argue, you two. We can do both,' was Sienna's answer.

So it was a pretty normal car trip with two young kids until we heard the weather forecast on the radio warn us that there was bad weather coming. They were absolutely right. They predicted hurricane force winds followed by a week of heavy snow. As we all know now it was a lot worse than that. Much, much worse.

When we heard the meteorological pronouncement we suggested that we stayed at my mother-in law's large house near Preston. Mother-in-law Mary would have none of it.

'You know that the forecasters always get it wrong. You are simply trying to sponge off my hospitality. You are taking me on holiday and that is all that can be said.'

Sienna agreed so I followed suit. That's the price one pays for peace in the family.

Rather than be caught out with a lack of supplies, and castigated for it by my witch-in-law, I stocked up very heavily at our friendly wholesale outlet. I have a card for the store due to my work as a self-employed electrician running my own firm. My work was another bone of contention with Mary.

'Why you couldn't marry a proper professional, I have no idea,' Mary had jibed constantly. 'Your father was an internationally respected Hospital Consultant by the time he was the age that James is now.'

'Yes, and he died just ten years later from overwork,' Sienna would reply each time she heard the same sorry comment.

Well, Mary has a point. I did have two university degrees but I had not pursued the obvious professional course after college. Physics and Astronomy degrees either lead to research, finance or lowly paid jobs. None of these appealed and a short electrician's course had been an easy option followed by regular work and a good income. Mind you, the work was hard and I did work long hours ... the bonus was that I set my own pace and I was my own boss.

So it all started in an uneventful way, considering what was to follow. We stayed the night at the witch inn, my name for Mary's house, and then took her with us up to Skye.

So here I was, aged forty, on the way to Skye in my 4 by 4 jammed full with food. Jimmy Scott and family. Including Mary the witch. My mother-in-law. The weather was delightful and I began to doubt the forebodings of the weather pundits. The sky was a beautiful blue with only a few wispy white cumulus clouds. It looked set fair for days but the radio told another story.

We crossed the Skye bridge at ten minutes to seven and the view was stunning. The sun was setting in the West and the sky was changing to a beautiful pink, highlighting the old volcanic Cuillin Mountain range. The sea was temporarily a deep lilac. The place was at peace.

Crossing to the cottage is never easy and is particularly bad at night. Mary complained, as we drove northwards through Skye, that she was bound to break her leg or worse.

'It's just your bad planning, James,' she stated. 'If we had left earlier we would have arrived in the light. As it is we should stop at a hotel overnight.'

I wasn't going to do that. The last time we had done so the witch had spent the whole evening telephoning friends and I picked up the bill in the morning.

'If the tide is right I'll get the rowing boat and pick you all up.' I replied. 'You'll have to wait by the car.'

'And the midges will bite me to death,' Mary answered. 'They always love me.'

'It's too early in the year for midges,' I replied, holding back an acerbic reply.

'I shall sit in the car to wait,' was all she said.

When we arrived at our parking place the tide was right so I took a torch and set off over the cliff path. I only had half a mile to cover but in the dark and over the edge of a wooded cliff ran the path I had to take. I was glad that I had no fear of the night. That was something that would come later.

I enjoyed the walk. I was wearing a backpack but my hands were free to carry the torch and catch me if I fell. I only slipped once when I was near the cottage. I was coming down the cliff at that point and this was the trickiest part, particularly at night. I located the right path to descend but missed my footing at one point. Luckily a hurriedly extended arm caught hold of a narrow sapling and I was saved from serious injury.

Mary was right. She could not have safely walked over the path in the dark. However, it was not my fault that we were late. She had insisted on meeting some of her cabal for her morning coffee and nothing would dissuade her. By the time she had finished gossiping, it was already time for lunch. This she would have been happy to forego, having consumed an enormous number of cakes (how does she stay so thin?) she obviously did not need lunch. But the rest of us did and that delayed us further.

I was mulling over this as I neared the cottage and the byre, wherein lay the aforesaid boat, but I was pulled up short by a bloodcurdling shrieking noise from close overhead. I looked up and a large dark shadow passed between myself and the moon. It took me a moment or two to recognise the vulture-like shape of the sea eagle, the largest raptor in Scotland. Was I right? Was it really an eagle? The moonlight played fanciful games with my sight and for a moment I imagined that I was staring at the shadow of a flying vampire. Not a vampire bat, but one of the living dead.

My rational, scientific mind clicked in and I reminded myself that such horrors did not exist whilst sea eagles certainly did. So sea eagle it was. Or was it?

- Chapter 2 -

The wind struck in the small hours of the morning. This part of the forecast was extremely accurate. Luckily the trip in the boat had been accomplished with no major problems. The rowing boat was a large plastic Pioner, double-skinned and very durable. I could pull the boat to the shore on my own and row it to meet the others.

On the way back over the water I rowed hard and looking between Mary and Sienna I could see two eyes in the water following my every move. If I rowed harder still the owner of the two eyes put speed on to catch us up. If I slowed down, it did the same. *That is a large seal,* I told myself, *a very large seal.*

We passed a small island in the middle of the loch. Upright shapes, almost still but occasionally shifting, could be seen grey against the black background. Herons resting on the place I always called Heron Island but which was really named after an ancient Scottish saint.

I looked behind me at the boys, sat in the prow of the boat. In the moon light I could see their excited faces. Sam's eyes were like giant saucers, lapping up the experience. Joshua was more thoughtful but just as intrigued.

When the wind came it arrived with a very large bang. A branch of tree or a piece of driftwood had been caught up in the first large gust and was smashed against the gable end of the building. The house shuddered but it was made of ancient stone and it withstood the bad treatment. This was followed by a huge howling gale with driving rain. Sienna and I considered that the best thing to do was to get down under the bedclothes and try to ignore the racket. It seems that the kids and Mary did the same in their own respective beds.

The wind had died down considerably by the time we arose at around eight in the morning and the rain had stopped. We looked out onto a scene of considerable devastation. On the far side of the loch over a mile away we could see the forestry commission land. All the trees in a broad swathe were down. I took out my binoculars and stared at the scene. It was as if a giant monster had come sweeping through knocking down the huge pines like so much dried hay stubble.

Nearer to hand I looked over at the forested cliff path. Again there were many trees uprooted and fallen. The area near our own cottage had survived well. The rowan trees between us and the sea were still intact and the fir tree behind the byre, planted by Sienna's cousin thirty years before, was pristine.

After breakfast we would take a walk up the hillside and survey the damage to the surrounding forests.

It might be true that the severe storms we have in Britain are not strictly hurricanes but they certainly pack a hurricane force punch. I considered this thought as I ate my porridge.

We climbed to the pinnacle. This was several hundred feet above sea level and the highest point of the headland. Down a dip and across the moor was the local mountain but that was a difficult climb for another day, perhaps. As for now the pinnacle would provide a good view of the surroundings and it was, in any case, a tradition to walk up there and sit on the rock we had always called "Granny's Seat."

My dear mother-in-law complained all the way up the hillside.

'I don't know why you want me to climb up here. I'm an old lady and very unfit,' she muttered this, whilst belying her comment by moving up the slope faster than any of the rest of us.

'I thought you should look at the effects of the storm, Mary.'

I wanted her to realise that staying put in Preston would have been the better option than travelling all the way to Skye.

'You are such a wimp, James. It's a nice day now and you don't know how bad it's been in Lancashire or in Bristol,' she sniffed. 'I'm sure Bristol is worse than this. It always gets the worst of the weather.'

I considered the last comment to be highly inaccurate but declined from further argument as the view had taken my attention. There was comparative devastation. Trees had been destroyed all around and quite a few houses had lost a roof. For now the weather was good but was this just the eye of the storm?

The boys were in good spirits and wanted to climb down to the beach on the other side of the headland but first I wanted to have a look at the ruined broch at the end of the promontory. Although I say ruined, the structure was in fine condition. A broch is a small hollow-walled fort of dry-stone construction built in the Iron Age. This one was typical as brochs go. It was about forty feet in diameter with walls ten foot thick. The outer wall was a complete circle with a small entrance. Some of the inner wall was missing but in one part it was complete. This made a tunnel which the boys had always enjoyed exploring.

The broch was completely unharmed by the wind as one would have expected. In the central area there was grass that had been recently grazed by sheep. The tunnel in the wall was beautifully dry despite the pouring rain of the night. We popped our heads into the dark place and promised to return with torches.

Down on the beach the sun had already dried the higher sand and the tide was on the turn. The kids ran down to the far end where a small stream ran. Another of our traditions, which Mary frowned on, was to dam that small stream just before it reached the sea. On one occasion we had managed to build a dam forty feet across and deep enough for one of Sienna's younger cousins to swim in.

There was to be no such dam today. The kids reached the

stream but immediately ran back down the beach to us.

'There's a dead bird by the stream,' Joshua exclaimed.

'That's hardly newsworthy,' Mary dismissed Joshua's enthusiasm.

'But Granny it's huge,' added Sam. 'It's really big and ugly and something has killed it.'

I ran back down the beach with them, intrigued by the news. Lying by the stream was a freshly dead white-tailed sea eagle. As the boys had imparted, the bird was not particularly attractive. Huge, perhaps eight foot in wingspan, the bird lay on its back with giant claw marks over its body. It looked as if it had been killed by another raptor. It had certainly not been killed by a human being, unless, of course, he had giant claws.

What was large and aggressive enough to kill a sea eagle? I had heard tales of the sea eagle killing other raptors but not of the sea eagle being killed. It was easily the largest bird of prey in Britain. So what had killed it?

We returned to the cottage by two in the afternoon and had a late lunch. I then phoned round a few of our neighbours. Many of them had trees down but all of our friends had escaped injury and their houses were intact. Johnny, a near neighbour, had some disturbing news.

'It's snowing very hard in the east of the Highlands and it will reach us soon.'

'You don't often get snow here,' I replied. 'It's not likely to worry us, is it?'

'Och, it may well that. The met office have put out a red warning that we have a cold front moving in from the North East with plenty of snow. Make sure you are snug and warm tonight for certain.'

I went over to the old brass barometer which had hung in the same position on the wall ever since I had known the place. The pressure was amazingly low ... lower than I had seen it before.

'That's nothing,' countered Mary when I remarked on this. 'That machine has never been reliable.'

Reliable or not that is a peculiarly low pressure. I thought this but said no more about it. Always best to avoid the argument.

The light faded and the tide rose. The weather was changing again and this was heralded by a large gust of wind that rattled the windows. Sienna made a point of getting torches and candles out in case of a power failure and we all went to bed early.

- Chapter 3 -

Parsifal X was angry. This was a normal state of affairs. He was an angry creature by nature and his advisers had let him down. They could not predict the future results of the activities he was undertaking. This was a course of action that he felt obliged to take and had been planning for years. Many, many years. They had known about his intentions for a long time and this was not the time to tell him that the outcome was unpredictable. He was not a gambler or, if he was, it was only when the odds were highly in his favour. He did not like uncertainty. He would not tolerate it.

*

I was woken by several large crashes, much louder than the noise the night before and the house shook as if this time it might really fall down. I switched on the light by the bed but nothing happened. Complete power failure. Sienna sat up in bed at the same time as me and passed a spare torch to me as she lit some candles. Our bedroom was downstairs, Mary was in the next room and the kids were in separate rooms upstairs. The crashing had seemed to come from immediately above us... a room that was empty.

I looked out of the window and saw a really fierce blizzard blowing. The wind was shrieking through the house as I ran upstairs. Within minutes the kids and Mary had joined us. Everyone but Mary had put on their clothes over their pyjamas. Mary was dressed immaculately as if nothing untoward was happening.

The room above us no longer had a roof. Instead it had a rowan tree, or, to be more accurate, the remains of one. Snow was piling into the spare room and the house was rapidly cooling. I closed the door to the room and put a pillow at the bottom to stop the howling gale that was rushing through the gap.

'Not much more we can do now,' I grunted, standing up and stretching my limbs.

'You should have pruned the tree last year,' replied Mary. 'I told you to do it.'

Along with a thousand other instructions, I thought to myself. *None of which would have made any difference in a storm like this.*

Downstairs Sienna had put candles around the living room. The stove worked with calor gas so we were able to boil a kettle and make a cup of tea. The four of us huddled together to conserve heat whilst Mary sat aloof and alone, apparently not noticing the cold. The house was shaking and I wondered whether it was due to an earthquake. There had been some fracking activity in the neighbourhood and maybe the combination of explosions for gas and hurricane force winds had set up a quake.

Dawn came and the light was feeble... the blizzard was still blowing and the sky was almost as dark as the night. Sam was staring out of the window at the sea shore. He picked up a pair of binoculars from the window sill and studied the view.

'Dad,' he started and then paused.

'What is it?' I replied

'Something's wrong with the sea and the houses round the harbour have gone.'

He handed me the field glasses. Portree, the town on the opposite side of the loch, had been devastated overnight. The houses were there but were almost unrecognisable as such ..... their roofs and walls had been destroyed and the harbour wall looked as if it had tumbled. More worrying was the sea, or absence of it.

'Quick, pass me the tide chart,' I requested. Sam immediately handed the chart to me and I looked at the dates and times.

'We are in the neap tides right now,' I was alarmed. 'The sea should not have receded so much.'

'Does that mean that there is going to be a tidal wave, Dad?' asked Sam, immediately realising the significance.

'You mean a Tsunami,' countered Joshua.

'It's the same thing, isn't it Dad?' replied Sam, his lower lip quivering

'More or less the same and I think you are both right. It might mean that there will be a tsunami,' I answered. 'Good thinking by both of you.'

'We better get out of here,' Sienna gasped. 'I'll grab a few supplies.

Mary was reluctant to shift but eventually we got her out of the house. We climbed wearily up the hillside in the teeth of the gale with snow swirling around us. Standing on the pinnacle we could just about see the loch but the visibility was poor due to the blizzard and the earliness of the hour. The wind whipped through us chilling to the bone.

I bet they're not taking off at Heathrow, I pondered. *Although it might be better down south.*

The sea was out as far as the horizon. I had never seen this before in my whole life.

'We might be better off in the broch,' suggested Sienna. 'It will provide some shelter and we will have almost as good a view.'

So we trudged off through the snow towards the top of the next hillock where the iron age fort commanded a view from the headland. The going was slippery and the snow was becoming deep making the headland path treacherous wherever it veered near to the cliff edge. The broch loomed into view, cold and forbidding, steeped in the mystery of ancient people and past ages.

*

'You are the best seers in the land and you say that the future is clouded?' Parsifal X had developed something of a tic, spoiling his otherwise perfect features. 'I won't tolerate it. So start being precise.'

'Mmmm, mumble.'

'What is he saying?' asked X.

'He says that is not really possible, sire,' an attendant to the seer translated the incoherent noise.

'Does he say why it's not possible?' demanded X.

'Cos Mmm, mumble, mmm.'

'Translate!'

'Due to chaos, sire,' the attendant translated the mumble.

'But I command chaos so it should be no problem.'

'Mut nnnt mumble three mmm. Cannot mumble mumble.'

'Why is he mumbling so badly?'

'Because you had his tongue removed, sire.'

'So I did.... but keep up and translate.'

'He said in this realm you control chaos but not in the other, sire, and three variables permits mathematical uncertainty. Your order cannot predictably control the chaos if there are three variables.'

'But only two variables meet, not three.'

'And yet there is a third, sire. There is a third variable.'

*

'Dad, the sea's coming back.'

I looked out in the direction to which Sam was pointing. His young eyes were better than mine in the poor light but I could tell that he was right. The sea was returning with the biggest wave I have ever seen, in real life or on film. As it entered the loch the water was channelled together and the wave grew bigger still. I clambered towards the broch through the deep drifts of snow and the quickly forming ice.

I never saw the wave hit the shore but at the last glance it must have been nearly a hundred feet high. I did not see the crash of the water or the spume reach up to the top of the headland and splash over Sienna, Mary and the boys before receding down the hillside sweeping away our byre and leaving the house in a total mess. None of this was observed directly because I missed my footing and fell, head first, into a crevasse in the snow and ice and then down through a crevice in the rocks.

I had walked this headland many times before so I knew no such crack had existed before the storm but as I tumbled it was clear to me that one was there now. I remember finding this a puzzle as I tried to grab hold of the side, hitting my head hard on a protuberance as I did so. Everything went dark.

*

'Bring me my best scribe. The diminutive seer,' Parsifal X was shouting again. He had eaten sparsely on shredded carrot and had drunk a mixture of mead and elderflower cordial and was now ready to go back to work. In reality he did not need such food but he enjoyed the flavours.

A small, wizened, gnome-like creature with a long white beard appeared at the doorway.

'You called me, sire?'

'Grab your quill and record my words,' commanded X. 'These are momentous days and I wish you to record my great triumph.'

'Yes sire, certainly sire, as you will sire. I will record all the words from your most estimable lips.'

The reply was so effusive that Parsifal looked sharply at the gnome. Was he being sarcastic? Surely he wouldn't dare for in this realm he, Parsifal X was the supreme and absolute ruler. Well, perhaps not absolute, an unusual flicker of self-doubt went through the ancient mind of this immortal ruler. It was just possible that another could challenge his power and that very someone could be hiding somewhere in the realm ready to displace him.

That is why I have to rule them with such a rod of iron, he pondered. *So that nobody can disrupt my rule and plunge the kingdom back into the chaos from which I carved it.*

- Chapter 4 -

I usually wake up to immediate alertness. Not this time. To a chorus of sledgehammers beating inside my skull, I blearily opened my eyes and then closed them again.

No, this cannot be real. I could not be strung up by my arms in a dungeon, the only light coming from luminescent moss growing on the wet stone walls. I must be hallucinating.

I cautiously reopened my eyes. The scene had not changed. How could I possibly be in an ancient place like this? I'm on the Isle of Skye, so is this Dunvegan Castle? It looked too old even for the seat of the MacLeods and they had been at Dunvegan for eight hundred years. This looked older !

There were rusty iron bands round both my wrists and a ball and chain were pulling at my ankles. I was hanging by my wrists. *This cannot be real. I am in a coma and this is not reality.*

I closed my eyes and passed out gratefully into a dark oblivion.

*

'Dad's disappeared,' shouted Sam. 'He's fallen through the snow and the ground has swallowed him up.'

'Don't talk nonsense,' came Mary's terse reply from some distance behind him.

I know what I saw, thought Sam. *Even if you think I can't be right.*

He wisely kept the thought to himself and simply pointed to the crevasse in the snow.

Joshua was the first to reach where Sam was standing and he looked down into the hole. They could see for at least twenty feet but no more as the gap was not straight and their view was blocked by sharp, jutting rock.

Sam stood there stunned as Sienna and Joshua shouted into the crevasse. There was no reply and to their horror they felt a rumble in the ground and were thrown into the snow. When they regained their feet the rift in the snow and rock had completely disappeared.

'Are you really sure that your father fell down into that hole?' asked Mary, still disbelieving. 'Perhaps he is just the other side of the broch and you imagined it all. I'm sure that he is just playing games with us. He can't have gone down the hole, it's such a silly thing to have done.'

Sam looked at his grandmother in amazement. He knew what he has seen but she was dismissing it as fanciful. He loved Granny but she could be so strange.

Sienna, after a few moments of shocked inactivity, was trying to get some signal on her mobile phone. The machine was fully charged but there was no service. She texted the emergency services, pressed send and that was all she could do. If a text couldn't get through then nothing could. She was wailing with anxiety and grief inside but for the sake of the children she tried to keep up appearances.

Don't crack up she told herself. *Keep it together or we are all doomed.*

Joshua was frantically shovelling snow aside with his bare hands and his feet, helped by a dazed Sam. Eventually they had cleared an area of several square feet but could find only a thin crack in the rock and no significant crevice. Their father had indeed been swallowed by the ground.

*

'Mmm, mumble, nnn,' grunted the diminutive seer, Parsifal having removed the gnome scribe's tongue as he had with the last prophet.

'Translate, damn it,' demanded Parsifal X. 'And tell him not to be so insolent in the future.'

'The realm has changed and the future is uncertain,' said the translator.

'Is that all he can say?' X indignantly brushed a wench to one side. He had no need of further refreshment and definitely did not require her other ample services.

'Mmmm, mmm,nnn.'

'The nemesis key is near us and it must fit the right lock,' the attendant translated before he could be harshly prompted.

'He talks in riddles. Take him away until he decides to be less obscure.'

*

I opened my eyes and kept them open. A very large rat was climbing up the wall in a fashion that I would have considered impossible. It reached my eye level and stared directly at me.

'Latha math, dè 'n t-ainm a tha oirbh.'

The rat was not trying to eat me. It was attempting to communicate. I shook my head and the pounding increased tenfold.

'I'm sorry, mister ratty, I cannot understand you,' I sighed.

'English, you speak English. Fascinating,' the rat was definitely talking to me.

Had someone given me LSD or magic mushrooms? That could be the explanation. Hallucinogens. None of this was real.

The rat continued.

'I greeted you in Gaelic and asked you your name. I assumed that Gaelic was your language as the last ones to come from your island spoke the old language. However, hey ho, English will suffice.'

'I'm Jimmy Scott and I'm strung up like a turkey,' I started to laugh. This was ridiculous. I was a physicist, and astronomer and more recently an electrical engineer. I was a practical man not a latter-day Doctor Dolittle.

'This is madness.' I laughed uproariously in disbelief.

The rat waited and just stared at me as I chortled away.

'No, that way lies the insanity of hysteria. Stop your laughter. I am your only hope,' squeaked the rat, angrily.

I stopped and stared at the rat. Nothing would convince me that I could talk sensibly to a rat, however large. Someone was having a game with me, a cruel game that involved the use of illegal drugs.

*

Sienna's mobile made a noise that indicated a text had arrived. The message was an automatic response from the emergency services.

"The British Government has announced a nationwide emergency. Your message has been recorded. Emergencies will be dealt with in strict rotation. You may have to wait for some considerable time so make local arrangements wherever possible."

Sienna showed the message to her mother.

'Whatever is that supposed to mean?' queried Mary. 'Surely the emergency services can't be that busy.'

'I suppose that they must be. Look at the town over there,' Sienna had taken the binoculars out of her backpack and now passed them to her mother, who, up until now, had shown no interest in the state of the town.

'I see,' replied Mary. 'Yes, this is serious.'

'What did they say?' asked Sam. 'When are they coming?'

'They're not,' replied Sienna, feeling really crestfallen.

'But Dad is down that hole. I saw him fall,' he let out a sob. 'I did see him fall.'

'There's nothing we can do Samikins,' replied his mother, giving him a hug. 'Look, Josh has cleared the whole area and there is no hole there now. The earthquake has swallowed Dad and then closed up again.'

'Come on Sam, we'll have to hide in the broch,' said Joshua. 'We can't stay out here. The storm is getting worse and the house is ruined. The broch is the only place that is dry.'

Joshua led Sam towards the opening of the outer wall of the broch. Sienna followed but Mary stood stock still.

'I'm not camping out in that ruined wreck. I'll catch my death of cold.'

'That's up to you, Mum,' replied Sienna. 'But I assure you it's colder out here than inside there. I have brought some provisions and Josh has a small camping stove in his backpack. I think we'll survive if we cuddle up close together to keep warm.'

*

'Tell me what kind of creature it is that has arrived in our dungeons,' ordered Parsifal X. 'And bring it to me.'

*

'I've received another text, Mother,' Sienna waved her mother over to her. 'It's awful. Things are getting worse.'

"The armed forces have been deployed to assist with the emergency. There are reports that over three thousand people have died and many more are reported missing. There have been widespread earthquakes unprecedented in the UK and the area to the north of Birmingham is blanketed by deep snow which is making rescue attempts difficult. We will update you when more information is available."

The two adults looked over to the children who were huddled together deep in the hollow wall of the broch.

'I was right that we could have been as badly off at my home as we are here,' commented Mary, smugly.

'That's cold comfort, Mother. My husband is missing and you are pleased that you were correct about bad conditions elsewhere.'

'I'm not pleased, Sienna. I'm just right. That's all.'

'But what are we going to do?'

'When it's light tomorrow we will have to start exploring. To see what has happened to our neighbours, find out if there are any salvageable items in the house. Perhaps try to get over to the town.'

*

A beautiful, slim, slight woman wearing a belly dancer's outfit appeared in the dungeon and the rat slunk, unnoticed into a dark corner of the cell.

I was convinced that the fantasy was improving until the belly dancer gripped my belt with one hand and effortlessly lifted me up in the air, dislodging my chains from the hook on which I was hanging.

Nobody could possibly be that strong. Especially not a young woman. I looked at her critically. Where would the fantasy collapse? The delusion shatter?

I could see no flaw....but then again how often could you take charge and dream lucidly? I know it only happens to me occasionally.

I was unable to protest as she dragged me unceremoniously up a flight of worn stone steps and into a grand hall. I could see the outside world through the windows. The sun was shining and small fluffy white clouds floated across the sky.

So I'm not actually underground I thought. *But maybe I am and this delusion is due to brain damage.*

In front of me was a large throne and sitting on the throne was a very handsome man. Tall and slim with clear skin and piercing blue eyes, the occupant of the throne would have been noticeable in any company. Here he was most certainly and definitely in charge. I looked closer. His body looked physiologically to be at a peak age of maturity ... somewhere between twenty-five and thirty years. But those blue eyes were disturbing, flecked deep in them was a dancing flame ! The eyes are the mirror on the soul and they were eyes with a worrying depth that told of countless years in charge. Age upon age.

- Chapter 5 -

The snow was still deep but the blizzard had stopped blowing when Sienna and Sam made for the cottage. Mary and her elder grandson, Joshua, set off over the cliff path towards the nearest house, which was less than a mile away but over rough terrain. Sienna's mobile phone was the only one with any charge left in the battery so they would be out of touch from each other until they returned.

The cottage was a complete mess. The roof had completely disappeared and all the windows were caved in. The only immediately salvageable items were a large stockpile of tinned food, mostly soup, and various tools. A few chairs and a table were scattered up the hillside where the wave had dumped them amongst other debris.

'Mum,' said Sam

'Yes, love.'

'Will we see Daddy again?'

His little lips were quivering and this was not the time to bluntly say no.

'I hope so but it may not be for a long time,' Sienna replied. *Which will probably not be until we get to heaven if there is such a place,* was her hidden thought.

'Daddy would have liked us to be safe, wouldn't he?'

'Yes, he would.'

'So he wouldn't mind if we used some of these things in a funny way.'

'How do you mean?' Sienna was puzzled. What was Sam thinking of?

'Well, I think we could use one of these chairs as a sledge but we would have to pull it to bits and use the back. We could then take all the things we have found up through the snow and take much more.'

Sienna looked at one of the broken chairs. Sam was right. They could adapt it and make a sledge. She put her foot on the seat of the chair and strained against the back until the chair came apart. The curve of the back created the runners and she strapped the seat flat onto it using part of a piece of rope that was in the debris. The remainder of the rope she strapped to the front of the makeshift sledge and then piled their various items onto it. She gave a tug on the sledge and it moved over the snow really well.

'Do you think the tennis rackets would make snow shoes?' asked Sam.

'Tennis rackets?'

'Yes Mum. Some of our old tennis rackets which we used to play with are here in the rubbish.'

Sienna looked. There were at least five old tennis rackets in amongst the wreckage and Sam was right. If they strapped them onto their feet they would make good snowshoes at least for a short time until they fell apart.

She smiled the smile of a proud mother. Their Sam was a bright kid, a really bright kid. It was the first time she had smiled since Jimmy had disappeared and the smile was quickly wiped away by that horrifying memory. Just trying to survive was all they had managed up until now and they had not had time to mourn Jimmy's death. There was no hope now of emergency services getting him out of the rocky grave he had fallen into. They had to fight on until things got better and Sam's idea about a sledge was a good one.

Thus resolving Sienna set to and pulled another chair apart, with perhaps a little more force than was really necessary. They could both haul sledges and both wear snow shoes. Things were already looking up thanks to Sam's ingenuity. However, she was missing Jimmy Scott. Oh, she was missing him.

*

'What kind of beast are you?' asked the man with the ancient eyes, the ruler on the throne.

The question was posed in Gaelic and I shrugged my shoulders. 'I'm sorry but I don't understand a word you are saying.'

'Ah, ha,' Parsifal X laughed. An attractive laugh with a tinkle of bells in it. 'So you speak English. You are English. However, I repeat, what kind of beast do you purport to be?'

'Pretty well the same as you, I expect. A human being.'

The tinkling laugh that had beguiled thousands over the centuries emanated from the so attractive but also so ancient creature.

'I doubt if you are the same as me. Are you also the absolute ruler of a plane of existence as I, Parsifal X?'

'Oh yes. This is all a fantasy, an illusion, a hallucination. You, Mister X, are a figment of my imagination and I'm inventing this entire plane of existence.'

Parsifal X leapt from his throne and slashed a thin cane across my face. It really stung.

'Is that imaginary, you fool? Did it not hurt.'

'I've been hurt in dreams before. It means nothing. It doesn't mean it's real'

'Answer me now. What is the nemesis key and which lock does it fit?'

'You might as well be talking Gaelic. It means nothing to me. Nothing'

Parsifal X grabbed the female guard who had brought me from the dungeon.

'Take him away. He is of no significance. His mind has already cracked such that he does not recognise reality. We will dispose of him when I see fit.'

*

Mary and Joshua returned several hours later. They were completely exhausted and were delighted that Sienna and Sam had made the broch more weather tight using the debris from the house and that they had prepared some lunch from their retrieved stores.

Mary reported that it had taken an hour to reach the next house which was deserted and in ruins. They had not been able to go any further in that direction because a large chasm had developed where there had previously been a small river. The bridge had disappeared and the sea had rushed into the chasm. They had spent the next two hours trekking along beside the chasm and along a new cliff edge. To their amazement they had discovered that the peninsula had been turned into an island by the earthquake.

There was no sign of our neighbours and Mary and Joshua had not been able to see anybody on the other side of the chasm. They followed the new shore round to the other side of the island where it reached the beach they had been exploring the previous day. They had then plodded through the snow and back up to the broch.

Sam's invention of sledges and snow shoes also cheered them as they drank some soup but Mary's next question pulled them all up short.

'So how are we going to get off this new island? We can't stay here for ever and this accommodation is not what I'm used to.'

*

The scantily clad female guard dragged me by my chains back to the dungeon. I did not try to resist. If she could lift me bodily with one hand there was no way that I could fight her.

I could have sworn that the dungeon was on the same level as the hall when she took me on the way out but we climbed down several flights of stairs to reach the cell on the way back. How could this be possible?

Simple answer. It couldn't. I was right. This was all a hallucination. I was detached from reality.

Mind you it was a very stubborn illusion

'Wake up, you fool, we've got to get you out of here.'

I awoke with a start. I was back in my chains hanging on the dungeon wall having been dumped there by the guard. The voice was once more coming from the huge rat. A rat that was impossibly hovering with its face at the level of mine.

'So you're back. What next? A rabbit with a pocket watch?' I laughed with a cracked sigh on the edge of total hysteria. 'Or perhaps you are my daemon and I can cut my way out of here with a subtle knife.'

The rat visibly flinched.

'So you still think this is not real. X is right. You are a fool.'

'Hey!' I replied. 'Who gave you illusions the right to abuse me? I demand a new hallucination.'

This struck me as hugely funny and, with my arms strung up by the chains and despite the sensation of water dripping down my back, I started singing the Python song. "Always look on the bright side of life, de dum, de dum" and I laughed maniacally.

The rat bit my ear.

'Ow, ow. That ruddy well did hurt. Ow,' I put my hand to my ear. For some reason the chains did not stop me.

'OK. I'm sorry I had to do that. It is important that you realise what is real and what is not.'

I looked at the rat with renewed interest.

Perhaps I should act as if the rat knows what it is talking about?

The rat continued. 'You are in a different plane of existence and you are in Parsifal X's kingdom. However, you are not really in chains and you are not really in a dungeon. They have made you think that you are and that much is an illusion.'

'It's all an illusion, rat.'

'No, it's not and I am not a talking rat.'
'What are you then?'
'I am an elf pretending to be a rat.'
'I'm sorry. That is no better than a talking rat. That's just ridiculous.'

'You may consider it to be ridiculous but we don't have much time and I need your help to get you out of here. If you don't try to believe me, X will finish whatever he is doing and give the order to have you disposed of, killed, destroyed, removed.'

'But why should an elf pretend to be a rat. I just don't get it.'

'I had to fit in with your illusion or you wouldn't have seen or heard me at all. I did not create your illusion. It is a standard trap set by Parsifal X. He has been using much the same type of trap for centuries and it is the only way that I have discovered of penetrating that trap.'

'So a rat is the only thing I can see?'

'Yes, you expect to see a rat in a dungeon so you can see me. Now concentrate. You moved your right arm when I bit you. The chains did not stop you. Now lift your left leg.'

I tried to move my leg.

'No, not that leg. That's your right leg. Move the other one. The one you think has a ball and chain on it.'

I could not move it even as much as an inch.

'Now imagine the chain is a paper chain and the ball is a balloon containing helium. That's better, much better.'

This time I was able to move both my legs.

'Now you must step down from the ledge that you are standing on.'

'I can't. I'm strung up by chains on my arms.'

The rat sighed.

'You are not strung up by your arms. It is an illusion spell. If you are strong enough to fight it you can see the reality. If not you will stay here and they will inevitably kill you.'

'OK,' I said, beginning to get the hang of it. 'Maybe this is a form of lucid dreaming and you are showing me how I can control my dreams. I'll try again.'

'Good, good,' said the huge rat and then it shouted in my ear. 'Put your arms by your side.'

I obeyed it and my wrists went right through the iron manacles. The chains and bracelets faded from sight and I could see that I was standing on a narrow ledge in a room lit by a couple of oil lamps. The walls were dry and plastered. Painted an institution green in fact .... not a piece of moss to be seen.

'Now we have to get you out of here,' said the rat.

'How are we going to do that?' I was perplexed.

'We are going to walk out.'

'Won't the guards stop us?'

'No, because you are a rat.'

The rat waved its large paws and I looked in amazement at my legs. The feet were turning into rat paws. My hands were doing the same. My nose was elongating and growing whiskers. I hunched down on the floor.

'What's happening to me?' I asked in a squeaky voice. 'What's happening?'

The rat sighed.

'I'm sorry. I should have warned you. It's another illusion spell. In order to be a convincing rat you have to think yourself into the part. It's like method acting.'

'But why must I be a rat?'

'The guards expect to see rats running around free and they will be fooled by the illusion.'

'But they'll soon see that I have gone.'

'It will take them longer than you expect. Look at the wall.'

I looked over to where I had been standing. Hanging on the wall was a breathing, twitching, life size version of myself.

'Another illusion?' I asked the rat.

'Not quite. It is a golem. I made it out of clay and brought it in with me.'

'How come they didn't spot it?'

'It was disguised as a rat, of course.'

- Chapter 6 -

Sienna, Mary, Joshua and Sam were working hard at securing the broch against the weather. It looked as if they would have to spend at least one more night on the new island. Joshua and Sam made several trips down to the ruined cottage wearing the tennis rackets as snow shoes and dragging any useful item up the hill on the sledges. Despite their depression due to the loss of their father, sledging down the hill had turned out to be good sport.

'Josh'

'Yes Sam'

'If Dad was here this would all be great fun,' Sam said this mournfully, after another slide down the slope

'Cheer up Sam. He may be in a cavern under the broch and reappear at any moment,' replied Joshua.

'Do you really think so?' asked Sam, excitedly.

'Not really but it might be true.'

'What would he live on if he was in a cavern?'

'He'd probably eat the wild mushrooms that grow there and the blind fish in the underground lake.'

'So he wouldn't starve?'

'No he would get by.'

*

'Ee ee ee' I squeaked.

'No, stay away from that. That is rat poison and it will harm you even though you are not a rat.'

I'm not a rat, I thought and started to stand up and stretch my arms and legs.

'Stop it,' whispered the large rat in my ear. 'Don't fight the illusion or you'll shatter it and they'll see you.'

I remembered what I was trying to do. I was attempting to get out of my prison by disguising myself as a rat using a self-delusional illusion. Put that way it almost sounded sensible. I imagined myself back into the shape of a rat.

'That's better. But stay away from the poison.'

We were out of the cell room and creeping slowly past the guards. Instead of looking like beautiful belly dancers they appeared to be hulking great brutes, perhaps nine or ten feet tall. I could have sworn that the nearest guard had only one eye centrally above his nose.

'Ee, ee, ee, ee ee, ee ee?' I asked the huge rat who I was tentatively following.

'Did you ask me where the sexy belly dancer is?' asked the rat who had told me he was an elf.

'Ee.'

'That's him there,' he pointed to the cyclopean monster.

'Ee e's e ee ee,' I said in rat speak.

'You're right. He's a cyclops. He wears the female belly dancer illusion because Parsifal X prefers him like that..... and what X wants he tends to get.'

I crept behind the rat-elf as quietly as I could. I felt sick to think that the sexy girl was really a cyclops. I tried to concentrate on my rat form so that the giants would not see us.

This may not be reality but I could damn well do with some cheese. This thought passed through my mind as we reached the door to the outside world.

*

Sam and Joshua had retrieved everything they could from the cottage.

'Mum, have you discovered anything else about the rest of Skye or the mainland?' Joshua asked the question that Sam had on the tip of his tongue. It was funny how Joshua frequently thought the same things as him.

'I haven't had any more messages.'

'Have you tried the radio app on your phone, Mum?'

'Good thought, Josh. I'll do it.'

They all sat down to listen to the phone set up as a radio.

"This is a recorded message from the British Government. All travel has been suspended and the State of Emergency has been extended. There is a curfew at twenty hundred hours and no travel is permitted beyond a two mile radius from your home at any time unless on official business."

This officious message was being repeated on all the BBC channels and between the announcements old popular music was being played. Even that repeated itself after just twenty five minutes.

'Let me have a go,' said Josh impatiently. Sienna reluctantly passed the cell-phone to her elder son and he immediately tapped in a different location.

"This is Hebridean Pirate Radio bringing you the latest news about the worldwide disaster. We'll tell you what is happening even though there is blanket censorship. This broadcast is a repeating message due to the continuing attempts to silence the station.

There is worldwide turmoil ever since the worst hurricanes and earthquakes since records began. The emergency was kicked off three days ago by severe winds and followed by quakes, tornados, tsunamis and a hail of meteorites...."

'Well at least we have been spared the meteorites..' Mary began. 'I told you..'

'Shush, Mum. We've got to listen.'

Mary was amazed at Sienna's instruction but shut up nonetheless.

"....a reporter on the scene said that millions are dead in Rio. This seems to be the case all over the world and in all the big cities."

There was a pause and pop music played from the mobile phone. Then the message started again.

"News from Hebridean Pirate Radio on the hour, every hour.

A leading geologist is blaming a shift in the magnetic poles for the emergency but other eminent scientists dispute that this is the only cause. They agree that the poles have shifted but also suggest that there has been a change in the universal constants, whatever that might mean.

In particular Ralph Breadstein, the eccentric Nobel prize winner, has stated that his measurements undertaken in difficult circumstances over the past forty-eight hours, suggest that alpha, the fine-structure constant, has shifted by one half of a single percent. He has argued that this is just within the limits that permit the sun to continue functioning. Any more and our star could have been snuffed out like a candle.

There have also been changes in dimensional physical constants such as G, gravity and c, the speed of light, but this may not be operationally meaningful. Breadstein says that there is nothing we can do about it even if they have changed.

This is Hebridean Pirate Radio bringing you the latest news about the worldwide disaster. We'll tell you what is happening even though there is blanket censorship. This broadcast is a repeating message due...."

Sienna turned off the phone. 'We have to conserve the battery and the message has started to repeat itself. We'll tune in on the hour to see if there is any further news.'

' Mum,' said Sam dolefully. 'Dad would have known what the constants are. It sounds as if the whole world's affected.'

'You are right, Samuel,' said Mary, before Sienna could reply. 'And we are definitely better off here than we would be near any of the big cities.'

Sienna nodded. It did seem that Mary was right this time. She nearly always was which had to be, in itself, frustrating and annoying.

*

Elf-rat crept ahead of me, through the outer doorway and past a huge ogre standing guard outside. I was beginning to think that we were free when elf-rat knocked the edge of a musket which fell with a clatter. The monstrous guard turned and stared at the rat,

'Well, well, well. What have we here. A nice fat rat.'

With speed that was incongruous in such a massive beast the ogre clapped a large metal bucket over the top of the fat rat.

'Run, get away while you can,' squeaked the rat to me.

'It's almost like it's trying to talk,' rumbled the ogre. 'I'll enjoy this one once I've roasted it. I'm partial to a large rat.'

'Go on, get away,' squeaked the rat to me. 'You are more important to the cause than I am. Forget me and run away. He has not noticed you.'

The last bit was true. I was crouching behind the ogre and I could just run away. The ogre had not spotted me and would probably be content with one large rat.

But, hey, what's the big deal? The fat rat's my only friend in this hallucination and I'm going to try to save it.

Thinking this, I cast aside the rat illusion and stood up.

'I'm your sovereign, Parsifal X,' I declared, imagining that I looked just like the supreme ruler.

The ogre groveled and bowed.

'Sire, this is a great honour, your great highness, sire. How can I be of service?'

'I am just here to inspect the prisoner but I've noticed you have caught a fat rat.'

'That is so, sire, I was hoping to eat the fat gobbler. Toasted rodent is my favourite.'

'Don't toast this one. Let it go.'

'Certainly, sire, but why should I be letting it go, with all due respect?'

'Are you questioning me?' I drew myself up with faked pomposity and anger.

'No, sire. Never sire,' rumbled the ogre. 'But I am curious.'

I was curious too. Why should he let it go? Inspiration struck.

'I've infected this rat with a nasty disease. It's called rat measles.'

'What might that be, sire?'

'It is an infection, a contagion. It will spread round the rat population and make them easier to catch. Unfortunately it can spread to ogres.'

'Shall I just kill it, then sire? I can just flatten the bucket and squash the gobbler inside.' The ogre lifted his huge left foot and placed it on top of the bucket.

'No, no,' I gasped. 'Stop that.'

The ogre looked at me quizzically. The illusion of Parsifal X was slipping and he was becoming suspicious.

'Here, wait a minute, you look like the prisoner.'

I stretched up and stared into his eyes.

'One more sign of insubordination and you die the death of a thousand knives after being skinned alive. Then I shall feed the pieces to the flying fish of Timbuktu,' I spouted this with a haughty expression on my face, nonsense spilling from my lips in a cascade of profusion.

'I'm sorry sire,' cringed the ogre, looking back into the room we had recently vacated, and beyond into the inner chamber. 'I've just looked into the cell and I can see the prisoner hanging on the wall and there is no resemblance.'

He lifted his foot as he said this and tipped the bucket over.

'Shoo along, fat rat, shoo along.'

The rat slowly moved away, looking for all the world like a sick animal.

'You're right, sire, the rat is ill. Thank you for saving me from eating it.'

'That's perfectly fine,' I answered. 'Now you stay here. I'll shoo the rat away. The disease won't affect me.'

I bent down and picked up the fat rat. It was much heavier than it looked but I was able to lift it and walk round the corner. The ogre stared after me and I saw it shake its head in confusion.

Out of sight I placed the rat on the ground. It barely moved.

'Rat,' I whispered in its ear. 'Come on rat, wake up.'

It stirred slightly.

'What's the matter with you?' I asked.

'I have a deadly disease called rat measles,' the fat rat squeaked. 'I feel dreadful and I'm going to die!'

'No you don't have a disease and you are not a rat, you are an elf.'

'So I am,' cried the rat-elf and to my horror started to change into a humanoid shape right in front of me. I shut my eyes and the elf grabbed me and started to kiss me passionately on the lips.

'Stop, stop,' I cried, opening my eyes again. 'Oh!'

I was very surprised and confused. In front of me stood the most beautiful girl I had ever seen and I had just stopped her from kissing me. She looked much like a younger Sienna, dark haired and seductive. She was perhaps eighteen years old, a bit slimmer and taller than my wife and had perfect skin. Her eyes were a deep, dark black and her ears were slightly pointed... And she was completely naked.

- Chapter 7 -

The night was very cold and the family were all huddled together in the hollow wall of the broch. The wind was being kept out by salvaged doors at either end of the tunnel. Sienna and Josh had nailed bars across the doors so that they slotted into grooves in the stone. They had then put another bar across the ends of each wooden bar and wedged those in place. It was possible to look out through holes at each end, both of which could be covered with wood panels swinging on a nail.

Sienna and Mary had decided that these precautions were necessary not only because of the weather but also because they had seen the spoor of a large animal which was also possibly trapped on the new island. The paw print was roughly circular with a posterior triangular pad and four toe prints. Indentations from large claws were visible in front of the toe impressions.

Sienna and Mary had argued as to whether the prints belonged to a large dog or to a wolf. Sam, however was convinced that he knew the answer. He had shown Joshua a place where the paw prints stopped and the naked prints of human feet took their place.

He whispered to Josh.

'It's one of those creatures that can turn into a human being or into a wolf,' he looked up with a start. 'We better warn Mum and Granny.'

'You mean a werewolf?' Joshua answered. 'They're only fictional.'

'So is being trapped on a new island in Skye and almost drowned by a tidal wave, Josh. But I do mean a werewolf. That's what it is, a werewolf.'

Joshua had leant down to examine the tracks.

'The dog tracks do stop and a man takes over,' fright was obvious in his voice. 'Perhaps there are such things as werewolves!'

They had run back to the broch as fast as they possibly could. Mary and Sienna would not believe the boys' ideas but they had immediately redoubled their plans to secure the hideaway.

The night was clear and frosty with a bright gibbous moon casting an eerie light on the snowy surroundings. Around two in the morning the huddled family could hear a distant growling and howling. The sound got louder and louder until they could hear sniffing right outside one of the blocked entrances to the hollow wall. The snuffling continued as if a large dog was determining the nature of the odours emanating from within the broch wall. The noise then shifted to the other end and scratching at the makeshift door could be heard. The family sat frozen with horror, stock-still in the darkness. Sam was certain that the pounding of his heart would be heard by the lupine creature. Lub dub, lub dub, lub dub ...... filling his head with noise.

Then a great howling started from the middle of the broch enclosure and Sam decided to risk looking out through the end of the hollow wall closest to the beast. He crawled slowly over to the door and carefully twisted the wood panel on its nail. Through the three inch diameter gap thus exposed he could see the enclosure. Sat in the middle, tilting his head to the swollen half-moon, was the largest dog he had ever seen.

Sam looked more closely. Was it a dog? It was more like a wolf. As he looked the shape quivered and changed and in place of the wolf stood an extremely hairy, naked man who came over to the makeshift door and shook it, testing it, twisting and trying to lift it. The door stood firm. He then ran away, out of Sam's vision, to try the other end. Again to no avail.

The man ran back to the centre of the enclosure, stood with his head held back in an unnatural position and howled at the moon before dropping down onto all fours and scampering off. As he disappeared Sam could see that the creature had changed back into a wolf. It was a werewolf. A mythological creature from Joshua's horror comic books.

*

Parsifal X had decided that he needed to question the man more closely. His majestic mind had been distracted by the man's mundane reactions. Perhaps the man was playing him on at a cleverer game than he had realised? So X glided down to the cell block.

'Who goes there?' asked the ogre guard.

'Don't you recognise your supreme leader? The ruler of planets, the decider of life and death?' asked X pompously.

'OK, if you are my commander, which I doubt, what happened to the rat? Tell me that,' demanded the guard. ' 'Cos if you don't I just might have to squash you.'

The ogre raised a huge solid fist above the head of Parsifal X.

'I can't be bothered with this,' replied X, waving his hand. 'If it's rats you want then it's a rat you can be.'

The ogre instantly shrank down to the size and shape of an average, rather weedy looking rat.

'No need to be like that, your honour, your highest eminence,' squeaked the newly created rat. 'I was just trying to do my job.'

'Perhaps too assiduously, my dear ogre,' smiled Parsifal. 'Try to keep out of trouble and in an hour you will turn back into your normal, beautiful self. Oh, by the way, this is not an illusion. I've used a shape-changing spell so if a cat gets you that's the end of it. You'll be feline nourishment and little else.'

'Ee, ee, ee!' exclaimed the rat, becoming, every minute, more rodent-like in its thought processes.

'No. You are right. It's not fair,' replied Parsifal X. 'But then I'm a tyrant and tyrant's make a habit of not being fair.'

- Chapter 8 -

Two cold days and nights passed on the new island. Each night they heard howling and each morning they saw the tracks of the werewolf. The news via the radio app was bleak. Sienna only tuned into Hebridean Pirate Radio occasionally, leaving the phone off the rest of the time to conserve the dwindling battery. On the morning after their fifth night on Skye the pirate radio station announced that martial law had been declared over the whole of the UK superseding the previous announcement of a state of emergency. The Queen had been taken to a safe retreat and a Brigadier Spencer Blenkinsop had taken charge. All parliaments and assemblies, local governments and statutory bodies had been disbanded.

"The Queen is perfectly safe folks, or so we are told, and the rest of the Royal Family are with her. Brigadier Blenkinsop can be trusted to look after the country.

Well, that's the official party line but confidentially, keep this to yourself mind, 'Blinkers' Blenkinsop is an odd choice of leader. What has happened to the full Generals? Who chose Blinkers to lead the country? Or did he, as rumour has it, choose himself? Listen to the news on the hour every hour. You won't hear this on the BBC."

'Things are hotting up on the mainland, Mum,' Sienna remarked.

'It won't be long before they come here,' replied Mary.

'To relieve us and take us to a shelter?'

'Don't be wet, daughter. They'll want this as a lookout base. It's strategically important.'

Before Sienna could reply there was a shout from Joshua who, with Sam, had been keeping watch over the harbour.

'Quick Mum and Grandma,' he exclaimed, 'Come and see this!'

They clambered up onto the top of the Broch wall. Joshua passed the binoculars to Sienna.

'That's a huge submarine,' she gasped. 'It must be a nuclear sub. What is it doing on the surface with a sail up.'

'Don't be daft, daughter,' countered Mary, grabbing at the field glasses. 'Nuclear submarines do not have that sort of sail.'

Sienna reluctantly passed the binoculars to her mother.

'Damn me if you are not right,' her mother countered her own argument. 'In fact it is from the Astute-class, the first of which was launched in 2007, commissioned in 2010. I can't tell from this distance whether that is the Astute or the second to be launched, Ambush.'

'How do you know so much about submarines, Mother? I didn't know that you were that interested in the navy.'

'See, Sienna, you don't know everything about me even though you think you do.'

'Mum, that doesn't answer the question.'

'Your father had a lifelong passion for submarines and I continued to take an interest after he died. I even went on the Astute on an open day.'

'And does it have a sail up, Granny?' asked Sam, itching to have a look himself.

'Yes it does, Samuel,' replied Mary, staring hard through the binoculars. 'I think that they must have made it out of bed sheets. What they made the mast out of, God only knows.'

She passed the glasses to Sam who at last was able to see what his brother had first spotted. His eagle eyes picked up another feature.

'There's a man on the top of the submarine trying to get people's attention in the harbour but there is nobody there to see him. He is waving like mad.'

Sam gave the field glasses to Joshua.

'I can see him, shall I wave back?' asked Joshua.

'No, don't do it,' cried Mary. 'They'll be over here soon enough without we draw attention to ourselves. I am certain that it will only cause trouble.'

'I think it might be too late, Grandma,' replied Joshua. 'There's another man at the back of the sub and he's got very powerful binoculars. He's staring right at me.'

'Come on down', instructed his mother, giving him a tug. 'Your Grandma may well be right. We should keep out of sight until we know what the military are up to.'

They climbed down from the broch wall but Sienna had a fearful apprehension that their relative peace, just the odd were-wolf, might soon be shattered.

But isn't that what I really want? she asked herself. *For the Navy to come and rescue us? But only if they really do rescue us,* her internal dialogue replied anxiously.

Then another thought came, unbidden, to her mind and she wondered whether the change in the value of the fundamental physical constants had anything to do with the nuclear submarine malfunctioning and having to use a sail. *Oh I do wish Jimmy was here. He would have known what to do.... and how does my mother know so much about submarines? I never knew she was interested in them. Nor my father for that matter....it's all so very strange.*

*

The sun was setting as the beautiful girl retrieved some diaphanous clothes from a niche in a wall and then led me to a small tavern in a dark side street. The small inn door was rudely flung open in front of us and a very small, thickset man was thrown out onto the street by a couple of slightly larger dwarves.

'Sorry ma'am,' said the larger of the two, tipping his hat to the female rat-elf and ignoring me. 'He's trouble.'

The smaller of the two 'bouncer' dwarves turned to face the

prostrate midget and shouted....

'And don't come back!'

He then beckoned the rat-elf girl and myself into the inn.

'Come in Lady Aradel, do come in. Bring your giant with you.'

So that was her name! Lady Aradel! I looked round for the giant and realised that the dwarf meant me. I am a respectable five foot nine inches in height but this was the first time anyone had called me a giant. The twinkle in the dwarf's eye told me that it was only a harmless jest at my expense.

This was definitely a dwarf public house. It reminded me of a mock-up of an old country inn that I had once seen at an "experience" museum but it was much smaller and more idiosyncratic. The ceiling was just a couple of inches above by head and I had to keep ducking and swerving to avoid the dark oak beams that criss-crossed the ceiling and the wooden pillars that held up the structure. The place was lit by oil lamps and there was a central round serving bar behind which there were tiny, broad-beamed barmaids serving mead, ale and cider.

Multiple curved tables encircled the bar and sat at the tables were scores of bearded dwarves clad mostly in tweed or tartan jackets and matching trousers. They were short, mostly around four feet in height, but very stocky and all sporting long white beards. When they saw us they started singing spontaneously and eventually the whole lot were rattling their mugs and chanting:

We don't like ourselves
But we all hate elves
They call us small but they grow too tall
Give 'em an inch, they take a mile
Tel 'em a joke, they never smile
Sing fi sing fo
We want them to go

The last two lines were repeated continuously and the whole thing turned into a round with some of the tables singing the opening stanza whilst the later bars were sang on the other side of the room. The dwarves were banging the tables in time to the chant and were clearly enjoying themselves. It was, however, very threatening. Our dwarf bouncers led us through the jostling throng and behind the bar. A wooden spiral staircase led up to another room above the saloon. This room had a slightly higher ceiling and a group of serious looking dwarves and elves were sat quietly discussing some plans that they had in front of them on a solid table of dark wood.

A handsome elf of indeterminable age looked up as we entered. His demeanor lightened immediately.

'Aradel.. you have returned!'

His words made the other people in the company look up also. They immediately greeted Aradel with smiles and laughter. The most venerable looking of the dwarves beckoned us to sit down and we joined them at the table.

'Lady Aradel,' he said in a deep, mellow voice. 'Your mission has been successful and we are all grateful.'

'It wouldn't have been a success but for gallant intervention on the part of Lord James, your highness.'

Lord James? Oh, she meant me... but how did she know my name and why did she call me Lord?

The venerable dwarf raised his eyebrows as he turned to me.

'Then we all thank you, Lord James. Indeed we do.'

The hallucination was most compelling and, out of politeness, I felt obliged to reply.

'Thank you, sir, but I got the impression that Percival had bad plans for me and it wasn't so nice being strung up. Thus the gratitude should be greater on my part for Lady Aradel's efforts in saving me.'

I stood up and bowed to Lady Aradel who blushed a most

becoming pink colour to the very tips of her pointed ears.

'Percival?' queried the venerable dwarf. 'Oh yes. You mean Parsifal X. The monster in charge of our realm.'

He looked round at the company.

'We are agreed on the plans so I am happy to explain them to Lady Aradel and Lord James. Would that be your wishes?'

The group of elves and dwarves nodded their heads in agreement. The elf who had first greeted us stood up and came over to Lady Aradel.

'Good luck, Aradel and look after our human well,' he kissed her lightly on the cheek. She smiled and went pink again.

Most of the dwarves and elves filed out of the room and exited via the spiral staircase, leaving just the venerable dwarf, lady Aradel and myself. The noise from below increased creating a general background hubbub of white noise punctuated by occasional louder grunts, squeals and chants.

What plans did they have for us? Perhaps I was about to find out or perhaps my unconscious brain was about to make the plans up.

*

Parsifal X was attempting to interrogate the prisoner hanging in the dungeon. The prisoner stood on a ledge with his arms raised above his head as if he was strung up by chains. He gave the occasional twitch but showed no other signs of life. Parsifal could switch in and out of the illusion seeing him one minute as a prisoner in chains in a dungeon and the next as a man standing on a ledge. However, there was no response to Parsifal's questioning or to his telepathic mindprobing.

Parsifal decided that he would have to touch the human being. This was something he always tried to avoid out of a general sense of revulsion. This time it was necessary. The man's arm felt as cold as clay.

What is this? thought Parsifal. *What is going on?*

This creature is clay!

Parsifal X realised he had been duped. Someone had taken the human being and replaced him with a golem. Golems were difficult magic requiring an enormous expenditure of time and energy and this was not just any old golem. It was a very effective simulcrum of the prisoner. So the human being had to be an important captive and now, he, the ultimate ruler of this sphere of existence, had lost him.

X extended his consciousness into the surroundings to look for the human being. He could pick up no trace in the surrounding town, the surrounding countryside, the country, the continent. Out, out, his consciousness spread. The whole world, the system. No trace, no trace.

Either the man had escaped the reality or he was being shielded. Parsifal X cried with rage and the heat of his anger burned his clothes off. He stood in the cell glowing white hot with flames licking around his body, engulfing the dungeon and the surrounding building. The guards were all immediately incinerated apart from one rat who was running away from an angry cat. The rat was hoping to last a few more minutes until the hour was up but he could not remember why.

*

It was just after midday and their usual victuals of soup and tinned ham, when Sam observed two rowing boats glide up to the shore in front of their ruined house. From each boat a mixture of soldiers and sailors climbed out into the shallow surf and, after securing the boats, started to climb up towards the headland and broch.

'We've got company, Mum,' he shouted to Sienna.

'Where? Are they definitely coming here?' she replied

'Looks like it and they're mostly soldiers I think.'

The armed visitors climbed swiftly up the hillside to the old dry stone wall at the top of the croft and jumped down into the snow drift on the moor of the headland. The family watched as the party from the boats marched up to the broch. The leader of the small expedition stood in front of the iron age fort and shouted out that the occupants should surrender.

Mary and Sienna clambered down from their vantage point on the broch wall and walked over to the army captain who was clearly in charge. Mary was bristling with anger at the intrusion.

'Surrender? What are you talking about man?'

'Madam, I am requisitioning this military stronghold for the use of the British Government.'

'Military stronghold! This is an iron age broch not a military stronghold and I think you mean commandeering rather than requisitioning.'

'Either way we are taking it over by order of the Brigadier Blenkinsop.'

'Young Blinkers! I'll have words to say with him when I see him. I'll have you know that this broch has been in our family for more than seventy years since my grandparents bought it on their honeymoon.'

'I'm very sorry ma'am,' replied the captain, somewhat taken aback by the verbal assault. 'But any strategic military position can be repossessed by order of martial law.'

'The army has never possessed this broch so it can't be repossessed.... what is more I'll have you know that my husband was civil consultant to the RAF with the rank of Air Commodore and that I am still an adviser to the Navy on engineering, with the rank of Commodore. Which easily outranks you!'

Sienna listened to her mother and tried not to show any amazement. She knew that most of the statements were completely untrue. Her parents had never worked with the armed forces. However, the army captain looked convinced.

'Sorry madam, I did not realise that you had a rank. That does make things more difficult because technically you are already in possession of the strategic stronghold and you do indeed out rank me. However I must insist that we leave a representative with you to liaise with our forces.'

'The female navigation officer can stay if you wish,' replied Mary in her most haughty manner, pointing to the young woman who was fiddling with some maps.

The army captain looked nonplussed at handing the task to one of the navy officers rather than one of his men but then agreed with a nod of his head.

'We were hoping that you could take us back to the main island since we have become cut off here,' interjected Sienna.

'No chance of that ma'am,' the captain replied curtly. 'No movement of civilians is permitted without express permission. There is nowhere particularly good for you to go to in any case. Most of the townsfolk are dead and the rest are in the community centre and school in makeshift refugee accommodation.'

'Do you know what happened to our immediate neighbours?' asked Joshua.

'No idea.' replied the captain, turning away to instruct his men.

'I do,' said the female navigation officer. 'They all survived the tsunami except for the people in the very next house to you who refused to be evacuated and are missing.'

'Thanks,' Josh replied, instantly worried about his missing neighbours even though they were not close friends.

'Nobody realised you were here,' continued the navigator. 'Not until our observer on the submarine saw you watching him with binoculars. He saw the glint of sunlight on the lenses I expect.'

'I'm also from the submarine,' interrupted a rather sallow individual, directing his attention to Mary. 'I work in the power plant and if you are an expert in engineering you might be able to tell us what has gone wrong with the propulsion?' He posed this as a question but it was clear that he, for one, did not fully believe Mary's story that she was an adviser with a high naval rank.

'That's an Astute class nuclear submarine, ' she replied without hesitation. 'I think, lieutenant, that it is possibly the Astute itself, the first of its kind. I suspect that the nuclear plant itself has stopped generating heat. Am I right?'

The naval engineer looked completely amazed at the reply. He was clearly expecting an evasive answer. Sienna and the boys were just as astonished.

'You are right, yes, completely!'

'Have you considered that it could be due to the shift in the fundamental physical constants?' Mary asked.

'The what?' replied the engineer.

'Ask Professor Breadstein, the Nobel prize winner. He's the one who has measured them. That's all that I can tell you without examining the power plant.'

I was thinking of that, thought Sienna. *I had to show an interest in such things because Jimmy was always talking about them but Mother has never had the slightest bit of interest in physics. She can't possibly know about the fundamental constants. It's just as if she were reading my mind.*

Sienna looked up to see Mary looking at her with her eyebrows raised. The grandmother turned her attention back to the army captain who had been most impressed with the exchange between the sallow engineer and the waspish woman.

'Are you intending going straight back now leaving the navigator with us and providing us with no assistance?' Mary asked

'Well yes, ma'am. That is my intention.'

'Then I suggest you wait for an hour or so. I believe that there is a hostile presence in the harbour water.'

The captain's incredulity returned.

'Hostile presence? What do you mean?'

'We have observed that there is something big in the water other than the submarine and the yachts. It is under the water.'

Sienna was again amazed. They had seen no such thing.

'Could it be another submarine?' asked the navigator.

'I don't know but I would urge caution.'

The army captain turned to the navigator. 'Wouldn't you have seen something big on your sonar?' he asked.

'The sonar packed up when the batteries failed after the generator stopped generating. So no, not necessarily unless we could have seen it when we were much further out.'

'But did you see anything when you were further out?' demanded the captain .

'No we did not, sir,' answered the navigator.

The captain turned to Mary. 'I'll be mindful of your advice, ma'am, but we shall set off immediately.'

So saying he turned heel and marched off with all but the navigator.

'I have a very bad feeling about this,' said Mary quietly. 'I was in deadly earnest about a malign presence. There is something evil out there in the harbour and it does not like us at all.'

- Chapter 9 -

The venerable dwarf, Lady Aradel and myself were left sitting at the table in the room above the bar. The noise generated by the dwarves below continued unabated.

'Lord James Scott finds it hard to accept that this realm is real,' Lady Aradel explained to the dwarf. The ancient figure laughed.

'I too have often felt that way but it might help if I explain the situation.'

Or it might not, I thought, *since I could be making up all of the explanation in my ever fertile semi-conscious brain. I expect I am in a coma.*

'I shall start at the beginning,' said the dwarf. 'Or what most folk would consider was the beginning. Reality doesn't really have a neat start and a conclusive end like a good story but I shall try to give some order to the narrative.'

Nicely put, I thought, *but still not convincing.*

'In your plane of existence the physicists study quantum theory. One explanation for the peculiarities of quantum mechanics is the many-worlds interpretation,' said the dwarf.

Wait a minute. I studied this during my physics degree. I'll see if my sub-conscious venerable dwarf entity gets it right.

'The explanation implies that the universal wavefunction does not collapse but that all possible alternative histories and futures are real. Is that not so?'

I was forced to answer.

'That is one explanation, yes. Not everybody is in agreement.'

'No, I would not expect them to be so,' replied the dwarf. 'What I have to tell you is that there are several parallel worlds, possible many. However, they were all united at one time not so long ago.'

'Do you have any idea how many different worlds there are?' I was being sucked into the delusion and was hooked by the dwarf's exposition of quantum theory.

'That depends on your scale of view, I suspect, but from your own world perspective there are at least two extra parallel worlds that are immediately significant. One is our own, which decays faster than yours. The other is a realm that lies from our perspective on the far side of reality and decays slower. You may consider it to be the eternal realm.'

'So there are only three?'

'Not really since we have you to one side of us and another parallel world to the other side, one that you probably don't need to worry about as they cannot reach your realm except through our own.... and this probably goes on ad infinitum.'

This is all very fine, I thought, *but it does sound exactly like a complex dream regression.*

Lost in my own thoughts I missed the start of the gnome's next sentence so I asked him to repeat what he was saying.

'...Ad infinitum. The difference between the parallel worlds is that the universal constants vary. This leads to differences in gravity, differences in the speed of light and in the application of science.'

Now I was fascinated.

'And in this realm magic rules supreme,' stated the dwarf boldly. 'Some of the inhabitants can wield enormous power by just the process of thought. You could say that this is simply science that we don't yet understand and I would agree with you.'

I nodded. I'd heard that before. Wasn't it a quote from Arthur C. Clarke?

The venerable dwarf stroked his white beard as he spoke.

'And this "magic" also occurred in your own world since we were all one and the same.'

'But there is no magic. It is all explained by physical laws,' I argued. 'There really is nothing that can't be explained by scientific principles.'

'As it is in this realm. However we are closer to the primordial chaos and the rules are more capricious, unpredictable. I expect that closer to order the rules are more certain than in your universe but that is beyond my ken.'

'And yet you say that we were once all one and the same!'

For some reason this annoyed me. I could almost accept that there could be a parallel world in which science appeared to act like magic but to suggest that this was the case in my own world felt like an affront.

'Yes. Your world was capricious also. Magic-wielding demons and fairies shared the world with human beings such as yourself . Dwarves and elves, sea monsters, vampires, werewolves. They were all present. Many of the creatures of power demanded obsequious obedience from the human population... and this was their undoing.'

'Why?' I asked. 'Why was it their undoing?'

'The priests and wizards amongst the human beings had always wielded some power on behalf of the entities they worshipped. But they learnt about the roots of the power...the magic in the stone, the power in the wood......'

Lady Aradel and myself were leaning forward listening to every word spoken by the venerable dwarf.

'.... And they were aware of the plight of the human race. They felt the race could be so much more without being tied to the whim of power hungry magic wielders. So they conspired to sever the realms.'

The noise of the dwarves singing below us carried up through the spiral staircase and interrupted the flow of the venerable dwarves monologue.

'Good, good,' the old dwarf murmured. 'As long as they continue we are shielded.'

'The dwarves are singing in a circle below us and their song is like white noise on the mental plane,' explained Lady Aradel. 'Parsifal X is an extremely powerful telepath who can stretch his consciousness throughout the world. The dwarves are shielding us from his telepathic probing. We are only a few miles away from him but he can't find us. The dwarves are also a good, loyal fighting force which could repel any physical attack from his army of cyclops and ogre guards.'

'That is correct, dear Lady Aradel,' agreed the dwarf. 'And our feigned dislike of elves and human beings means that this is the last place that they would look for you anyway.'

This was all too convincing for my own dreams. Was it real?

*

The soldiers and sailors marched off down the hillside through the slushy snow that had been churned up by themselves on their ascent. The navigator and the family watched them push the boats out and set off rowing across the broad loch towards the ruined harbour.

Mary continued to watch using the field glasses. The navigator took from her pocket a pair of powerful prismatic binoculars and also observed what was happening. Sienna and the boys looked on with their naked vision.

About three-quarters of the way to the harbour over the very deepest water there was a disturbance beneath the surface and first one boat faltered and tipped and then the second. The occupants were thrown into the sea and started swimming for their lives. A giant mass swept over them.

'What is happening, Mum?' asked Sienna.

'There is some giant mass upturning the boats and chasing

them. These field glasses don't provide sufficient magnification for me to tell what it is,' answered Mary.

The navigator whispered hoarsely. 'I could see!'

They looked round at her.

'What was there?' asked Sienna.

'It was a huge sea monster. Like the Loch Ness monster. Something like a plesiosaur,' the female naval officer replied.

'Plesiosaurs died our sixty-five million years ago,' Mary crossly announced. 'Sixty-five million years ago.'

'But that's what it looked like,' replied the navigator belligerently. 'And it destroyed both boats.

*

'I shall continue,' the dwarf shifted in his seat and beckoned us closer to him. He whispered the next part of the tale. 'The priests and wizards constructed an amplifier that would augment their limited powers. The initial amplifier was made out of wood in a giant circle.'

'When was this exactly and where?' I asked, curious.

'Some five thousand of your years ago, about one thousand of ours,' answered the dwarf.

'Have you any idea where?' I persisted.

'Well yes, it was deep in the South part of what you call the British Isles on a great chalk plain.'

'Salisbury?' I suggested.

'I believe you are correct,' concurred the dwarf, introspectively consulting his memory. 'Well done. Yes, it was on Salisbury Plain.'

The songs of the dwarves continuously filtered up to us. A stumpy barmaid clambered up the stairs bringing us liquid refreshment in large pewter tankards.

'Thank you, my dear,' the dwarf addressed the barmaid before continuing to enthrall us. 'The wooden henge was built to provide sufficient power for the construction and shielding of the larger, stone amplifier.'

'Stonehenge!' I exclaimed triumphantly.

The beautiful elf-girl, called Lady Arudel, smiled at me and the venerable dwarf positively glowed with satisfaction.

'Yes, indeed, Stonehenge,' agreed the dwarf. 'On mid-summer's day, about five thousand years ago, the words of power were spoken in the circle and the magic was amplified. With a great upheaval the worlds were separated. To one side was order, to the other the chaos and in the middle was your own world, the complexity.'

'But we still talk about fairies and goblins, dwarves and giants,' I pointed out.

'And we still sometimes cross over into your realm. We do so at places that break the circle. Places of power such as arcs of stone. You might call them fairy bridges. Also temporary portals such as toadstool rings in the forest,' said the dwarf.

'It is easier for us to cross over into your realm than it is for you to enter ours,' stated Lady Aradel.

'Why should that be?' I asked.

'Because we are more insubstantial than you are,' she replied

'Then how come I'm here?'

At last. I had caught them in an illogicality. This could prove the non-existence of this shadow kingdom.

'Parsifal X has decided to recombine the realms and you were caught in the process,' stated the dwarf.

Damn, I thought. *They got out of that one.*

'So what you are saying,' I recapitulated. 'Is that this is the fairy kingdom, the other side is heaven and in the middle is my universe. Also that Parsifal X is powerful enough to recombine the fairy kingdom and earth.'

'That's about it,' the ancient dwarf nodded. 'But I wouldn't call it the fairy kingdom, I might call it the dwarf-lands, Lady Aradel thinks of it as the elf-lands. It has been called the never,

never land or the middle earth or perhaps the shadow kingdom despite the fact that we are no more in shadow than you are. But you are certainly not in Kansas anymore.'

The dwarf laughed at his little joke and Lady Aradel joined in. I was still puzzled.

'But is the side of order our heaven?'

'Heaven, Valhalla, Asgard, Beulah land, the shining kingdom, my father's house, the bosom of Abraham,' the dwarf reeled off a list of names and then pronounced. 'What is in a name? But details I can give you none. That kingdom is closed to the dwellers in the dwarf-lands.'

'Elf-lands,' corrected Aradel.

'Yes dear,' agreed the old dwarf, patting Lady Aradel on her hand.

'So how do you know all this about the priests and Stonehenge, five thousand years ago?' I asked the venerable dwarf.

'Oh, that's easy to answer,' replied the dwarf. 'I was there at the time.'

- Chapter 10 -

'Mmm, mmm, mumble.' The old gnome seer, was once again in the presence of Parsifal X.

'Oh, I'll have to restore your tongue, I suppose' X grumbled and waved his hand.

'Thank you, your great highness,' the seer felt his mouth with his right hand. His tongue was firmly back in place.

'So what do you have to say, fortune teller? What will the outcome be of my great enterprise?'

'The nemesis key must be found and deployed.'

'But what is the key?' asked X.

'That I do not know but perhaps the family of the human prisoner can tell us if he can't.'

'The ex-prisoner, fool. He has escaped.'

'Even more reason to interrogate the human family.'

'Thank you, seer.' He dismissed the soothsayer with a wave of his perfectly groomed hand.

I am pleased that I have already sent a portion of myself as an avatar over to the realm of complexity, thought Parsifal X. *And it can capture the family, torture, question and destroy them. I shall enjoy that.*

*

'Have any of the crew survived?' Sienna asked the navigation officer from the submarine.

'I don't think so,' gasped the navigator. 'It's a complete disaster.'

'I warned them and they wouldn't listen,' remarked Mary in an almost nonchalant manner.

'But Mother, how did you know?' asked Sienna. 'You hadn't

told me that you saw something in the harbour.'

'That's because I hadn't seen anything,' replied Mary. 'It sounded more convincing than saying I could detect an evil presence in the harbour water.'

Sienna looked at her mother quizzically. Was Mary psychic? How did she know these things.

The light was beginning to fade and the family took shelter in the broch wall. The navigator insisted that she would stay outside to keep watch over the harbour.

'That's what the army captain would have liked me to do,' she said firmly. Sienna and the boys explained about the werewolf but the navigator was very sceptical. Joshua was irritated by this.

'You saw a sea monster,' he argued 'And expect us to believe you and now you won't accept that there is an equally unlikely land monster. You are not being logical.'

The navigator would not listen and climbed onto the top of the broch wall to scan the loch with her binoculars.

*

'But that would make you five thousand years old by my reckoning,' I protested to the venerable dwarf.

'Only one thousand by our years,' the dwarf replied.

'That is still preposterously old.'

'Nowhere near as old as Parsifal X,' the venerable dwarf countered. 'Now he is really old.'

'So what is Parsifal X and how come he is so powerful?' I asked.

For me this was the million dollar question. Perhaps if I knew what he was I could think of a way to defeat him? I then added a bit more.

'And why does he want to combine the realms when he is so powerful and in such a good position in this one.'

'Answering the second question first,' replied the dwarf. 'He wishes to combine the realities because this realm is dying.'

'Dying? In what way?'

'It only has a few more hundred years before the sun runs out of energy. To a creature as old as Parsifal that is almost no time at all. He has been planning this action for some considerable time.'

'Wait a minute, the sun shouldn't run out of energy so soon. I recall that it is good for another five billion years or so not just a few hundred years.'

'Your sun is good for five billion years. Ours is much shorter lived. Our plane of existence has different parameters and Parsifal believes that the only way for him to have a continuing kingdom is to combine the two. But something is going wrong and the third realm is also colliding.'

'I remember something from my physics and astronomy degrees about a very new theory. Someone suggested that our four dimensional world is restricted to a membrane or brane within a higher-dimensional space called the "bulk." The idea was that the universe could have come into existence by the collision of two branes,' I squeezed my eyes tightly as I recalled this, trying to conjure as much as I could from my memory. 'It is an alternative theory to the standard cosmic inflation theory.'

'Yes, young man, and I remember suggesting something very similar about three hundred years ago. Fifteen hundred by your reckoning. I called it the ekpyrotic universe.'

I stared at the dwarf, flabbergasted.

'You dreamt up brane theory fifteen hundred years ago?'

'About that, yes,' replied the venerable dwarf. 'And in answer to your first question. Parsifal X is an ancient creature who went by many other names in the past. He is an evolved energy creature. An intelligent complexity of plasma drawing his power from the centre of the earth. Some of your scholars might call him a fire demigod or possibly even a Balrog.'

'A Balrog! That's surely something out of Tolkien?'

'Ah, Tolkien! A good chronicler of future events, I believe,' answered the ancient dwarf.

*

The navigator stood shivering on the broch wall and refused Sienna's entreaties to come inside. As the night progressed distant howling could be heard. The noise came closer and closer and eventually the navigator's nerve broke. She jumped down from the top of the wall and banged on one of the makeshift doors.

'I can't see anything out there because it is too dark. The clouds have covered the moon,' she said when they let her in. 'And the howling is really spooky.'

'Come right in and we'll bar the door,' said Sienna, opening the portal fractionally to let the shivering naval officer inside.

'Perhaps I can keep watch through the peep-hole?' asked the officer.

'More than welcome,' replied Sienna. 'But don't open the door whatever you do. This is about the time that the werewolf comes to the middle of the enclosure and starts howling even louder.'

The navigator clambered in over the various barriers and Sienna carefully re-barred the door.

'We've not really been properly introduced,' the naval officer held out her hand. 'My name is Hannah Lee.'

'Pleased to meet you, Hannah,' Sienna politely shook the proffered hand. 'I just wish the circumstances were better.'

Mary had uncharacteristically made a cup of tea on the primus stove and she thrust it into the hands of the shivering navigator.

'Thanks,' the girl smiled. 'That is most welcome.'

'You need not expect me to make it for you every time,' grouched Mary. 'However, this time you need it. You are not really wearing the right clothes for this weather.'

'No, we weren't expecting conditions like this……'

The navigator was interrupted by howling right outside the

recently barred door. She jumped up and looked out through the peep hole at yellow eyes that stared back at her. The werewolf was outside scrabbling at the entrance, howling and whining as it did so.

*

'If the years are different here, how long a period of time has elapsed since I arrived?' I asked the dwarf.

The venerable being discussed this with Lady Aradel for a few moments.

'It can vary depending on how you came here but we reckon that it has been about six days or a week. No more,' the ancient dwarf replied.

'If this is reality I am very worried that the family will think that I am dead,' I stated. 'And if I am in a coma it would be helpful to get a message to them that there is still some brain activity continuing in here. Is there anything you can do?'

'I've sent a messenger to talk with them,' answered the dwarf. 'I did so as soon as I heard that you had been captured. I can do no more....and you must accept that this is reality for your very life depends on that acceptance.'

*

Sienna, Mary and the boys lay down to sleep at one end of the tunnel in the wall. The navigator had borrowed a spare sleeping bag and was lying down at the other end. As dawn broke Hannah, the navigator, got up and peeped through the small hole in the door. The werewolf was nowhere to be seen.

Hannah shook Sienna's shoulder lightly.

'I'm going down onto the shore to see if there is anything I can do for the people who were attacked by the sea monster. I didn't have the nerve to go before but I have to do it.'

'I'll come with you,' Sienna was rapidly putting her clothes on. 'There may be bodies on the shore and we would need help to bury them if there are.'

The two ladies clambered down through the remainder of the snow to the shoreline. A broken boat had drifted up and lay upside down amongst the kelp. At first glance it appeared empty but when they turned it over there was a body beneath it.

The submarine's engineer, thought Sienna, *the sallow one who didn't believe my mother. Mind you I didn't believe her either*

The navigator turned the body over and jumped back in total surprise as it twitched and rolled its eyes. The engineer sat up.

'I survived!' he looked at himself in amazement. 'I was certain that I was drowning. A monstrous sea creature overturned the boat and I went down to the bottom. I don't know how I ended up here.'

He coughed a little and stood up shakily.

'I'm not even a very good swimmer,' he continued. 'So I have no idea how I got away. However, I would appreciate some assistance.' He staggered and almost fell.

Sienna and the navigator both went to help him and he leant heavily on the naval officer. They looked around the foreshore but could see nothing else from the two stricken boats. The three of them climbed back up the hill to the iron age fort.

Mary had been making "brunch" from the various tins that they had salvaged. Sienna looked on with some amazement. Her mother was becoming quite domesticated .... and was enjoying this in a strange way.

'We have enough stores for about another week, Sienna,' stated her mother as they entered the broch with their salvaged engineer. Mary looked up and saw the survivor with them. 'I was basing that on three adults and two boys. Perhaps only five days if there are four adults.'

'We shouldn't be imposing on you like this,' said the navigator, Hannah Lee.

'But there isn't much else we can do,' said the naval engineer.

'I don't suppose there is,' Mary looked at the engineer closely in the gloomy flickering candle light. 'But we must make plans to get off here. This tiny island is not sustainable.'

Mary continued to stare at the sallow naval man. There was something about him that worried her. Perhaps the near drowning had made him sick? His colour was becoming even more unhealthy... it had originally been a wan yellow but there was now a tinge of grey and he had a grumbling cough that every so often erupted into a paroxysm of forced exhalation followed by a whooping inhalation. He may have survived the harbour water but he was clearly very unwell.

*

'It is time we were moving on,' said Lady Aradel. 'The shielding effect of the dwarf singing will only suffice for a short time. We have to get you back to your own realm. You must then rejoin your family and travel down to Salisbury Plain.'

'What are we going to do when we get there?' I asked, puzzled.

'We don't know,' the venerable dwarf answered. 'But our seer has told us that it is essential to get you all down to Stonehenge. Otherwise the collision of branes cannot be stopped nor can the deterioration of our own reality be contained.'

'So how do I get back to my own reality?' I asked, eager to start, keen to get home. 'Can you just bounce me back in some way as quickly as I came here?'

'I'm sorry to say that we can't. You will have to trek to a place where the two realities meet. The nearest such gateway may be known to you. It is the Macleod Fairy Bridge.'

'Do you mean the abandoned bridge at the foot of the Waternish peninsula? Between Dunvegan and Edinbane?'

'Yes, that's right,' replied the dwarf. 'But you say it is abandoned. That will weaken its power.'

'I think it's maintained as a tourist attraction but the road bypasses it now,' I added.

'It was still a functioning portal when I passed through it ten years ago,' Lady Aradel commented.

'But that is fifty years ago, in their time, my dear,' the dwarf reminded her. 'However, it is still our best chance.'

'We shall have to ask permission of Oberon and Titania's ambassadors,' Aradel pointed out.

'That is only a formality in your case,' said the dwarf.

'Yet out of politeness I must do it,' she concluded.

Oberon and Titania? The King and Queen of the fairies? This was getting more peculiar by the minute.

*

During the day Sienna and the boys salvaged wood off the shore. They were attempting to make a raft so that they could move across the relatively short gap where the chasm had appeared. It would not be easy as the current through the gap was fierce at certain times due to the river and the tide. Having seen the devastation caused by the sea monster they were not keen to risk the open waters but Mary had reported no further premonitions of disaster and it was clear that they could not stay much longer on the tiny island.

Whatever the conditions were like on the main island they would have to try their luck. The curfew and restriction on travel was a problem but the navigation officer had agreed to provide written permission explaining the impossible conditions. Moreover it was obvious that the naval engineer was sick and needed help which could not be obtained by sitting still and doing nothing.

As the day progressed the engineer became progressively more ill. He was shivering despite sitting next to the bonfire of driftwood they had burning in the broch enclosure. It was clear that he was feverish and in the late afternoon his condition was very bad. Sienna decided that it was worth using up some of the precious battery on her mobile phone to text the emergency services but no text came in reply.

Throughout the night the werewolf could be heard howling outside the enclosure but, whether due to the bonfire or whatever, the monster did not enter as he had done on the other nights. Every time the howl went up the engineer stirred and sweated more.

In the morning the engineer rallied but by late in the evening he was so feverish that he was hot to the touch. Sienna had never felt such hot skin. She had nursed sick children many times but had never felt someone so hot that touching them was uncomfortable.

As Joshua sat next to him in the night the man suddenly sat up on his makeshift bed, looked around him, stood on his bare feet and pushed Joshua to one side. He went to the door and started to dismantle the barriers. Joshua cried out for assistance. Sienna and Hannah the navigator came to help Joshua constrain the engineer but his feverish strength was too great. They tried to grab him but could not hold him..... he was so hot that his flesh appeared to be steaming.

He now had the door partly open and he grabbed Joshua under one arm and Samuel under the other. With superhuman endeavour he threw the temporary door to one side and started to run off with the boys.

From the outside of the enclosure their came a deep, menacing growl. In the light of the fading bonfire and the bright moon they could see the large dog-like shape of the werewolf leap at the engineer. The feverish naval man dropped the two boys and turned on the werewolf, lifting it in the air and dashing it to the ground in a flurry of remaining, drifted snow. The engineer then picked up an impossibly large boulder and attempted to smash it on the werewolf's head but the lycanthrope monster, twisting with fury, leapt up and sank its teeth into the man's raised arm.

The boys had scrambled out of the way and were watching

the fight accompanied by the three adults. It was now the turn of the naval engineer to show his anger and he screamed with rage. He ripped at his clothes and jumped up into the air. Suddenly, spontaneously, his clothes were on fire and even his hair and skin were aflame. He pointed his finger at the werewolf and a jet of combustion shot out to engulf the creature. The werewolf yelped in pain and rolled over in the snow, dousing his burning fur.

The lycanthrope turned tail, chased by the flaming engineer. Just a few yards further on they could see a deep puddle where snow was melting. They saw the werewolf stop in front of the pool, turn and face the flaming man. As the man ran at the werewolf the doglike creature shrank down and then sprang at his feet. The momentum of the man's run caught him out and he toppled over into the pool. The super cold water immediately doused the flames that had been engulfing the engineer and to the astonishment of the onlookers the man completely disappeared. They stared into the moonlit scene wondering whether this was just a trick of the light but they could see absolutely no trace of the engineer. The werewolf turned and looked at them malevolently and they all shrank back in fear.

*

'Ahhhh, the pain,' cried Parsifal X. 'They will all suffer for this.'

*

'So would the King and Queen of the fairies be in charge of this land if it were not for Parsifal X?' I asked, curious to understand the politics of the land.

'They used to be in charge of part of the land, that is true,' answered the dwarf. 'But they have become too involved in the complexities of time travel to join our opposition group. They have not been seen for some time. Their ambassador will suffice.'

'So are the tales of the fairy bridge true?' I queried.

'Up to a point. The Chief of the Macleod's did marry

a princess from Faerie and received permission to do so from Oberon. She returned to us because she was unhappy in what you would call the real world, not because Oberon said she could only stay there for a year and a day.'

'And the Macleod's fairy flag? What was that?'

'Sure, it is her shawl.'

'So the Macleod's are part fairy?'

'Very diluted, but yes, part Faerie. That is so.'

'So are you the leader of the opposition?' I asked. 'And was the opposition elected by anybody?'

The venerable dwarf gave a belly laugh and then spoke through his merriment.

'No, there are no elections. We don't believe in the rule of the fool here.... and I am not the leader. I am merely the Arch-Chancellor.'

'Do I get to meet the leader before Aradel and I set off?' I asked.

'You have already met the leader, young man,' replied the dwarf.

I thought of all the people I had met. The cyclops, the dwarf bouncers, the midget who had been thrown out, the barmaids. Surely not the ogre?

'Don't tease him any more, Kinsman Iron-builder,' smiled Lady Aradel. 'This reality is difficult enough for him without playing games.'

Thank you, Aradel, I thought. *At least the rat-elf is on my side.*

'Our leader is Lady Aradel,' he replied. 'The Queen of the Elves.'

*

The werewolf crept towards them, as if stalking the group of frightened human beings. As they watched it turned into a hairy, naked man standing on two feet. He shook his tousled head and spoke.

'So sorry about the lack of attire. Can't carry clothes with me when I'm in the wolf form. I've tried various ways but none of them is truly successful.'

The family group and Hannah, the navigator, stared at the lycanthrope in complete bewilderment. The werewolf had an upper class Oxford accent!

'I was a bit disorientated when I arrived here but I've been trying to get your attention for days with no success, don't you know,' said the creature. 'The name is Ardolf Mingan, but you can call me Ard. Ard as nails.' He laughed slightly at what he considered to be a bit of a pun on his own name and then added, politely. 'How do you do-oo?'

Despite the varsity accent the last bit of the sentence came out as a slight howl. This was, after all was said and done, still the werewolf they had been barricading themselves against for the last five days. Mary was the first to recover her wits.

'So why are you here and why were you trying to gain our attention?' she asked, then added as an afterthought. 'We do have some spare clothes if you would like some?'

'Clothes? Spiffing idea. It's really chilly when I'm in my human form,' Ardolf the werewolf drawled. 'I was sent by the Arch-Chancellor of the Dwarves to tell you that Lord James Scott is safe but that you must all travel with me to meet him.'

Again they stared at him in amazement.

'Jimmy is safe?' Sienna shouted. 'That's great news. But where is he?'

'That's harder for me to explain, dear folk,' replied the werewolf. 'Would you mind if I put the spare clothes on and we sat round the bonfire? I can then tell you everything I know.'

- Chapter 11 -

'Lady Aradel?' I looked at her in wonderment. 'You are the leader?'

'Yes, Lord James, that is so.'

'But you are far too young,' the words slipped out and I bit my lip. 'Sorry that I said that but you don't look older than eighteen years, twenty at the very most.'

The Arch-Chancellor laughed. 'It's not polite to ask a lady her age but Lady Aradel is older than I am.'

Lady Aradel gave the dwarf a chagrined glance.

'Kinsman, you should not have told him that. Now he will be embarrassed that I kissed him and that he saw me naked.'

I stared at her too overwhelmed to say a word and she continued.

'We don't have time for any more of this. We must move out. The dwarves will create a diversion and we will start for the fairy bridge.'

'I have to point out that I am feeling very tired.'

I had become resigned to treating this as some form of reality even if it was not mine and the tiredness hit me as I accepted that as a fact.

'We have to get away now but we will find somewhere on route for both of us to rest,' she answered.

I could hear a ruckus beginning downstairs. I looked out of a tiny mullioned window at the courtyard below. Wrestling dwarves spilled out from the tavern, apparently having a blood fight. Some of Parsifal X's troups emerged from the shadows. Clearly they had targeted the inn as being suspicious and were waiting to act.

Whilst their attention was taken at the front, Lady Aradel led me down the spiral staircase and opened a hatch under the bar. Further steps led down from there and a short tunnel led under the street into an adjacent cottage. We emerged in the dark in the small house and let ourselves out via the back door. We could see the guards trying to break up the fight and they could probably have seen us if they had turned to look.

In the backyard there were two horses. We untied them from their rail and jumped upon their backs. I had very little experience of horse riding but I was not about to tell Lady Aradel. I would have ridden a hump-backed whale to get away from the cyclopean monster guards of Parsifal X. If this was real, and I was now convinced that it was, the monsters were that much more scary.

We were riding away to save our lives as well as attempting to save the various realities. I have to admit that the less glorious of the two, saving my own skin, was uppermost in my mind as we rode off into the night.

*

'I am a representative from another reality,' began Ard, the werewolf, as they sat in a circle close to the roaring fire, enjoying the heat. 'I have been sent here to tell you that Jimmy Scott, Lord James, is safe and that you must all join him on his quest.'

'Do you really mean all of us?' asked the Hannah, the navigator. 'Am I included?'

'I think that all really does mean all, dear soul,' replied the lycanthrope.

'So we should up sticks and follow a werewolf through the terrible snow and against the diktats of the military government. Is that what you are proposing?' asked Mary archly.

'Just about, I daresay,' replied Ardolf, the werewolf.

'OK, I'm game!' replied Mary.

Sienna and the two boys looked at Mary in amazement.

I did not expect that, thought Sienna, *I was convinced she would complain.*

No, you didn't expect that came the thought reply from Sienna's mother.

Sienna sat up with a start.

Did my mother really put that thought in my head?

She again glanced over to Mary who nodded her head as if to say.. *Yes I did.*

*

'If the problem lies with a third variable on the far side of reality then we need to negotiate with the rulers of that variable,' surmised Parsefal X, the fire demigod, who sat on his throne passing himself off as a handsome, beautifully clad, male human being.

'That would seem appropriate,' agreed the dwarf seer. 'Though I must add that the future following collision of three realities is very difficult to read.'

X laughed a mirthless laugh. 'Such weaselly words won't help you if your advice is wrong, soothsayer. I won't just rip out your tongue ... I'll extract your entire nervous system intact, keep it living and stimulate the pain fibres until they burst into flame from overuse.'

The little mage shuddered. The future was indeed difficult to see and he was playing a dangerous game with the fire demi-god. The prerogative of those who can foretell the future is that they can usually back the right horses and bet on the right teams..... but they can't be right all the time however hard they try.

*

We cantered away in the light of two full moons and stars that I, an astronomy major, could not identify. The road out of town was initially cobbled but soon gave way to muddy cart-tracks. They had obviously never heard of tarmac in this alternative world or if they had they had could not understand the relevance of it.

Horse riding is not easy when you are as inexperienced as myself. Initially I found that I was fighting the rise and fall and a terrible pain developed in my private parts as I thumped up and down. I pushed up a little from the stirrups and leant forward so that I was riding in a position that I thought was similar to the Grand National jockeys I sometimes watched. The horses both reached a galloping pace and the ride became smoother, even enjoyable. Occasionally small branches whipped at my face and on one occasion I had to duck right down under a large branch.

I had read somewhere that horses can only truly gallop for a few miles at best. In this reality things were different. We galloped for half an hour and covered at least fifteen miles. When we stopped the horses did not look at all tired.

Lady Aradel took a sugar lump from a hidden pocket in her flimsy gown and proffered it to her grateful steed. She passed a second one to me and I gave it to my own horse. I was convinced that the horse whinnied 'Thank you' in reply.

'We have arrived at a place of natural power and there is a safe house here owned by a distant cousin of mine. We shall stay here for the night in perfect safety,' Aradel explained to me.

A couple of servants came and took the horses from us and Lady Aradel led the way into the house of her cousin, a high elf from the North.

*

'So what do you know of the far realm?' asked Parsifal X, the energy demi-god.

'Not a large amount, your highness. Just one tentative contact,' answered the gnome-like seer.

'And.....'

'And that creature is a trickster. Very powerful but out of kilter with the order in the rest of the domain.'

'But powerful, you say?'

'Certainly powerful. In control of its own large domain within that reality.'

'And will this creature assist us in combining the realities?'

'It has offered to do so at a price.'

'What price? Speak up seer or lose your tongue again!'

The old, bearded, gnarled gnome quivered in fear before replying and then answered

'It was something to do with pledging our eternal souls, your royal greatness, highest of all, mightiest of masters.'

The fire-demigod threw back his head and laughed.

'Ha! Such considerations may concern mere mortals but not one such as I. This reality is doomed and yet I am immortal. Unless I combine the realms I am doomed to eternal darkness, aware but unable to act. I have no eternal inner being, no eternal soul ... I am eternal. I am eternally damned.'

As he laughed, the demon or demi-god began to smoulder and smoke. The gnome quickly retreated. He knew full well what would happen if Parsifal X lost control. The flames would engulf everything around him including one gnome-like seer. This was one of the circumstances the gnome could foresee without using his sixth sense.

Parsifal X slowly regained his human form and shut down the flames. He looked around him for the gnome, considered the various residues and concluded that the seer had escaped the conflagration. X cursed quietly to himself. For years he had been drawing power from the sun as well as from the centre of the planet. This was one of the reasons that the sun was aging so quickly, not just due to the different constants and Parsifal knew this. If his plans went ahead successfully he would once again have unlimited energy for a very long time. With the power of the real earth's yellow sun he would be able to expand his influence to the nearest stars. Over time his rule could extend to the whole of the galaxy.

However, first he must contact the rebellious demi-ruler of

the far realm and once again he needed the help of the diminutive soothsayer.

*

'There is a boat at the end of the beach on the other side of this small island,' Ard, the werewolf in human form, imparted the knowledge with a slight, mischievous sniff, as if he really wanted to go round sampling the odours of all the people seated round the bonfire.

'A boat! That's good news but why didn't we see it?' asked Sienna.

'It was probably covered in debris,' replied the lycanthrope. 'It's full of water but appears intact.'

'What does it look like?' queried Joshua.

'Quite small, red. I think you would call the material plastic.'

'That's our boat,' Joshua declared. 'Double skinned plastic. Almost unbreakable.'

'We better retrieve it straight away in case it floats off!' exclaimed Sienna.

'It's dark now and it would be better to rest before our trek,' answered Ard. 'Besides, I have already tethered it to a rock so I doubt if it will break free.'

'And this trek,' started Mary, smiling. 'Which you say we must go on ....'

'....Starts first thing at dawn,' said Ard finishing the sentence.

Sienna looked in amazement at her mother. She actually appeared to be relishing the prospect.

*

Lady Aradel's cousin came to greet us in the hallway of his house. To call it simply a house is to abuse the term and grossly underestimate the nature of the dwelling place. It may have been technically a manor house but to my untutored eye it was a small castle. It was a startling combination of function and beauty, residence and fortification. The outer fortifications consisted of a high turreted wall standing proudly above the adjacent road, which was, like that in the town, cobbled with ancient stone. Beyond the outer hallway was a grand hall with many smaller rooms off it, a minstrel gallery at one end and a chapel leading off at the other. I did wonder what form of worship pertained in the chapel and resolved to ask the question when the moment was opportune.

Next day I was to discover that the castle walls also enclosed a large courtyard, stable blocks, servants quarters and armoury and that the other side of the castle was a sheer cliff down to a sandy beach. But tonight it was too dark for such a tour and we were exhausted. The cousin, Lord Ethdriel, gave us some refreshments and then led us to adjacent rooms which, to my delight, had modern en suite facilities. Up to now one of my major complaints about this reality was the basic nature of the plumbing...apart from being dragged here in the first place, strung up in a dungeon, chased by cyclops and ogres, abused by singing dwarves and obliged to take part in a quest, that is.

I thought about all of these things as I lay down to my first comfortable sleep in a long time. I lay in the large four poster bed within sheets of beautiful satin and my head on a soft feather pillow...... and sometime in the night Lady Aradel tiptoed into the room and snuggled up next to me!

*

The eastern sky was bright blue and the west a beautiful pinky-violet just after dawn as the family climbed down to the beach to retrieve the plastic boat. It took a matter of moments to tip out the water and debris. Joshua and Samuel had each carried an oar down to the beach. These had been salvaged from the byre remains after the hurricane and earthquakes had passed but up until now, without a boat, had been of little value.

The family and Hannah, the navigator, had brought supplies in their backpacks and they climbed into the boat.

'We must start off as soon as possible, if not earlier,' Ard the werewolf had told them on awakening them at dawn. They were taking him at their word.

There was just about enough space for the three adults and two children with their backpacks. However, it was not going to be possible to fit the werewolf into the boat without a major struggle and overloading the craft.

'We can do it in two trips,' suggested Sienna.

'Time is of the essence,' answered the werewolf. 'Already I can detect that the town is beginning to wake up and that the soldiers are on the prowl.

Sienna looked over towards the distant harbour. She could not see any movement but did not doubt the lycanthrope's words.

'I can feel them prowling, as well,' agreed Mary. 'But if you are not in the boat, how will you reach the far side and where exactly will we be going?'

'I suggest that you go as short a distance as possible in the boat,' Ard replied. 'It is rather conspicuous. The best route would be to go into the new passage, which is out of sight from the town, and then climb up the cliff and over the moor.'

'I think we should stay away from the roads, at least initially,' suggested Hannah. 'The authorities are being very strict about the curfew and the travel restrictions.'

'Just my thinking too, dear heart,' concurred Ard, the lycanthrope. 'As for me, I shall swim across. It's not far.'

'Will you be changing into your wolf shape?' asked Sam, excitedly. 'And if you do, shall I take your clothes for you?'

'Good thinking,' agreed Ard, stripping down and passing his borrowed garments to Sam. 'And stop staring, ladies. I only look small because of the cold.'

The werewolf plunged into the water in his human form, pushing the rowing boat out as he did so. Then he underwent the strange transformation into a huge wolf and swam alongside the vessel.

Sienna and Hannah were rowing and finding it hard to keep up with the lupine creature.

'He didn't look small to me,' whispered Sienna to Hannah.

'He looked large, from my experience,' replied the navigator, keeping her voice down so that it would not carry to the rest of the family.

Sienna caught her mother's disapproving look and realised that, once again, Mary had read her thoughts.

*

'The contact in the far reality is proving elusive. Something about sacrificing innocents, I understand,' said the gnome soothsayer.

'Just tell him that the sacrifice will take place at the time of the conjunction of realities,' replied the fire demigod.

'I'm not sure that the contact is male, sire,' the soothsayer was perturbed. He did not like sacrifices. 'Or whether the innocents were to be male, female or even human.'

The fire demigod laughed, singeing his outer garments as he did so. 'It makes no difference to me. There is nothing human or humane about me except the appearance.'

Much like most of my employers thought the gnome.

*

The morning came too quickly for me. I had enjoyed the warm bed, the clean sheets and the beautiful girl lying next to me. I knew that she claimed to be over a thousand years old but she still looked as fresh as my first girlfriend... and her perfume was divine.

I lay there with my eyes closed, wondering whether this was reality or some kind of Freudian wish fulfillment. The girl looked very much like my wife, was younger looking and just that scintilla more beautiful ... and she claimed to be very old which made me lose my guilt over her young appearance. Definitely fulfilling some deep-seated urge from my id, I decided. I could have lain there happily for ever.

However, independent of any volition on my part she opened her eyes, looked at the brightness of the sky and exclaimed. 'We must up and away!'

Now that was a very strange thing for my id to have longed for and I once again reluctantly decided that I did not control this reality. This was an alternative reality to my own and we did have to set out on a dangerous quest to save my own world and this realm.

We arose, did our ablutions, dressed and went along to the great hall. The place was thriving with elves of all ages and this was the first time I had seen children. I mentioned this to Lady Aradel.

She looked at me with mild amusement. 'Children are rarer here because we live so long but there were plenty of children in the Dwarf Tavern at the Port of the King.'

'Where?' I asked. 'I didn't see them and I saw precious few female dwarves... only the barmaids'

She smiled again. 'Perhaps you didn't recognise them. They all have beards even when they are very young. Some have grey or silver hair at the age of two.'

'And the female dwarves, do they have beards?'

'Of course,' she replied. 'Except the barmaids who shave the beards off, for some reason.'

How did the dwarves tell them apart, I wondered, and was that the reason for the low number of kids?

The breakfast was very light ... mostly fruit and a form of delicious, sweet yoghurt. Despite being light it was surprisingly filling. Lord Ethdriel hugged his cousin tightly and told her to be careful. She smiled warmly in return. Lady Ethdriel put in a short appearance and also wished us well. Aradel explained that her 'cousin-in-law' was busy helping to maintain the shielding from Parsifal X's telepathic gaze so she had little time to spare for socialising.

We readied ourselves for the journey by putting everything we had into a couple of backpacks. Lord Ethdriel then looked at me as if measuring me up. He disappeared over to the armoury and returned with a couple of swords.

'This is your favourite, Aradel,' he announced handing her a gold-handled sword with a bright silvery blade.

'And this,' he handed me a much more dour looking weapon. Longer and with a dark black blade it was slightly curved, rather scimitar-like, with a single cutting edge. There was a fancy guard, a leather grip and a pommel. In the end of the pommel was a single large diamond.

'This,' he continued. 'Is for you, Lord James. It is called Morning Star and belonged to my Great, Great, Grandfather.'

I took the sword and swished it around a little. I had fenced with épée and sabre when at school so I did not feel completely out of my depth. However, this weapon was different ... it was so beautifully balanced that it felt like an extension of my arm.

'Beautiful strokes, young man,' said Lord Ethdriel. 'But in a real fight don't forget to fight dirty. We are fighting for our lives so use anything that comes to hand.'

I nodded in agreement, fervently hoping that we would be able to evade our pursuers as we had done up until now and thus avoid any real fighting.

The sword slid poetically into its scabbard and two serving wenches helped fasten the scabbard around my waist on a strong leather belt. We were led to the front door by a procession and as we went the musicians in the minstrel gallery started to play and sing.

The mournful bird was singing
As the wagtail went a winging
Leaving home
Fi diddle eye
Leaving home

The little skylark
Plucked her harp
Leaving home
Fi diddle eye
Leaving home

Off they went birds of a feather
But they came not back, alone or together
They found a nest in a far, far world
And the rest of the tale cannot be told
Fi diddle eye
Diddle eye
Di

It was in a strange mode and all seemed very doleful to me but the elves were enjoying it. I would have preferred a bit of the Rolling Stones, U2 or Legion of Many. That would have livened them up.

We reached the portcullis at the front of the castle, a feature I had not noticed when we had arrived, and I looked round for the horses.

'Where's our transport?' I asked Lady Aradel, wondering what had happened to our mounts.

She smiled at me. 'The horses have to stay here. They will provide too much of a psychic signal where we are going.'

'So we go forward on foot?' I tried not to sound too daunted.

'Indeed, Lord James, and I know that you and your English compatriots are great walkers. I think you call it "to ramble". I did a lot of it with a family when I was there last.'

And that was fifty years ago, I thought. *We've become a lot lazier and fatter since then.*

'Yes, that's true,' I agreed wryly and somewhat dishonestly.

'I'm worried that I will not be able to keep up with your pace,' she added. 'So go easy on me, Lord James.'

- Chapter 12 -

The small red rowing boat reached the other side of the chasm with no great difficulty and Ard, the werewolf, helped pull it up the short bank, pulling the tether rope with his teeth. He then climbed out of the water in his wolf form and shook himself vigorously. Sam was standing near by with a pile of clothes and just about avoided being inundated with the spray.

They climbed the new cliff and then joined the old road that led round to the village. Sienna wondered what had happened to their car. It had been parked down at the end of the road and the parking space had disappeared into the chasm, presumably taking the vehicle with it.

'So where are we going?' asked Hannah, the navigator.

'We have to reach the fairy bridge by sundown tomorrow,' replied the werewolf.

'The old bridge on the Waternish peninsula?' queried Sienna.

'That's correct,' answered Ard. 'It is about twenty miles away.'

'And we have to walk? We can't take a car?' Sienna was asking the questions again.

'That is correct. There are restrictions on travel and there is a curfew.'

'I'm not sure that Mary and Sam can make it,' Sienna said, glancing at them.

'We can!' they chorused together, the oldest and the youngest.

The werewolf looked with amusement at the unlikely couple.

'That's settled then. We must set off.'

*

'The Prince from the far realm has agreed to stabilise the realities and give the control of the middle realm to you in return for your soul and two specific innocents,' reported the seer.

'How do you know all this?' asked Parsifal X, becoming suspicious rather late on.

'I conjured a meeting with an avatar of the prince using a pentagram and the blood of a goat,' answered the gnome. 'You still have to find out what the nemesis key is and put it into the correct lock.'

'Yes,' Parsifal X took some time over the word. 'I think you could help me there. Perhaps as part of the bargain the Prince of the Far Realm could find the family and the escaped man for me?'

'Why should he help you in that way, sire?'

'I understand from my avatar that the family includes two young boys. Since the Prince has not yet specified whether the innocents need to be male or female they could suffice. That might entice the Prince.'

'So you want me to conjure the Prince again?'

'Just his avatar, gnome. Just his avatar.'

'I will do that, sire, but could you tell me what happened to your avatar?'

Parsifal X grew angry at the mention of his own remote incarnation. His skin began to heat up and his eyes blazed.

'Perhaps you already know what happened to my avatar, soothsayer?' X began to smoke and his clothes started to steam. 'Perhaps you were partly to blame for its destruction?'

'No, no, I had nothing to do with it,' the gnome furiously tried to back away from the demigod whose temperature was rapidly rising. 'You need me to contact the Prince of the Far Realm. Kill me and you will never stabilise this reality.'

The fire demigod allowed his body to resume its accustomed human shape.

'You are right. I do need you at present ...but if the time

should come...' his voice trailed off but the warning was palpable.

The gnome shivered despite the heat.

*

They followed Ard, the werewolf, up to the gate at the top of the old private road. The signs saying 'Private Road: No Parking' and 'Dogs must be kept on a lead' still hung on the gate but the gate itself was dislodged from its hinges and lay in a crumpled heap across the roadway. Ard shuddered as he looked at the second notice.

The house next to the gate had clearly been inundated but was otherwise intact. Our friends who lived there were not at home but there was a note pinned to the door inside an envelope. Sienna went up to read it out of curiosity and discovered that it was addressed to Jimmy and herself.

Dear Jimmy and Sienna
Thought you might make it up to our house. We can't get to you, though we have alerted the emergency services.
We saw you arrive late two nights ago. Since then we have had the earthquake, hurricanes and tsunami. We knew that you were cut off and may not have received the warnings. We all escaped to higher ground and are staying with Margaret's sister. There is now going to be a curfew and restriction on travel. Before that kicks in we wanted to leave you some supplies and an open invitation to join us. You know the address.
Love Margaret and Hamish
PS If you want to you can stay in the house

Sienna smiled. They were such lovely neighbours. It was typical of them to help in times of trouble.

She handed the note to her mother, who read it, nodded, and passed it round to the others.

'Where would they have left the supplies?' asked Ard. 'I've just realised that we may need them. We don't have to reach the fairy bridge for just under a week.'

'I thought we had to get there by tomorrow evening!' Joshua exclaimed.

'I was confused. The passage of time is different in this reality from my own. A day in the Faerie realm is equivalent to five days here, more or less,' replied Ard.

Sienna pondered for a moment and then answered the werewolf's question.

'I expect they have put them in the shed behind the greenhouse.'

She led the way as she said this, around the shattered glasshouse. The door to the shed looked padlocked but closer inspection showed that the lock had not been pushed together. It had been deliberately left unlocked. Sienna pushed open the door. Much of the shed was in a terrible state from the flooding but, sealed in a large plastic bag, were the supplies, mostly tinned food but also some fruit and a loaf of sliced bread. The latter was a bit hard and stale, having been there for the best part of a week, but it was welcome nonetheless.

'I don't suppose there is any dog food?' asked the werewolf. 'Your food is OK but it is a bit bland for the likes of me.'

*

As we set off I marveled at the view. We were walking along a dirt track, the cobbled road having petered out only a few yards from the castle, and at points it meandered close to the edge of an enormous cliff. Below us the sea crashed against the rocks and way in the distance, on the horizon I could see blue-green mountain peaks topped with snow.

Aradel followed my gaze. 'The Eastern Mainland,' she answered my unspoken question. 'But we must go West.'

Turning a corner I saw a tremendous waterfall crashing down

to the sea from a river that flowed from the mountains to the West of me. It reminded of Kilt Rock in Skye. Was it possible that this was still Skye?

Aradel again read my thoughts. 'No, this is not the Isle of Skye as you know it. There are close similarities and points where the two realities meet and combine but in between there are major differences. This is an island but it is much larger and more extensive than Skye. It extends for several hundred miles south and we call it the Western Mainland.'

It figures, I thought. *After all there are two moons and the stars are different.*

'Yes,' agreed Lady Aradel, continuing the conversation as if I had spoken out loud. 'There has been a lot of discussion about the difference in the constellations. Our natural philosophers declare that the changes are the result of the decay and disappearance of stars. Some of this leads to formation of new stars but overall the number of stars has been decreasing ever since the two realities parted company.'

'The build up of entropy and the decrease in organisation,' I replied, this time out loud. 'In this reality entropy is increasing more rapidly than in mine and the stars are dying. It will lead to an early heat death of your universe.'

'Heat death?' queried Aradel. 'It was our opinion that the reality would get gradually colder.'

We walked on as I replied.

'It's just a name for the state of the universe when it has reached a condition of no free thermodynamic energy.'

'Your terms are strange to me, Lord James, but I understand the concept,' replied Lady Aradel. 'No more work could be done because everything would be at the same energy level.'

By jove, I think she's got it, I thought to myself.

'Pygmalion by George Bernard Shaw,' stated Lady Aradel, instantly. 'I was at the opening night at the Hofburg Theatre in

Vienna in 1913.'

I looked on in amazement and she continued.

'Mind you, that was in German. The opening night in English was April 11th 1914 in London and starred Mrs Patrick Campbell as Eliza Doolittle.' Aradel paused and looked at me triumphantly. 'I was at that premiere also!'

'It led to a musical and a film called My Fair Lady,' I told her. 'But it must have been wonderful to see the premiere of the original.'

'It was,' she enthused with girlish delight. 'I so much enjoyed it. Shaw was such a good playwright. Not as good as William but a better lover.'

'Which William?' I asked, suspecting immediately who she meant.

'The Stratford one, of course. The greatest English Playwright,' she paused, lost in her reminiscences. 'I spent many happy days with William Shakespeare discussing the accuracy of his historical plays. I thought it important but he didn't really. He was more concerned with the legitimacy of the emotions he was portraying.'

I listened attentively. This was exactly how I wished my English Literature lessons could have been when I was at school. But was it just more wish fulfillment?

'No,' said Aradel sharply. 'There is no point questioning reality again. It is a pointless solipsistic, egocentric thing to do. We are here and that is all there is to it.'

She shocked me with the sharpness of her words and the way in which they were delivered. Her general manner and looks so belied her enormous age that even her tales of opening nights one hundred years ago had not broken the illusion. However, I now felt like a schoolboy who had been rapped over the knuckles with a ruler by his piano teacher.

The beautiful, mercurial, magical elf soon smiled at me and

the world felt perfect again. I ventured a question.

'Do you think, in retrospect, that Shakespeare was right to alter the history to fit his plays?'

'Oh yes,' she replied. 'I've never managed to scribble anything of note despite frequently trying. He knew how to engage his audience and he purposely altered the stories so that he could get a message over about the times he was living in.... and they certainly realised that.'

'Did he write them all himself?' I'd often wondered this.

'Mostly, though he used a lot of contemporary writing by other authors to provide him with the plots. There wasn't the horror of doing that in his day as there is now in your reality.'

She was quiet for a moment.

'Or at least that was the situation fifty years ago when I was last in your realm.'

We walked on, each of us deep in our own thoughts but not trying to communicate either telepathically or by spoken word. After a long pause I finally asked the question that had arisen in my mind

'Why were you in my reality fifty years ago? Was there a particular premiere you attended?'

Lady Aradel smiled. 'No, nothing of that sort. I was in London with seventy thousand marchers demonstrating against nuclear weapons.'

'The Aldermaston March!' I had heard about that in my history lessons. The history master was a lifelong member of the Campaign for Nuclear Disarmament.

'That's right,' Aradel agreed. 'The CND. A good idea but too much involvement by KGB.'

I was once again amazed. The depth of knowledge exhibited by this highly intelligent and beautiful elf made my own thought processes feel truly inferior.

If she and her friends could not help solve the problems of this

realm why did they think that I could be of assistance?

*

'I shall be present next time you conjure the Prince of the Far Realm,' said Parsifal X.

'He may not like that sire,' replied the gnome seer. 'The Prince is unpredictable.'

The fire demigod laughed, scorching his clothes again.

'If he does not like it I shall not worry. I shall not worry at all.'

'Perhaps you should sire, he is from the eternal realm.'

'And.....'

'His power may match or even exceed yours!'

Parsifal X puffed up his body, his plasma reality scorching through the material of his clothes and drawing on the heat from the centre of the planet.

'Exceed mine? EXCEED MINE?'

The gnome had run for cover as soon as he realised that he had said the wrong thing. Working for demons and demigods was a worrying trade. It was only his ability to predict the future that kept him alive and yet it so frequently led him in to danger pondered the diminutive soothsayer as he knelt down in his bolt hole.

*

'We couldn't have stayed on the tiny island very much longer,' said Mary to the werewolf. 'We were running out of supplies. With your appetite we would have run out completely in a couple of days.'

'I don't normally eat that much,' protested Ard. 'But I had very little to eat for the two or three days I was outside your fortress trying to get your attention.... and this cold weather makes me very hungry. It's only as cold as this up in the mountains where I come from.'

'Then you should be used to it,' concluded Mary.

'I am, but I still get hungry.'

This conversation is getting nowhere, thought Sienna, I'd better steer it to more useful conclusions. 'So should we go and join Hamish and Margaret at her sister's place or what?'

'Wherever we go we have to be very circumspect,' interjected Hannah. 'Is your friend's house out of the way?'

'Her sister lives up in the hills behind Staffin,' replied Sienna, looking for the address in a little book. 'I'm pretty sure we can find it and it is certainly a remote spot.'

'But it is a good twenty miles from here, Sienna,' said Mary. 'It would be hard to make it in a day ....'

'.... There is another friend we could stop at on the way out of Portree,' suggested Sienna.

'... and I was going to say that it is not en route for the fairy bridge,' Mary finished her point with a look that reminded the family that she did not like to be interrupted.

'That may be a good thing,' mused the werewolf. 'I think that the direct route from here to the fairy bridge is going to be well guarded. The ruler of my domain is looking for you and he is bound to have made alliances with the authorities in your own reality. We have a difficult task ahead of us so we will have to work together as a team if we are to win through.'

*

'When will I meet the Prince of the far realm?' Parsifal X directed the question at the timid gnome.

'Tonight at midnight is the earliest time that augers well, sire.'

'I will accept that. Go and arrange the conjuring,' X turned to his nearest cyclopean guard. 'Bring the Brigadier to me.'

The guard hurried out and came back almost immediately with Brigadier Spencer Blenkinsop holding his hand.

'This really is most frightfully nice of you, old boy,' said the Brigadier to X. 'And this little girl is a delightful companion. Where do you get them from?'

'From your fertile imagination, I expect,' replied Parsifal.

'Eh, what?' the Brigadier adjusted his glasses which were attached to a string around his neck. 'Ah, yes, one of your little jests. Very droll.'

'Droll indeed,' Parsifal rolled his eyes skyward. 'Now we need to sort out the stabilisation of the space-time continuum.'

'It's well beyond me, I'm afraid, but I'll do whatever you say,' answered the Brigadier and then, in a conspiratorial whisper, he added. 'Do you know, I wasn't even aware that your special unit existed until the emergency. The United Nations Reality Engineering Activity Liaison. Sounds very grand. Bad acronym mind you ..Unreal. You might think of changing that.'

'Thank you. But we think it's most apt,' replied Parsifal. 'Gives people a clue as to what we are doing.'

'Well, you boffins know best. How is the work progressing?'

'We still have to find Professor James Scott. His work is crucial to the project.'

'You say he was holidaying in Skye? They had a bad time of it, I understand. The tsunami hit them centrally. Do you think he is dead?'

'I'm certain that he isn't, Brigadier. He just doesn't know that we want him so badly.'

'My army will do anything they can to find him, Professor Parsifal, anything at all.'

'That will be all, Brigadier,' said the fire demigod turning to the guard as he said it. 'Take him back to the cell.'

'Cell, ha, ha. Very droll,' laughed the Brigadier and he patted the hand of the huge cyclops. 'We better get back to our work. Come along dear. We have some letters to dictate and orders to send out and we mustn't get behind.' He patted the cyclops on its huge bottom and then gave it a squeeze. 'Have I told you what a delightful behind you have, dear.'

'Yes,' growled the cyclops in a deep bass voice, leading the

Brigadier out in chains. 'You have, several times.'

'And what a beautiful,sweet, lilting voice.'

'That as well,' the cyclops groaned as they disappeared towards the cell block.

- Chapter 13 -

The morning passed pleasantly enough although I was disturbed by rumblings underfoot. In the far distance to the south and west I could see cone-shaped mountains with their tops shrouded in clouds. As we walked I watched the mountains for some time, noticing lightning and odd belchings of smoke. Lady Aradel noticed my preoccupation.

'They are active volcanoes,' Aradel told me. 'And the rumblings you feel are small earthquakes. This land is a very active one and that is where Parsifal shows his power. If he knew we were here and if he wished to do so he could open the ground and swallow us up. Luckily he does not know where we are.'

The scenery was otherwise delightful, the weather remained fair and Lady Aradel was great company. She regaled me with stories of her trips over to my reality which had been more frequent in the past when the faerie realm had greater stability. They spanned several thousand years and I had to stop her flow of conversation at many points to clear up misconceptions that I had gained regarding the history of the United Kingdom and elsewhere. For example I had not realised that King Harold in 1066 did not get an arrow directly in his eye but just beneath it. He was subsequently cut down and killed by one of William's warriors. I also had not understood that Oliver Cromwell died from malaria. Aradel had seen it all or had known people who could provide primary source information.

We stopped for a short break at noon. As we started off again Lady Aradel told me that our easy passage would end soon as we would be leaving elf lands and entering the fairy kingdom.

'I thought that you called the whole thing Faerie?' I pointed this out, confused once again.

'Yes, but within the Faerie realm there is a much smaller part that is the fairy kingdom,' replied Aradel as she spelt out the difference. 'And the fairies can be very difficult to please. They will tolerate me as they are in a loose alliance with us but they will have a lot more of a problem enduring your presence within their fiefdom.'

'Why should I be a problem?' I asked surprised and confused, a condition I had been in frequently since I had arrived in the alternative reality.

'It's not you personally. It's what you represent.'

'So what do I represent? I'm a pretty average human being.'

'That is the problem. You represent centuries or even millennia of persecution of fairies. Originally by the religious fraternity and latterly by scientists.'

I laughed. 'Scientist don't persecute fairies. They don't even believe in them. Or is it simply that every time we say we do not believe in fairies, a fairy dies?'

'No. It is more complex than that and I will explain it after we have discussed your passage through their territory with the fairy ambassador.'

As she said that we turned a corner in the lane. In front of us was a barrier in the road and a small tollhouse. It had two stories but was under two metres from the floor to the top of the roof. Perhaps it measured six feet in toto... just a few inches more than my own height. A soldier peeped his head out of the door and stood up straight. To my surprise he was taller than me. His uniform was rather like that of the praetorian guard and the buckles on his shiny black shoes shone and glistened in the midday sun.

'Stop. Who goes there?' asked the fairy guard. 'Friend or foe.'

I had an insane urge to reply that I was foe but countless experiences with border officials had taught me not to try and joke with them.

I better treat them like the American Immigration officials, I thought to myself. *And their absurd visa forms that ask you whether or not you are a spy.*

Yes, you had better do that! came a loud telepathic reply from my elf companion.

'Friend,' I replied loudly and Lady Aradel's exactly similar reply resounded in unison with mine.

'Then you had better meet the ambassador,' intoned the guard in a disappointed voice.

So saying he beckoned with his hand and another figure appeared from within the tollhouse. This unfolded to reveal a rather statuesque, beautiful lady of indeterminate age but a very rough guess would have been fifty-five. She was running a little to the plump side and the only really unusual features were a wand in her right hand, a pair of gossamer thin wings which kept fluttering and the fact that she was hovering about two feet off the ground.

'Hello Lady Aradel,' she said in a very modulated voice that seemed to harmonise with itself. 'We were told you were coming and warned that you had company.'

I looked closely at the fairy ambassador. She looked exactly like a fairy godmother or perhaps the tooth fairy.

Fairy godmother, came the telepathic reply from Lady Aradel. *The tooth fairy is blonde.*

OK, I thought. *Godmother it is.*

'Who is that travelling with you?' asked the fairy ambassador in her beautiful voice.

'This is a human being called Lord James Scott,' answered Aradel.

'A human being?' growled the fairy. 'We do not want their type in our kingdom.'

'Woooah!' I said holding up my hands. 'I've got nothing against fairies. I've never even met any.'

'That is not the point.' said the fairy ambassador. 'And don't speak until you are spoken to.'

I was inclined to protest further but Aradel telepathically told me to desist.

'This is no ordinary human being....' she started to reply to the fairy.

Yes I am, I thought to myself. *Very ordinary indeed.*

Stop it Lord James, Aradel replied. *Leave this to me and don't interrupt whatever I say.*

She continued her conversation with the ambassador with scarcely a pause in the flow.

'........ I can personally vouch for him and he is part Elven in origin.'

Me? Part elf?

Quiet, Lord James

How is he Elven?' asked the fairy.

'Down through the maternal line from the Elven princess who married a Lord of the Macleods,' answered the elf.

'The elf princess who was your second cousin?' queried the fairy.

'Indeed!' came the reply.

'Then by rights he is an elf and may enter,' the fairy ambassador grudgingly concurred and then turned to me. 'Welcome to our kingdom, Lord James, Elven prince of the Macleod line.'

'Thank you,' I bowed deeply as I said this and the fairy ambassador curtsied to me in turn. Even the toy-town guardsman smiled as he pulled the barrier to one side.

I waited just inside the fairy kingdom as Lady Aradel went into a huddled conversation with the ambassador before joining me on what looked suspiciously like a yellow brick road.

When we were out of sight of the tollhouse I asked Aradel about my Elven connections. I was aware of the fact that my mother had claimed Macleod blood and could understand that descent however I had heard the myth that the Macleod lord had married a fairy princess not an Elven princess.

'My second cousin is definitely not a fairy. She is an elf.'

'She's still alive?'

'But very old and infirm.'

'So where did the story of a fairy princess come from?' I asked.

'She was a princess from faerie land. FAERIE,' she spelt it out for me as she had done earlier.

'I get it,' I replied. 'But what is the mystery about the fairies that you were going to tell me? And why do they hate human beings so passionately?'

'Because they are insects,' replied Lady Aradel. 'Elves, dwarves, ogres, cyclops and even gnomes are closely related to human beings but fairies are not. They are closest genetically to fireflies. They are highly intelligent very powerful insects.....'

'But the ambassador looked just like a human being with wings,' I said in surprise.

Lady Aradel smiled '....And they are great masters of deception and illusion. Even better than I am.'

*

The family, the werewolf and the navigator walked quietly along the road that led over the river and round to the town and harbour. They would have to pass near to the town but at this time of day the curfew was not in operation. Restrictions on travel to just two miles were theoretically a problem but they had close friends just the other side of town. Once they were within two miles of their friends property they reckoned they could claim to be staying with them and simply on their way to rejoin them. Sienna and Mary were sure that the friends would cover for them and lie to protect them although, at best, they did not want to put them into that position.

They had walked about a mile and a half and were still

considerably more than two miles from their friends' house when they saw a checkpoint in the distance. They immediately veered off the road into the forestry commission trees to the west of the road. Many of these had been blown down by the huge hurricane force winds, snapped off like so many discarded lolly sticks. They did however provide cover as the party sat down to decided what to do.

'I could use up my cellphone's remaining battery power and try to contact my friends,' suggested Sienna.

'I have a bad feeling about that,' said Mary immediately.

'I agree,' said Ard. 'There is no doubt that the authorities have been alerted to look for you. The ruler of our domain did have Lord James Scott in his power but he has escaped and is free. Our despotic ruler is trying to recapture him and he believes he can do that more easily if you are in his grasp.'

'I could phone your friends,' suggested Hannah. 'My mobile is still functioning. It's a cheap old one and so the battery lasts for ages.'

Mary had no objections to this so Sienna gave the phone numbers to the navigator. Hannah sat down and tried to contact the friends with no success. Eventually she gave up.

'We'll have to think of something else,' said Joshua.

'What about creating a diversion?' suggested Sam

'What sort of diversion would draw the soldiers away from the checkpoint?' asked Sienna.

'We just have to get their attention in another direction whilst we sneak by,' said Joshua.

'I know this sounds cruel,' said Mary. 'But if we were able to entice some of the highland cattle into the water it might attract that sea monster. Surely something that looks like the Loch Ness Monster would attract all the soldiers' attention.'

'Do you think it is still out there, Granny?' asked Josh.

'Oh, it's still there without a doubt....' replied Mary.

'....I have a better idea,' Ard interposed . 'Rather than involve highland cattle or sheep, both of which would be unpredictable, why don't I go into the water in my wolf form, splash around a bit until I get the monster's attention and then swim away before it can reach me.'

'Because it might catch you!' Sam exclaimed. 'And you are our friend and know what we need to do.'

'You know the plan now,' countered the werewolf. 'Just get to the fairy bridge by seven days time and wait for Lord James. He'll know what to do after that.'

'It is a plan that has a high potential for success,' Mary stroked her chin whilst she considered Ard's suggestion. 'But for it to succeed we must act very soon. Every moment of delay makes the chance of success decrease.'

'It is decided,' said Ard. 'I go immediately.'

'Put your clothes in a polythene bag around your neck,' said Sam handing Ard a plastic bag. 'Then you can change back into them when you get out onto the shore.'

'Thank you, Sam,' replied Ard. 'Remember, whatever happens we are a great team. I shall be able to keep warm when I get out.'

If he gets out, thought Sienna and she caught the eye of her mother who was clearly thinking the same way.

*

'The Church hated fairies because their magic really worked whilst the miracles from the Church usually didn't,' explained Lady Aradel. 'And the scientists indiscriminately killed insects with compounds such as DDT because they had discovered that they were vectors of disease. In addition human beings with their wars, their pollution and their massive overpopulation have destroyed many habitats in the real world where the fairies used to live comfortably. So, almost extinct in your world, the fairies have retreated to the fairy kingdom, here in faerie land. But they have not forgotten their hatred of mankind.'

As I listened it did make sense. Before I had fallen into the crevasse I would not possibly have imagined that human beings could have destroyed magical creatures such as fairies without even having realised they were there. However I did know that we were causing extinction of species on a massive global scale and that we barely knew a few percent of the species that were present, particularly amongst the smaller creatures such as the insects.

After all, I pondered, it was only very recently that we discovered the Archaea, a domain of single celled organisms distinct from bacteria and which, in plankton, probably made up one of the largest groups of organisms on the planet. So maybe we really had been killing off the fairies with our insecticides.... and maybe they did have a good reason to hate us.

We walked along the yellow brick road. In the fairy kingdom the colours seemed brighter than in the elf-lands. The elf landscape consisted of muted violets, heather, lilac and green but this environment was one of primary colours. The sky was a uniform blue and the clouds were not really quite like the usual summer fluffy clouds ...they were more like cotton wool.

It was when I noticed a gingerbread house, a slinking wolf and, in the distance, three bears dressed in finery, that I began to be suspicious. I had become convinced of the reality of the faerie realm but now the fairy kingdom was very odd.

'You are right,' Lady Aradel answered my unspoken question. 'It is not real. There is a road under our feet but it is not the bright yellow colour that you imagine. There is a house but it is not made of gingerbread and there are three people in the distance but they are not bears dressed in finery.'

'And the wolf?'

'Well, there was a real wolf slinking along watching us.'

'So this is another illusion?'

'I told you that the fairies were masters of illusion. They are providing you with the illusion of the fairy kingdom that your subconscious desired.'

'Can I see the reality?'

'You could try asking the fairies if they would mind you seeing the reality.

'How do I do that?'

'Just speak to the fairy that is hovering next to you.'

I turned slightly to my right and saw a fairy flying along next to me as we walked along the road. Until Lady Aradel had pointed her out to me she had been completely invisible. Now she appeared to be about six inches in height with iridescent wings and a small wand.

'Hello fairy.' I started to ask politely. 'Could I please beg a favour of you?'

'Lord James, of course you could. Whether we grant the favour is a different matter,' replied the fairy in a sweet, melodious, tinkling voice.

'I would like to see the reality we are passing through, please,' I requested.

'You will be disappointed,' answered the fairy.

'Then that will be my loss and I will have to bear it.' I replied.

'So be it.'

The fairy waved her wand and I took a few moments to orientate myself. The yellow brick road disappeared, replaced by dirty brown cobbles of a similar size and shape. The sky returned to a natural blue and the clouds, white and grey, were drifting in a normal manner, some blacker ones even looking as if they might rain on us.

The gingerbread house was made of stone, wood and tiles and the bears were three normal sized folk who waved to us. In the distance were the muted greeny-blues and mauves of the mountains. Adjacent to the road and running off down into a valley were strips of heavily cultivated land looking for all the world like allotments. The people working them were mostly dwarves and they were clearly taking delight in growing large pumpkins, huge carrots and a variety of beans and other vegetables. Although it was a lot shabbier than the illusion I had to admit that I preferred the reality. It was more inviting and comforting .... more home-like.

Tell them you prefer the reality. Lady Aradel was talking to me telepathically again. *They will be pleased.*

I turned to the fairy again. She had shrunk to the size of a very large dragonfly. Her wings were still iridescent and they caught the sunlight in a dazzle of colour.

'You really are beautiful!' I exclaimed with delight. 'And your land is fine. I prefer the reality, it reminds me of home.'

The fairy buzzed around me happily and settled on my shoulder.

'I am really glad that you like our land, Lord James, and we are very grateful that you are trying to help us save the Realm.'

We walked on at a steady pace. Despite my misgivings I was not finding the going too tough and this was, perhaps, due to the slight decrease in gravity in this different reality.

'We shall soon reach a place where you can take refreshments....' the fairy started to say this when there was a sudden increase in the rumbling underfoot and a swaying of the ground. This developed into a sizeable quake. We fell to our knees and saw cracks appearing in the road. Cracks which focussed on us, creeping in our direction from all sides.

'The illusion,' shouted Lady Aradel, 'Reinstate it. Do it now!'

The fairy sprung from my shoulder and waved its antennae. Instantly the shiny yellow colour of the road reappeared, followed by a change in the sky. The fairy doubled in size and sprouted a wand. More worryingly Lady Aradel and I shrank down, fell onto all fours and turned into rats.

The rumbling died down and the cracks in the road came together.

'That,' said the fat rat to me as we continued along the road. 'Was an attack by Parsifal X. The illusions were protecting us and when the fairy dropped them we were exposed to his searching consciousness. Luckily she was able to reinstate the environmental illusion and I could change us into rats.'

'Couldn't we have been something other than a rat?' I asked. 'A bird would have been nice or even a cat or a dog.'

'That would have taken more time. Convincing illusions are difficult to prepare' replied the fat elf-rat. 'And time was something we did not have.'

The rumblings had now ceased completely and Lady Aradel judged that it was safe for us to turn back into our usual forms. It was with some relief that I regained the familiar shape of Jimmy Scott, aged forty, electrical engineer and sometime physicist and astronomer. The fairy maintained the illusion of the kingdom around us. I presumed that as long as we were not seeing the reality the fire demigod could not read where we were from our consciousness.

*

The werewolf changed into its lupine form and jumped into the water with the bag of clothes round its neck. It swam around near the shore for a few minutes and then doggy paddled further out in the loch towards the harbour. Even the sight of a dog in the water drew the attention of a few of the soldiers guarding the checkpoint. Then from a deep water area closer to the harbour a ripple could be seen in the otherwise calm sea. This disturbance moved towards the werewolf and then broke through the surface. The head of the plesiosaur appeared .... two large jaws, a long neck and a huge bulk of body. The monster was fast. It swung its neck round in a loop and down towards the werewolf. The family stared at the ensuing drama, caught up in the moment.

'We must move,' said Mary, pragmatically. 'All the soldiers are watching the action and this is our best chance.'

'But we've got to know the outcome,' said Sienna.

'And make his sacrifice worthless? No, we must move,' demanded Mary and they all reluctantly turned away from the scene and slid quietly through the trees lining the road adjacent to the checkpoint.

When they had reached what they deemed to be a safe distance beyond the barrier they looked out to sea again. The monstrous reptile was swimming away towards open water. The werewolf was nowhere to be seen. Despondently they walked along the side of the road and as they did so they heard voices coming along the road behind them. Sienna looked around.

'Quickly,' she suggested. 'Get behind the trees.'

They stepped into the forested border as a couple of soldiers came running up in full kit, talking to each other as they did so. The soldiers, out of sight from the officers at the checkpoint, paused for a rest just as they came next to the hidden party.

'Never seen nothing like that before,' said the first soldier between panting breaths.

'Blinking Loch Ness Monster, I reckon,' replied his companion. 'Did for that big dog, though. Did you see? Dragged it right under.'

'No hope, no blinking hope at all,' agreed the first. 'Still, we better get on. We've got to report to HQ.'

After a few moments the two soldiers resumed their jogging pace and disappeared round a bend in the road.

'Sounds like bad news,' said Sienna.

'That horrible sea monster got our friend Ard,' Sam had tears in his eyes. 'First we lost our Daddy and now we've lost our dog.'

'You mean our werewolf,' corrected Joshua. 'He wasn't really a dog.'

'He was and he wasn't. I'm right aren't I, Mum?' asked Sam.

'Ard was very special and I'm very sad that we have lost him,' Sienna pulled Sam close to her and gave him a hug. 'Cheer up!

Ard wouldn't want us to be miserable. We are still a great team.'

But when will these disasters stop? Sienna asked herself.

Not for a considerable time yet, replied her mother, telepathically prophetic.

*

'I almost had them, I could feel them and smell them,' growled the fire demigod. 'Aradel and my prisoner were inches from my grasp and now they have disappeared again.'

Parsifal X was sitting on his throne surrounded by cyclopean guards. He called for the gnome who instantly appeared from behind the throne.

'Are you prepared for the conjuring this evening?'

'Yes,' replied the tiny mage. 'The chalk pentagram has been accurately drawn. I have a live goat ready for sacrifice and I have obtained a crucifix from the real world and placed it upside down,'

'A crucifix? That has significance?'

'It does seem to, your highness, your most powerfulness, sire. Yes, it does seem to,' the gnome soothsayer was amazed.

Parsifal X did not understand the significance of the crucifix. Did that mean that he did not understand the power and glory of the far realm either? This was a significant omission in X's knowledge.

- Chapter 14 -

We walked along the yellow brick road and reached a small woodchopper's cottage. Next to it was a beanstalk that grew unsupported way up into the clouds. A little old lady came out of the cottage and waved the three of us over to a picnic table.

'Dear wayfarers, partake of my humble fare, please do,' suggested the old lady.

'Is this safe?' I asked Lady Aradel. 'I've heard about fairy food before now.'

Lady Aradel smiled.

'We are their guests so it is perfectly safe. Even though it is not always what it seems, it will be nutritious.'

We sat down and in minutes the table was groaning with food and drink. After thanking the old lady I started to tuck into the repast. Sometimes what looked like an appetising morsel, a piece of chicken or a prawn, would disappear from my plate just before I could pop it in my mouth. I looked over at Lady Aradel's plate and several times saw the food land on her platter. At one point it disappeared just as I had it at the lips, whipped away from me by the Queen of the Elves.

'Lady Aradel,' I asked. 'Do you have a magic snatch? How does the food move so quickly?'

Some of this food although wholesome may not be to your liking, she replied in my thoughts. *For instance I doubt that you would enjoy toad's eyes in roasted bat's milk. So I'm taking the pieces you would not want.*

'But it even smelt of fish. I thought that would be a particularly juicy prawn,' I argued.

The illusion is not only visual. It involves all the senses. Just eat up and don't worry about it. I'll remove anything that might not suit you.

Aradel was doing a good job of sorting the food. Whatever I ate tasted delicious and I soon felt satisfied and ready to continue on our journey. Lady Aradel and our accompanying fairy also indicated that they were happy to move.

'How do we pay her?' I asked. 'We can't just waltz over to her house, take her food and leave.'

'You honour her by your presence but a promise of future help in time of trouble would be sufficient payment,' replied Aradel.

I leant over and kissed the old lady's hand and offered to help her if I could be of any assistance at any time. The old lady thanked me and we left to carry on with our pilgrimage.

*

It was bitterly cold and it had started to hail as the team progressed along the loch-side towards Portree. Further down the road to town there was a visitor's centre. By sheer chance none of the fallen trees had hit the centre but unfortunately the quake had damaged the front wall of the building and there was a gaping hole. The centre was empty so the family, accompanied by Hannah, took shelter inside to have a late lunch.

As they sat eating the first bread they had eaten in days they looked out towards their cottage, the other side of the loch on the headland that was now a new island. As they watched they saw several large helicopters land near their ruined family house.

'Is that the emergency services belatedly coming to help Jimmy?' asked Sienna hopefully. 'Perhaps I should call them on my mobile.'

She went to take her cell phone from her pocket but Mary's hand stopped her. Mary had already taken the field glasses from her pocket and was staring at the helicopters.

'What is it Mum?' asked Sienna. 'Why don't you want me to

phone them.'

'They don't look all that friendly. That's all,' replied Mary. 'Take a look.'

Sienna stared through the binoculars. 'There's a load of soldiers piling out of those helicopters. Does you expertise in military matters extend to helicopters too?'

'No it doesn't,' answered her mother, tetchily.

Inside the large plate glass window of the centre there was a telescope pivoted on a stand. In order to use the machine Joshua put in a twenty pence piece and was focusing the powerful machine on the helicopters.

'They're Chinooks Mum. Transport helicopters. I can see three of them and there must be at least a hundred soldiers, maybe more. They've looked in the house and they are beating their way up through the grass and bracken. They've gone up into the woods and they're searching through there, now,' Joshua kept up a running commentary. 'I can see some on the top of the pinnacle and on the broch now.'

Hannah was staring at the scene through her powerful prismatic binoculars. 'That's a large SWAT team,' she stated, still staring intently. 'Special weapons and tactics. Counter-terrorism unit. They're not there to help you. They are there to capture or kill you. Believe me it is a good job that we got out when we did.'

It just gets worse and worse, thought Sienna. *Will it ever stop?*

*

Parsifal X was furious. His latest clothes, a particularly expensive suit he had obtained several years previously from a Saville Row tailor, were already beginning to smoulder.

'So you say that Brigadier Blenkinsop sent soldiers onto the island on which I had marooned the human's family? Is that right?'

'Yes sire. The brigadier did what you said and organised the army to invade the island,' replied one of the cyclops.

'And nobody was there? How did they get away?'

'We don't know sire. They can't have gone long. The army found the remains of a bonfire and it had only just died down.'

X by now was smoking badly due to overheating. 'Get them to extend the search to the entire neighbourhood and get Blenkinsop up here again. We must find the family.'

The cyclops changed into an illusion of a young female belly dancer and disappeared to fetch the brigadier, returning a few moments later with the military ruler of Britain on his arm.

'Thank you, Professor X, for agreeing to see me,' said the deluded brigadier. 'I would say that things are going well.'

'And your communications with the leaders of the other significant countries ... USA, Germany, Russia, China, Japan, Brazil. Have they agreed to my terms?'

'They've accepted your kind offer to set up an institute in each country and are delighted that you will share with them the, shall I say, fruits of your research.'

'I'm sure they are,' said X, urbanely. 'When will the leaders be coming to a conference?'

'They weren't keen to come to Scotland but they favour meeting in London,' replied the Brigadier and X, thwarted in his favoured choice of venue, started to smoulder more.

'By golly it's warm in here,' remarked the brigadier. 'Have you turned up the central heating?' Blenkinsop looked at the giant cyclops which he perceived as a belly dancer wearing just a thong and brassiere and continued to talk. 'She'll have to take off her remaining clothes if it gets any hotter, what ho!'

'And then eat you,' said the fire demigod.
For just a moment 'Blinkers' Blenkinsop looked perturbed at the turn of phrase then he smiled.

'Ah, yes. One of your scientific jokes, I imagine. Must get back to work.'

'Before you go, have you any further advice about the family

I am seeking? The SWAT team were unsuccessful. The family has fled.'

'Fled? Oh, you mean from the tsunami and earthquake. I suppose they must have done if they are still alive. You have tried to trace their mobile phones, I imagine? Being a scientist I expect that was the first thing you did.'

'Mobile phones?'

'Cell phones, communication device. Here, look at mine,' the brigadier pulled a phone from his pocket. 'You must have been shut away in your lab for a very long time if you've not seen one of these.'

'Of course I've seen mobile phones,' lied the fire monster. 'Here is mine.'

He conjured in his hand a device that looked very similar to Blenkinsop's machine.

'Oh, that's a new type. What sort of apps does it have?'

'Apps?'

'Applications. You know, programs so that you can use it for all sorts of things. Look mine has a camera, still and cine, game center, passbook, calendar, piano keyboard,' the brigadier was flicking across the screen of his phone as he listed all the apps. To him, due to illusion, it appeared as if the phone was working but to the onlookers it was blank. He looked up with his usual inane grin.

'And you can even use it as a phone. What can yours do?'

'All the things yours does,' replied Parsifal. 'And more ...'

He copied the scrolling action that the brigadier had used and three dimensional pictures appeared in front of his camera. Then wine poured from a jug into an instantly conjured glass. Blenkinsop looked on in amazement. Parsifal X was enjoying this. He pointed the machine at a small chair on the other side of the room and used his own powers to teleport the object over to where they were standing.

'Amazing, quite amazing! Japanese, I daresay,' said the UK's military leader. 'I had no idea they were so advanced. It uses holograms I expect.'

'No doubt,' replied X. 'And the answer to your question is yes. Yes we have been trying to locate them using their phones.'

The fire demigod turned to the cyclops guard who was holding Blenkinsop's hand.

'Take him back to his cell,' he commanded the guard. 'Then return here.'

'Cell! You are such a droll wit, professor, you really are,' said the brigadier. 'Come along dear.' He was now addressing the guard. 'We really must get back to work. Tempus fugit, you know.'

Within minutes the guard had returned. X was smoking again.

'Why didn't we know about mobile phones,' he fumed. 'And why haven't we searched for the family and for James Scott by locating their phones? Why?'

'It shall be done, sire,' replied the cyclops. 'It shall be done.'

Parsifal X ruefully looked at the sleeve of his beautiful jacket. He had ruined another perfectly good suit by becoming too hot.

- Chapter 15 -

The team set off through town. The houses along the shore were in complete ruin but further back the wave had not been so destructive. The school was on the other side of the road at a higher level and although there was evidence that the water had reached the lower story the rest of it was unharmed. They could see people milling around inside the school.

'This is where some of the folk have taken refuge. This is an unofficial site,' Hannah informed the family. 'The community centre and the church are official centres for refugees. Food is being distributed from the large co-op on the outskirts of town. Basically, all the rest of the shops are closed.'

'Shouldn't you be rejoining your ship-mates?' asked Mary, looking at Hannah sharply. 'Now we are in town they may be looking for you.'

'I think that I will be better employed helping you,' replied Hannah. 'And Ard the werewolf told me that I must stay with you as long as possible.'

They walked quickly past the school keeping out of sight as much as possible. The centre of the town looked deserted but they skirted round the side streets. Looking down into the harbour they could see into the tops of the destroyed houses .... just the bases were left, the roofs having all been washed away but the wave did not seem to have reached such a height on the harbour side of the loch as it had done on the far side where the cottage was sited.

The sudden invasion of the headland with the SWAT team had disturbed the family and they were trying to avoid contact with other people. The house belonging to their friends was not a great distance on the North side of town but progress was relatively slow. They reached the road to the house and could even see the large monkey puzzle tree in the garden when a couple of soldiers stepped out in front of them. They had clearly been having a furtive cigarette behind a tree but should have been standing watch.

'Halt!' said one of the pair. 'Do you have identification on you and where are you going?'

'They are with me,' replied Hannah, the navigator, who was still in her naval uniform even though it was, by now, rather dishevelled. She took out her military pass and smiled at the soldier.

So close to the house and we get stopped thought Sienna.

That may be too our advantage replied Mary.

'There is a two mile travel restriction,' the burlier of the two soldiers informed them, nodding at Hannnah's papers. 'So where are you going?'

'About sixty yards,' replied Mary in her haughtiest tones. 'And you are fully at liberty to come with us.'

Mary marched past the soldiers towards the house. At the gateway she turned and waved the rest of the team in. The soldiers stood on the threshold to the property and watched as she banged on the door. Luckily Charlotte, the family's friend heard the rapping. Her eyes almost popped out of her head when she saw who was at the front door.

'Come in, come in!' she exclaimed and, seeing the soldiers at the gate, gave them a wave. They turned and walked back to their watch post.

'How in the name of glory have you all just appeared?' asked Charlotte after Hannah had been introduced to her. 'And where have you been?'

She paused and looked us up and down.

'No, before you answer you must come in and get warm. I'll find you some dry clothes. You all look drenched. There's a kettle on the wood stove, I'll make some tea.'

She ran ahead of the team into the kitchen and they could hear her rattling cups and taking out some cake from a tin. She then disappeared upstairs, returning with a bundle of clothes.

'There's the bathroom,' she indicated with her hand, 'You can put these on and tell me what has been happening.'

*

'Now, Blenkinsop,' said X as urbanely as possible, having insisted that the brigadier be brought back again. 'What do you know about the eternal realm?'

Parsifal X had realised that there was a lot that he did not know about the Earth and its reality let alone the far realm. The middle realm of the normal world was closer to the far realm than he was in the faerie realm so perhaps, he wondered, the occupants of the normal world would know more about the far realm than he did?

Brigadier Blenkinsop looked surprised at the question. 'Funny question for a scientist,' he remarked. 'Thought you weren't religious.'

'No, no. I'm not religious,' replied X, fully aware of the fact that whole swathes of the faerie realm had been forced into worshipping him over the previous four millennia. 'I just wanted your opinion.'

'A load of poppycock,' replied the brigadier. 'Mind you I am C of E. Church of England, what?'

The fire demigod was confused. *If the soldier was not religious why did he claim to belong to the church?*

The brigadier noticed his confused expression..... an expression that Parsifal X had studied over the centuries and could now perfect on his handsomely created human construct.

'Sorry, I've confused you there,' the brigadier apologised. 'Of course I do attend my local church. Christmas, Easter, weddings, funerals. Particularly enjoy harvest festival.

> *"All is safely gathered in,*
> *'Ere the winter storms begin."*

The brigadier started to sing in a passably good baritone. Parsifal X waited impatiently and eventually "Blinkers" Blenkinsop stopped his singing.

'Sorry professor,' said the military ruler of the United Kingdom. 'You didn't come here to listen to me singing. I'm sure you had a much better reason for leaving your laboratory. Now what was it you were asking me?'

'I was asking about the eternal realm. What do you know about it?'

'Probably no more than you do, old boy,' answered the soldier. 'Heaven, hell, maybe a bit of purgatory. That's about it really.'

'And the crucifix? is that significant?'

'Certainly as a symbol. Rising again on the third day. All that stuff.'

'And one that is upside down?'

'I should stay away from that sort of thing, if I were you, old boy,' answered the brigadier. 'Don't believe a word of it myself. Superstitious nonsense. Demons and devils, gods and angels. No. Don't believe in the supernatural. Never have done.'

Blenkinsop turned to the large, ugly cyclops standing next to him. 'Now come along dear, we mustn't keep Professor Parsifal from his work.'

He patted the cyclops on the hand and the monster docilely trotted along with him out of the door.

*

'And that's about it,' said Sienna, having finished a resume´ of their misadventures. Mary, Hannah and the boys had supplemented her account.

Charlotte had kept quiet the whole time but now she spoke.

'That sounds as if you have had a horrendous time,' she shook her head in sympathy. 'And you say that Jimmy was lost down a crevasse?'

'Disappeared without a trace,' Sienna wiped a tear from her eye. She had not cried about her husband up until now... there had been no time. To distract herself from the sad thoughts she asked Charlotte how they had been.

'Joseph has been worked off his feet. He even got me to help him though I've not nursed for twenty years or more,' Charlotte replied. 'He's out on his rounds now. He is also acting as the medical officer for the armed forces that are stationed here. They say they are here because of the nuclear submarine to stop it getting into the wrong hands but we don't think that they are telling us the whole truth......'

'They put a SWAT team down on the headland near our cottage,' Joshua interrupted Charlotte's flow of conversation.

'We saw that,' Charlotte grimaced. 'What were they looking for?'

'Us,' replied Sienna.

'And there was a monster in the harbour and you had a werewolf as a companion? Now you think the SWAT team were looking for you. If it was just you saying that, Sienna, I might think that you had cracked up,' said Charlotte.

'I'm afraid that it is true, Mrs. Burns,' said Hannah. 'I witnessed a lot of it.'

'You are welcome to stay here, of course,' said Charlotte. 'We have only one spare bedroom, perhaps the three adults could share that and the kids could sleep down here on the sofas. It will be warm enough.'

'Warmer than a stone-cold broch, Aunty Charlie,' said Sam, smiling for the first time in ages.

'Who is in the other rooms?' asked Sienna, aware of the fact that it was a five bedroomed house.

'Didn't I say?' asked Charlotte. 'The army has billeted some of their troops here. We have six soldiers staying with us.'

*

We walked on through the fairy kingdom. Despite the fact that I knew it was an illusion the kingdom was definitely enchanting. Down below us I could see a field in which three billy goats were grazing. As I watched, the smallest goat trotted down to a small hump-backed bridge over a river. I could see that it was trying to get to the other side to graze in the grassier, untouched field. The goat reached the middle of the bridge and, as I half expected, a huge troll appeared from under the bridge. There was some sort of discourse going on and I expected that the little goat would trot onwards and the next size of goat would follow. But no, the troll in one giant sweep of its arm grabbed the goat and pushed it into its huge, yawning chasm of a mouth.

'That's not right!' I exclaimed. 'That's the billy goats gruff and they outwit the troll.'

'Not every time,' said the fairy. 'Otherwise the troll would starve to death. Keep watching and it will start again.'

I waited for a good forty minutes before the cycle restarted. There were once again three billy goats in the field and this time, sure enough, the little goat did outwit the troll and the story progressed to the next stage. The troll ate the middle-sized billy goat. A further half hour went by before the cycle was repeated and the large billy goat gruff tossed the troll down the river.

*

The family relaxed during the remainder of the afternoon but Sienna fretted about the soldiers who would be returning soon. Mary told her not to worry so much.

'It might even be in our favour,' she said to Sienna. 'They are less likely to look for us when we are right under their noses.'

The soldiers, the team were told, did not normally return until eleven in the evening. Dr. Burns appeared at eight o'clock.

Joseph Burns was the local family doctor and he had worked solidly all day. His skills included obstetrics and some surgery and he would be going back to work after supper .... this later work would mostly be with the army.

'I don't know whether they are looking for you but they are definitely trying to find Jimmy,' he said when the family had told their story. 'The narrative they are putting out is that he is a research physicist and they need him to help in this crisis.'

'But that isn't true,' protested Sienna. 'He stopped doing physics years ago!'

'That's what I thought,' said Joseph. 'I've been wondering why they have put in so much effort to find him. It doesn't really make sense.'

'The werewolf told us that there is a merging of realities happening and that the creature commanding the faerie realm is the person who is really after Dad,' said Joshua.

'And you really think that the person was a werewolf?' asked Joseph. 'Are you sure that it isn't some kind of mass hysteria or delusion.'

The family protested that this could not be the case but it was Hannah who convinced the doctor.

'The rest of my colleagues on the rowing boats were killed by a sea monster, the werewolf saved us from a flaming devil and then changed from wolf to man and back again several times in front of our eyes before sacrificing itself to save us,' said Hanna, in a slightly exasperated manner. 'If this is hysteria it is affecting me the same way that it is affecting, Sienna, Mary and the boys. I've concluded that it is really happening.'

'OK,' replied the doctor, putting his hands up in submission. 'You've convinced me ..... and I have something to add to your story. Some of my patients today told me that they have seen the sea monster. They say it looks like the Loch Ness monster and today they said that it was being controlled by a man. I didn't know what to make of it but your story puts it in context.'

'What do we do about the soldiers billeted here. Won't they shop us to the authorities?'

'Not if I say you are my cousins from in the town,' said Dr. Joseph. 'And that your house has finally fallen down. Hannah will have to stay out of her uniform if she does not intend returning to the navy immediately.'

'According to Ard the werewolf, we have to get to the fairy bridge in just under a week's time,' said Mary. 'We were thinking of moving to Staffin from tomorrow.'

'Better if you stay here and I will take you to the fairy bridge when you need to be there,' answered the doctor. 'I am one of the only people allowed to move around, disobey the curfew and travel more than two miles from base.'

*

It was now late in the afternoon and we were nearing the fairy bridge which was to be our portal from the faerie realm to my own reality. The fairy who was accompanying us told us to keep walking along the road whilst she flew on ahead to scout out the land.

We did as she said and half an hour later she returned bearing bad news.

'Parsifal X has taken control of the fairy bridge. I got as close as I could disguised as a ladybird but I was almost swatted by a giant cyclops.'

Lady Aradel was very perturbed. 'The rest of your family will be coming here soon and they will be walking into a trap.'

'Can we get a message through to them some way?' I asked.

'I will try but my messenger has not reported back for some considerable time. I don't know what has happened to him.'

- Chapter 16 -

The soldiers billeted at the Burns' house did not return home until gone midnight by which time the Scotts and Hannah Lee had long gone to bed. Over the next five days Hannah and the Scott family got up late and went to bed early, keeping out of the way of the soldiers, who had been told that relatives from town were staying.

Charlotte and Joseph, were busy each day looking after Joseph's patients. The local hospital was full of people of all ages injured during the storms, earthquake and tsunami. The electrical power was inoperative until the fourth day when an intermittent supply recommenced for half of the town, including the Burns' house. More worrying to Dr. Burns was the fact that the water supply was also intermittent. This had ramifications for drinking and cleaning but also for sewage.

'There will be outbreaks of cholera if this is not sorted soon,' Joseph said over supper on the third night that they were staying. 'It spreads by the oro-faecal route. Poor sanitation is the cause of its spread. You just need one person to start it off and there will be an epidemic. I've heard rumours that it is already killing millions round the world.'

'What are the first signs that you've got it, Uncle Joseph?' asked Joshua.

'It can start with constipation but usually starts suddenly with profuse diarrhoea and vomiting,' answered the doctor.

'What does that mean, Uncle Joseph,' queried Sam.

'Having the runs and being sick, of course,' said Joshua before the doctor could reply.

Marvellous, thought Sienna. *Here we are eating our supper and all they can talk about is vomiting and diarrhoea. Typical medical conversation. Just like dear old Dad.*

'What happens next?' asked Joshua.

'Unless the patient is successfully treated they become dehydrated and die,' answered Dr. Burns. 'They may go a strange bluish-grey colour from the loss of fluids.'

'Can you treat it, Uncle Jo?' asked Joshua.

'As long as my medical supplies continue, yes. But when they are finished we will all be in trouble.'

'Is anybody sorting the situation out centrally now?' asked Hannah. 'What has happened to Brigadier Blenkinsop?'

'He is still in charge, so I've heard,' replied the doctor. 'But his orders are becoming very erratic and he will only let people see him occasionally.'

'Not a good way to run the country,' said Mary firmly. 'We need to get the proper government back in charge as soon as possible. Martial law is acceptable for only a very short time.'

Phew, thought Sienna, eating her food. *At least we have got off the subject of wayward guts.*

You're just a wimp, came the thought from her mother.

*

Lady Aradel and I had a hasty conference with the fairy. Overlooking the fairy bridge was a fairy castle that had not been occupied by the fire demigod's cyclopean guard. The plan was that we should set up a base and watch the bridge whilst Aradel tried to contact her agent in the real world.

The castle was made of a pale pink stone that looked suspiciously like icing sugar. In shape it was a sumptuous gothic construction with multiple castellations and pointed roofs. In the centre was a bright green dome. We were inspected by the fairy guard at the gatehouse and permitted to walk across the drawbridge and under the portcullis.

'What does it actually look like when the illusion is removed?'

I asked Lady Aradel.

'Try not to think about that. It may damage our protection,' replied Aradel and then added. 'But it is much like your Castell Coch in Wales.'

Whilst I sat eating more fairy food, with the occasional piece being snatched from my grasp as before, Lady Aradel was deep in thought. Eventually she looked up and smiled.

'Lord James, I have done my best to get the message through. It may not be enough. It is now up to my representatives in the real world.'

'Nobody can do better than their best,' I answered. 'And if a job is worth doing, it's worth doing badly.'

'Paraphrasing G.K. Chesterton in his wonderful book: What's Wrong with the World, published in 1910?' asked Lady Aradel.

'Really?' I was disappointed. 'I thought I had made that up based on the proverb if a job's worth doing it's worth doing well.'

Lady Aradel laughed. 'I've heard a lot of people claim that they made that up. But what about the opposite.... If a job's not worth doing it's only worth doing well ?'

I paused to think about that for a minute then asked for an example.

'Certainly,' replied Lady Aradel, 'Imagine that I had a beautiful cut glass vase. Would it be worth painting?'

'On it or of it?' I queried.

Lady Aradel shook her head with my obtuseness and her eyes flashed with a measure of annoyance or was it simply amusement?

'Painting on it,' she said. 'A picture. You doing a painting on it for instance.'

'No, I would only spoil it. It would not be worth doing.'

'And yet I saw Leonardo da Vinci paint the most exquisite portrait on a cut glass vase. So there was an example of a job that you agreed was not worth doing but because somebody else could do it really well it became a worthy project. So with that one example I can prove my statment.... If a job's not worth doing it's only worth doing well.'

I disagreed.

'That's only one example. It's not a universal truth.'

'I will reply with a paradox,' answered Lady Aradel. 'There are no universal truths.'

*

How the family would get to the fairy bridge had been a topic of discussion ever since they had arrived with the Burns. They had no idea what would happen when they got there and only had Ard's word that it was what they had to do. The werewolf had sacrificed himself in order that they could continue their quest which redoubled their certainty that it was, indeed, necessary to continue to the bridge and to do so on the correct date. As the doctor pointed out.... 'The times are very strange but in strange times you must do strange things.'

Walking was not going to be sensible as they would undoubtedly be stopped at some point. Eventually the family planned with the Burns that in the early morning of the seventh day of the team's stay the good doctor would smuggle the family into the garage. There he would load them into his huge 4 by 4 people mover. There was room for all the family and Hannah to hunker down between the seats with blankets over them. Mary was getting progressively more worried and said that she had very bad premonitions. However, Dr. Burns was certain that they would have no trouble at the checkpoints.

'They've not stopped me once,' he said confidently. 'They just wave me through. If we get up early enough it will be too dark for them to see anything even if they do take a glance.'

They arose at 5.00 am, a good hour and a half before dawn, and readied themselves for the trip. At 5.30 a.m. the doctor and the team were ready to move out. He kissed his wife and she whispered good luck in his ear. As they walked towards the back door there came a very insistent knocking at the front. The doctor peered out through a window and could see people in uniforms standing on the front step. He then ran through to the back. There were soldiers there also.

'Quick,' he said. 'Go back upstairs and get into bed. Undress and pretend to be asleep. Feigned innocence will be our best protection.'

'There's no other way out via a side door?' asked Mary, acutely aware of the problem.

'We can't get away,' said the doctor. 'We will have to let them in and try to talk our way out of this one.'

Hannah and the family fled upstairs. The knocking was becoming more insistent and Mary reckoned that it was only the respect that the doctor was held in that was stopping the soldiers from summarily breaking the door down.

Dr. Burns went to the front door and made a point of slowly opening it with the chain on. By this time the noise had woken the soldiers billeted in the house and they were coming down the stairs.

'What's the matter doc?' asked one of the more friendly soldiers, who, truth be known, had all enjoyed their time in the house.

'Don't know,' replied the doctor. 'I was just getting up to go out on an emergency visit.' As he said this the door was thrust very hard back towards his face and would have hit him but for the chain.

'Open this door at once,' came a very harsh voice. 'Or I shall order my soldiers to break the door down.'

'Hold on, hold on,' replied the doctor calmly. 'There's no panic.'

'There will be if you do not have the door open this instant,' came the reply.

'I need to shut it first in order to take the chain off,' replied Dr. Burns and the soldier reluctantly pulled his foot out of the way.

The friendly soldier was standing next to the doctor by now and looked at him, questioningly. Doctor Burns shrugged his shoulders expressively and swung the door back. A very bulky soldier wearing a red cap and sporting three chevrons marched in. Behind him came several soldiers in combat gear and at the back, apologetically, came a man in the naval uniform of a commodore.

'Hey,' shouted the friendly soldier. 'You can't just barge in on the doc like this!'

'Shut up,' replied the military police sergeant and back-swiped the soldier with his hand. The action was remarkably quick and the power deceptive. The friendly soldier was flung back against the wall and crumpled in a heap. The other soldiers billeted in the house pulled back in horror.

'Now, now, calm down,' the doctor spoke gently. 'There's no need for violence.'

'There will be more violence unless the fugitives are brought to me right away,' growled the ugly sergeant.

By now the soldiers in combat gear had moved into the front hall and had started to search downstairs.

'And which fugitives would that be?' asked Dr. Burns. 'I am not aware of any fugitives in this house.'

'Number one, a Lieutenant Hannah Lee,' replied the military policeman, he consulted his notebook. 'Seen entering this house one week ago. She is absent without leave.'

'I haven't gone AWOL,' said Hannah from the top of the stairs. 'I have been pursuing my duties using my own initiative.'

'Not what I have heard,' replied the red cap. 'Walk slowly down the stairs and stand up against the wall.'

Hannah reluctantly obeyed the bullying soldier who again consulted his notebook.

'Number two. The family of James Scott. Scott is wanted for action against the State and his family are implicated.'

'I thought that he was needed to help the Government's scientists with their theoretical physics problems,' said the doctor. 'That's what I heard and......'

Before he could finish his sentence the red cap backhanded the doctor. Joseph Burns slumped down bleeding from his mouth.

'Come on now, sergeant,' said the Commodore. 'That was definitely not called for. You have no right to treat civilians that way.'

'Shut it, captain, or you are next,' the sergeant growled. 'Now get the family down here.'

'There is no need for that sort of behaviour,' Mary's strong, powerful voice came from the top of the stairs. 'You must desist.'

The sergeant hesitated, pulled up by the power of command in the voice but then, more quietly replied.

'Come down here now, please.'

The family gingerly walked down the stairs. Mary came last.

'That's better, a bit calmer,' said Mary. She had her arms behind her back and appeared to be carrying something as she walked down towards the military policeman. The soldiers moved to one side as she walked past. This was clearly an encounter of significance but nobody wanted to get caught in the crossfire between the two powerful characters.

'Where is James Scott? Tell me now,' demanded the sergeant.

'We asked the emergency authorities to help us find him two weeks ago,' she replied. 'And now you ask us?'

'So you won't answer,' replied the sergeant. 'Well the first to die will be this deserter, followed by your daughter and then your grandchildren.'

The sergeant twisted round blindingly quickly, pulling out a large gun as he did so. He fired off two shots at Hannah before anybody could stop him. Almost simultaneously a hirsute figure, clad in army uniform, sprang between the sergeant and Hannah the navigator. The hirsute soldier took the bullets full in the chest and bright red arterial blood spurted out in profusion, splattering the horrified onlookers. Taking advantage of the distraction Mary brought the object she was carrying from behind her body. It was a jug containing fluid which she instantly hurled over the military policeman.

'Now go back to hell where you belong!' she screamed.

To the astonishment of everybody the sergeant screamed, clawed at his face and steam arose from his body.

'No,' he cried. 'Not again. No, no!'

His clothes started to smoulder and his eyes turned to flame but this faltered and the figure shrank and shrank, finally disappearing completely with a squeaky popping noise.

They turned to the bleeding soldier who was trying to get up. The doctor had recovered from his injury and told the man to lie down whilst he examined the wounds.

The hairy soldier whispered in his ear.

'Please tell everybody to turn round. I don't want them to see this.'

The doctor turned and addressed the throng.

'OK, you heard what he said. Give him a little space. Please turn round and don't look.'

He turned back just in time to observe the wounded man transform into a large lupine figure.... a huge wolf which initially lay in front of him, bleeding and panting but fairly quickly recovered. The wolf then underwent the opposite transformation back to a man and put his clothes back on.

'Ard!' screamed Samuel, running across and hugging him.

The werewolf was back.

It was clear that most of the soldiers were watching and a gasp of amazement was heard after an initial awed silence.

'Lieutenant Lee,' commanded the Commodore. 'Could you please tell me what is going on?'

'Certainly sir!' replied the navigator with alacrity. 'As you can see it is very complicated and I had no intention of being absent without leave. You sent me to go on watch and investigate any strange happenings and I have been doing so for the past week.'

The Commodore dismissed the soldiers, who were reluctant to leave but had to respond to the considerably higher rank of the navy man.

'Now I could do with a nice cup of tea whilst you give me a full report,' suggested the Commodore. 'And I need to hear everything.'

- Chapter 17 -

Lady Aradel was busy discussing the possible course of action with our accompanying fairy and a number of other unusual looking figures who had joined them. I was not party to the discussion and it was conducted in a language that I did not understand. I stood up from the table at which I had been sitting, eating my food. I nodded politely to the company, thanked the chef who had been standing in attendance and asked if they would mind me looking around the castle.

Aradel looked up from the discussion. 'Go ahead,' she agreed. 'But don't go outside the castle walls.'

I wandered around the great hall first. On the walls were paintings of previous occupants. I half expected that the people depicted would turn and stare back at me or move around. They had done that in the Magic School film I had recently seen but thinking about it I realised that, before the recent disasters, many posters on the London Underground had done that as well and that it was possible to work out who I was by using my smart phone and the pictures could personalise messages to me. Once again magic could be seen simply as science I did not understand.

'I think you are underestimating us,' said a large portrait. 'All paintings are part of reality and all reality is part of a whole. I am a painting but I also capture something of the pattern of the person I represent.'

'And is it magic that animates you?' I asked, aware of the fact that talking to a painting could have me locked up back in the real world. Or would it now, given that many people walked along apparently talking to themselves but actually in deep conversations via their cell phones? I was not sure.

'It is magic, yes indeed,' replied the painting. 'But stop looking so glum. You don't have to understand it all to use it. Nobody does understand it all. They can't. The all is far too large. So even to the cleverest person some of what happens has to look like magic.'

The very paintings were trying to cheer me up. There was something in what the portrait said. Much of my life I had imagined that there was somebody somewhere who did understand everything. The realisation that this was not the case had been partly instrumental in making me take up a job as an electrician rather than continue as a physicist and astronomer.

'Just try to enjoy yourself,' said a rather jolly looking portrait of a plump fairy.

'That's difficult to do when it all seems to be going wrong,' I replied grumpily.

'It's still worth trying, dear,' answered the picture.

I walked on past the talking paintings and stood looking at a large mirror in an ornate gilt frame. In a moment of mischievous fun I stood and asked the mirror the standard question.

'Mirror, mirror on the wall. Who is the fairest of them all?'

'Difficult,' replied the mirror. 'Could you be a bit more exact? Do you mean who has the blondest hair, who is the most attractive, who is the most..... ? '

'.... The most attractive, I suppose,' I answered.

'Male or female?'

'Female,'

'All species, human, pan-human?'

'Try human,'

'Tri-human, planet Zorg. Probable answer is mezcarto ß 2, given that she has mated with both the other sexes the most times and given birth to the greatest number of progeny.'

'No, I think you misunderstood me. I meant female human,' I tried to frame my question for the magic mirror more exactly.

'Who is the most attractive human female?'

'Of all time or just the present day?'

'All time?'

'Reputed to be Helen of Troy.'

'OK, now present day, living now.'

'Shabana Azmi.'

'Shabana Azmi? Who is she?'

'Bollywood actress, appeared in 120 Hindi films. Attracted more people to see her than any other actress therefore the most attractive,' replied the mirror.

'OK,' I sighed. 'Last attempt. Who is the most beautiful, adult, female, living human now.'

'That is much more difficult as history has not had a chance to make its mind up,' answered the mirror. The mirror raised its voice. 'You're still making up your mind on that one aren't you, history?'

A ghostly voice wafted back.

'Not yet decided.'

'Is that the best you can do?' I asked the mirror.

'On the same subject or on any subject?' asked the mirror.

I did not reply and the mirror continued.

'For example I can do a lot better on simple factual problems. Such as the distance from here to the nearest of the twin moons or the age of the sun.'

'Not interested,' I said. 'What about predicting the future. Can you do that?'

'Sometimes,' the mirror was rather petulant. 'If the question is posed correctly.'

'OK,' I said, thinking hard about a question that might be useful. 'Can I cross the Skye fairy bridge safely?'

'Yes,' answered the mirror instantly.

'When and how?'

'When it is too late after the cyclops guards have gone.'

'Is there any way I can cross it now and not be caught?'

'No,' came the reply from the mirror.

At last! I thought *Useful information. This fairy bridge is not the answer. We will have to go somewhere else.*

I thanked the mirror and walked quickly back the way I had come until I reached the enclave of various fairies, elves and Lady Aradel who were still in consultation together.

'I know what you are going to say,' said Aradel as I neared them. 'The mirror has told you that the fairy bridge is closed to you and that you must go elsewhere.'

I nodded in agreement.

'We are presently discussing how you will do that. Most possibilities are unpalatable but we have reached a decision....'

I looked at her questioningly.

'....We shall go South,' she continued. 'We will have to travel over the southern mountains.'

'The active volcanoes?' I questioned in alarm.

'It is not the volcanoes that are the main problem. We can, mostly, avoid them,' she paused and I waited to hear the bad news. 'No. It is the dragons.'

'Dragons?' this place never ceased to amaze me. 'There really are dragons?'

'There are poisonous dragons in your world,' Lady Aradel pointed out.

'Yes, Komodo dragons,' I agreed. 'But not mythical, fire-breathing, winged, flying dragons.'

'Well there are such dragons here,' she answered, 'And they live in the southern mountains.'

*

Hannah had almost completed her report to the Commodore. He had sat listening intently to his lieutenant's story, only interrupting occasionally to ask her to elucidate a point or expand on her narrative.

'....And then you appeared, sir, with the military police and you know the rest.'

'Amazing story but I've seen much of it with my own eyes now,' replied the Commodore. 'I'm very sorry about the way that red cap behaved. He was completely out of order.'

'It wasn't really him, sir.'

'No?'

'It was like the engineer, sir. He had been taken over by a fire god's avatar. Or something like that. Ard could tell us.'

'I'd like to speak to that young man myself,' said the Commodore. 'As a naval man the Nessie bit intrigues me most. How did the werewolf get away?'

'I don't know, sir, but if he hadn't I wouldn't be here now,' Hannah looked over to Ard as she said this.

'We should ask him,' said the Commodore. 'If he doesn't mind, of course.'

Ard looked up and caught Hannah looking at him. He came padding over. In the soldier's uniform he could pass as any other human being .... except for his excessive hairiness.

'Can I help you, Hannah?' he asked.

'I am eternally grateful to you,' replied Hannah with a surprisingly coy smile. 'You saved my life and endangered your own.'

'I don't think I was in any danger, as such,' Ard shook his head. 'No. The sergeant didn't have silver bullets and I am a magical creature. It did hurt, mind you. Really hurt.'

Hannah grabbed the hairy man and gave him a big kiss and a hug.

'Thanks,' she said and hugged him again.

The werewolf pulled back in embarrassment.

'I've a vixen and five cubs in Faerie,' he explained. 'She would be very jealous.'

The Commodore cleared his throat.

'Ahem. We were wondering how you escaped from the sea

monster. Would you be so kind as to tell us? If it's not too much bother, of course.'

The Commodore was obviously rather wary of the werewolf but was very keen to hear Ard's version of events.

'Certainly sir, no problem at all,' Ard said this politely in his incongruously posh accent. 'You have heard that I met the family over on the new island?'

The Commodore nodded his agreement and Ard continued.

'I had been sent from the Faerie kingdom to protect the family of Lord James Scott and to deliver a message. We escaped from the island but had to find a way around the soldiers without alerting them. I decided that the only thing to do was to create a diversion by drawing the attention of the sea monster that has recently been living in the loch.'

'What sort of monster is it?' asked the Commodore.

'It is a plesiosaur,' replied Ard, still speaking beautifully but with the occasional hint of a growl or a howl. 'It was displaced into this world when the most powerful being in Faerie, Parsifal X, moved a mass of water during the attempted combining of our two realms. The monster is about twenty to thirty meters in length with a large body, shortish tail, four large flippers and a large head on the end of a long neck. It has jaws as big as the largest crocodile.'

The audience listened agog as Ard continued.

'I swam out in my lupine form and attracted its attention by thrashing around, barking and how, how, howling. I soon saw the bow wave created by its huge head as it swam in my direction. I then tried to swim away but it caught hold of the bag of clothes I had around my neck. It dragged me under and the only way I could escape was to change back into my human form. That form, incidentally, is much more vulnerable and does not heal as well as the wolf shape which is why you saw me change into my lupine form after I had been shot.'

The people crowded into the Burns' house were listening very attentively as the werewolf continued his story.

'When I changed I was slimmer and smaller and therefore able to slip out of the monster's grasp. The creature was so startled by my change in appearance that I was able to frighten it away by screaming at it and splashing my hands.

From then on it was simple. I swam under water for a while and then emerged on the shore. I found a soldier's uniform in a house and I have been watching the good doctor's residence ever since. When the military police arrived I mingled with the crowd of soldiers and came into the house. I was too slow to stop the red cap shooting at Hannah ...... I had not realised that he was another avatar for Parsifal X ... but I was able to juxtaposition myself between the sergeant and Hannah. You know the rest.'

'You make it seem all so easy,' the Commodore was impressed with the tale. 'But you are an amazing hero. Well done soldier... err...I mean werewolf.'

The Commodore clapped Ard on the back and the werewolf almost purred with pleasure before sitting up straighter and speaking again.

'....And please do not go to the fairy bridge. It is in the hands of hostile forces and Lord James will not be coming through that way.'

'Then what should we do, Ard?' asked Sienna

'We have to go to the Isle of Man. There is a fairy bridge there that also acts as a portal between the two realms. Lord James may be able to make the crossing there.'

'How can we do that?' asked Mary. 'There are major restrictions on travel. We can't just pop on an aeroplane.'

The Commodore stood up and shook his uniform straight. 'I would be delighted to take you, if you don't mind confined spaces.'

'I thought the submarine was not working. Has it been

mended?' asked Joshua.

'You are right, young man,' the Commodore nodded again. 'But we do have diesel submarines and I am in charge of them also. We will take you in a diesel sub.'

'By the way mother, since we are clearing up mysteries what was in the jug? What was the fluid you threw over the sergeant?' Sienna asked Mary.

'It was only water. Why what did you think it was?'

There was an embarrassed hush from all of the family.

- Chapter 18 -

We took our leave of the guardian fairy at the edge of their kingdom. We would be initially crossing the territory of the wood elves who had sworn allegiance to Lady Aradel. Then, my beautiful rat-elf told me, would come a testing section of mental swamp. Quite what she meant by that I had no idea. This led to the foothills of the southern mountain range and the home of the dragons. This was the section that had perturbed Lady Aradel.

'Dragons,' she informed me. 'Are beautiful and capricious. Powerful and easily provoked. They swear allegiance to no-one.'

'Some of that could apply to you,' I riposted.

Her eyes flashed.

'These creatures could be our undoing. I lived with them at one time and their minds are huge. Their intelligence is greater than any humanoid and they exist for thousands of years. But they have no ambition except, like a magpie, to collect pretty things and sleep in their warm caverns under the mountain. They hate being disturbed.'

We set off at dusk. We would be staying in the wood elf princedom overnight and Lady Aradel led the way with a jolly swing of her arms.

'The matriarch of the house we are coming to will be very pleased to see us. Her husband is an old friend of mine and he has a large happy family. He is away at the moment but I can bring her news.'

'They are wood elves?' I asked.

'Wait and see,' she replied.

The forest started off much like any other I had seen but as the dusk deepened I began to notice strange murmurings. The trees grew taller and taller and I started to stumble over roots and shrubbery. Low branches felt as if they were purposely brushing against me.... not to hurt, perhaps, but to see what kind of creature I was. Lady Aradel was having no trouble walking in the dark but I could not even see the path I was trying to follow.

I looked up from one particularly painful stumble and found that Aradel, lost in her own happy thoughts, had left me behind. I could see no further than a few inches in front of me. Looking up there was still some light in the sky but underfoot was impenetrable blackness.

Around me the murmurings had become progressively louder and more menacing. This was supposed to be a friendly forest but I was lost and had no idea which way to go. In the distance, then getting closer, I could hear the howling of wolves. I stumbled forward and found that I was in a clearing. Suddenly I could detect eyes staring at me from all around, twin moonlight glistening from six pairs of eyes. Huge grey shapes were closing in on me.

No point trying to run, I thought. *They can easily outrun me and I have no idea where I am supposed to be going.*

So I sat down on a log.

'Hello doggies,' I said in a lighthearted way, picking up a small branch and throwing it over the head of the nearest wolf. 'Go on, fetch it for me. That's a good boy.'

The wolf, the biggest of the pack, came in closer and a deep growl emanated from its jaws.

I reckon I made a tactical error, I thought. *Perhaps they don't like being called dogs?....*

....You are right there, Lady Aradel's reply cut in on my thoughts. The elf was clearly not far away and had been observing my progress. *You'd better apologise or we may be in for a rough night.*

'Sorry about that,' I said standing up and addressing the wolf. Apologies were something I had never had difficulty in producing

... I had plenty of experience. Being a bit of a maverick and trying to keep my own business going meant that whenever anything went wrong, whether I was to blame or not, I found it easiest to accept the liability. 'In this gloom I can't see very well but now I am able to perceive that you are a very noble wolf.

....Werewolf, you idiot.

'Thank you Lady Aradel. A very excellent and handsome werewolf. I am delighted to make your acquaintance.'

The animal was much mollified by my comments and six wolf noses came up close to sniff around and over me. Satisfied they led me towards a hollow at the base of a giant redwood tree. I followed towards their den just a little cautiously.

...Are you really sure this is a good idea? I asked Lady Aradel telepathically.

....Of course, these are my friends. We are staying with them for the night.

I looked at the tiny entrance into the hollow of the tree. If I crawled in there would I ever be able to crawl out? I wondered how the huge wolf could get in there. The largest wolf was bigger than a pony and smaller ones were the size of wolfhounds. The largest led the way, scrambling down into the den, followed by the others.

'Get in there!' commanded Lady Aradel to me, out loud. 'I'll bring up the rear.'

'Are you really, really sure?' I asked again.

'Do it, don't hang around,' came the reply.

I got down onto all fours and put my head into the hole. Instead of being a dark tunnel the inside of the den was spacious and light. I was able to pull myself in and sit comfortably on some sheepskins on the floor. Lady Aradel followed me and the largest wolf pulled another sheepskin over the entrance.

'How is the place lit?' I asked Aradel.

'Look more closely and you will be able to tell,' she replied tersely. Since we had left the fairy kingdom her mood had perceptibly changed. I wondered what could have made her so tetchy.

Lady Aradel stood up and moved away from me in a huff......

I am not moody, came her telepathic reply interrupting my thoughts.

Sorry, I thought. *My mistake.*

YES IT WAS, she almost screamed at me in her thoughts. *And the room is lit by fireflies as anyone with half a mind could have seen.*

I looked closely at the lights which had gathered together on branches which had been positioned across the main room of the den. Lady Aradel was quite right. They were fireflies. Larger than any I had ever seen before but definitely fireflies. I sat quietly feeling rather forlorn and sorry for myself... something I had always tried to avoid being.

Lady Aradel came back and sat down beside me again.

'I'm sorry I was so irritable,' she said. 'It is not your fault and they are very large fireflies.'

'What is the problem, Aradel?' I asked. 'Perhaps I can help?'

'You are helping and you have been very uncomplaining,' she answered. 'I am worried about the dragons but I have an even greater premonition that something is about to go very wrong but I do not know what it is. Still, we should be safe tonight. Parsifal X has never penetrated the wood elves mental barriers and this den is secure so we should make an early night of it and then move on with the dawn.'

Whilst we had been chatting the werewolves had moved into another room. From that room emerged a tall, handsome woman, three boys and two girls, ranging in age from ten to about fifteen. They were clad in furs but I got the distinct impression that they did not usually wear anything when in their human form. They all had very shaggy hair on their heads. The boys were extremely hirsute but the woman and the girls had beautiful smooth skin with no facial hair.

'Welcome to our forest den,' said the woman in a distinctly distinguished and educated accent. 'I am proud to present my three sons and my daughter.'

I stood up and bowed to the lady.

'I am honoured to be here as your guest,' I said taking her hand and kissing it. 'This is a most delightful residence.'

I found that I really meant it. What was there to dislike? It was clean, dry, warm, slight doggy smell but not too bad and, with the sheep skins covering the floor, very comfortable.

'Peter will show you the facilities,' said the lady werewolf. 'But first I will introduce you. Here are Era, Cinder, Arth, Jangle and Peter. ... and my name is Celestia.'

I bowed to all of them. Peter, the youngest, came over and quietly suggested that I might like to know where they did their ablutions. He led me outside the den by a different route and to a small turf hut.

We came back into the den and Celestia poured mead into fine glasses. Lady Aradel, Celestia and I toasted the success of our venture and Aradel then told Celestia that her husband, Lord Ardolf Mingan, was safe but they did not expect to see him again until we reached the Isle of Man. She also told Celestia that she had a very bad feeling about the night and that a guard needed to be put at the door all night.

'But Aradel,' Celestia replied with a slight smile. 'We have never had trouble here. In the winter den, yes, but that is out in the wild lands. Here, it has always been peaceful. We are very friendly with the wood elves.'

'I know,' replied Aradel. 'But times are changing and I fear that I have brought danger to your door.'

'We are magical creatures and we do not fear for ourselves,' replied Celestia.

'Nevertheless, I fear for you,' answered Aradel.

*

'It is nearing midnight,' intoned Parsifal X. 'Is everything ready for the summoning of the lord of the far realm?'

'Nearly,' replied the gnome seer. 'But the far lord did not want goats sacrificed this time.'

'Well, that saves us some trouble,' replied X.

'Not really,' whispered the gnome. 'He has asked for two dwarves. They must be sacrificed exactly on the stroke of midnight.'

'Do it then,' replied Parsifal. 'Little bearded monsters. Why should I care? There are far too many of them anyway.'

'I would rather not sacrifice dwarves,' said the gnome. 'They are humanoid sentient creatures.'

'Barely sentient, I would say,' said the fire demigod. 'And they are far too ugly. Do it or I will sacrifice you!'

The gnome scurried off accompanied by several large cyclopean guards.

- Chapter 19 -

At the stroke of midnight in the Port of the King in the Faerie Realm two huge, ugly cyclops brought down steel swords onto the necks of a pair of innocent dwarf victims. The dwarves died almost instantly and their blood ran into the pentangle that had been marked on the ground by the gnome seer.

The gnome was, himself, hiding behind a rock, trembling with fear. His last encounters with the Lord of the Far Realm had left him exhausted and extremely anxious. The more he thought about it the more fearful he became. He had certainly not wanted to see any dwarves sacrificed ... they were, after all, nearly his cousins. However, he could not stop Parsifal X and the die was cast. He had to follow this through to the end game. Anything else would be fatal.

Parsifal X was lounging to one side of the room waiting for the Far Lord to materialise. He did not have to wait very long. A long sighing sound, like the last breath of a dying man, filled the room followed by a horrific discord. An acrid smell of brimstone filled the room and smoke appeared within the pentangle. A writhing dark figure was gradually appearing .... two cloven hooves, the tail of a dragon, a hairy body, a goat's head. Then this monstrosity disappeared and a tall, sinister looking man stood there, clothed in a white dinner jacket and white trousers. He was wearing a crimson red shirt and a diamond bow-tie. His hair was jet black and around his temple the hair flicked up on either side giving a semblance of two horns. His feet were clad in cowboy boots but incongruously smoke was still emanating from around his ankles. Despite the human clothing the man gave off a palpable air of evil.

'How do you do?' said the Far Lord.

'Well, thank you,' replied Parsifal X, not at all put out by the somewhat unusual appearance of his guest. After all, he could do similar things himself.

'To what do I owe this summons?' asked the tall sinister figure.

'Not so much of a summons as a request, really,' replied X. 'I need help finding something I have lost, a nothing really, just a man who was my prisoner.'

'I was under the impression that rather more was at stake,' said the dark-haired sinister man. 'The merging of realities and the selling of immortal souls. If that is not the case my time has been wasted and I shall go.' The creature started to fade.

'Stop, stop. You are right. We are merging realities and we need your help,' shouted Parsifal X, worried that they would have to wait for another twenty four hours or more before they could talk again.

The white clad figure solidified.

'That's better,' he said. 'Maybe we can do a deal.'

The fire demigod outlined what he wished to do with the realities and how the Eternal Realm, or the far realm as he described it, was preventing the full integration of the worlds.

'I do see that there are opportunities for myself in this,' said the white clad figure. 'So I shall help you find this individual. I shall also help you to avenge your loss of avatars and will assist in the integration of the realities. In return I will require your soul and that of two innocents. It will become apparent to you exactly who the innocents are but you must find them.'

Parsifal X had already lived for thousands and thousands of years. He knew he had no hidden inner soul and he was therefore happy to accept the first part of the bargain.

'I would like the two innocents to be the two members of the family who have thwarted me and assisted in killing my avatars,' stated X. 'We could work together on this since you have agreed to avenge the loss of my avatars.'

'You have chosen well. They are the innocent human beings I require. We will work together,' said the figure in the pentangle. 'We have a contract.'

The figure stretched out two long arms and slashed his left palm with the sharp nails of his right. Brimstone and lava bubbled out in place of blood. Parsifal X was at a loss as to what he should do next and looked round for assistance from his gnome seer. The little soothsayer peered out from behind his rock.

'You should do the same with your left hand and clasp his hand in a handshake,' the gnome instructed Parsifal X, his voice hoarse with fear as he did so.

'Certainly,' said Parsifal, thinking that all this theatrical behaviour was of no significance.

He stretched out his own left hand, pierced it with a dagger held in his right fist and allowed white hot plasma to burst out from the wound.

The demigod and the white clad figure clasped their hands together.

'Before I let go I need to know your name,' said X, grasping the creature in a cosmic powered grip.

'That is no problem,' replied the creature, slipping away with deceptive ease. 'Some knew me as Loki, others as the Serpent. Others the Adversary, the Slanderer, Shaytan, Satan, Beelzebub, Old Scratch, Old Nick and the Devil. But I prefer Lucifer. Me nombre es Lucifer. Lucifer. Lucifer. Je m'appelle Lucifer. I AM LUCIFER!'

The figure expanded to fill the whole room laughing in a louder and louder multi-timbral voice until the noise made the gnome's entire body ring with pain. Then Lucifer had gone.

Parsifal X stood looking at this spectacle. 'Quite an actor, that one,' said X. 'But will he actually deliver?'

Running into the room came one of the cyclopean guard.

'Sire,' he shouted. 'A strange mark has appeared on the map. It is a burning configuration of the man who was our prisoner.'

'Really?' said X. 'Maybe he isn't just hot air. Interesting.'

He walked into the next room where four huge maps covered the walls. On one of the maps there was indeed a writhing, burning image of the man X knew from his avatars' reports was called James Scott.

'So he is staying in the forests of the wood elves in the company of werewolves,' Parsifal X examined the map. 'The wood elves have frustrated my plans for too long. It is time I destroyed their haven and recaptured this man. He has the secret of the Nemesis Key and he will reveal it to me. And then he shall die.'

*

Midnight, deep in the forest and Lady Aradel sat up with a start. We had been sleeping for about two hours, snug on a sheepskin rug, curled up together like two spoons in the cutlery drawer. I woke up, bleary eyed.

'It's not dawn already, is it?' I asked.

Lady Aradel did not answer. I looked at her. She was wild-eyed and distraught. She climbed up from the mat and looked around her.

'A great evil has come to our land,' she muttered. 'An evil so great that even the stone cries out against its presence. I have felt its fleeting touch before but never so strongly.'

'Could it really be worse than Parsifal X?' asked Celestia, who had now also stood up.

'The devil we know?' queried Lady Aradel. 'Yes. this is worse. This is the devil we don't know and should never have to know.'

'What should we do?' asked Celestia.

'Run,' replied Aradel. 'This evil has told Parsifal X where we are and we must all flee. They will be here very soon and we are not safe, you are not safe. The wood elves and the very trees are not safe. We must all flee.'

'The trees cannot flee and the wood elves will stay to protect them. We shall stay to help the wood elves,' stated Celestia.

'Then we shall all die and the quest will be in vain. The realities will merge catastrophically and the greater evil will walk the Earth,' Aradel replied.

'You must flee but we will not flee with you,' answered the vixen werewolf. 'We do not fear Parsifal X. We are creatures of magic.' She crouched down and changed into her huge wolf shape, ran over to the entrance and put her head outside. She sniffed the air and returned.

'Yes,' she said. 'They are almost here. I can smell the guards and the monster X. I can even smell the little gnome who is always with him. You must go. Peter will lead you by a safe route whilst we fight to prevent your capture and to protect the forest. Now we must warn the forest folk.'

Peter was already in his wolf shape, having slept that way, so we followed him out into the forest clearing. The other wolves joined in a circle as we were led away and I just got a glimpse of them all sitting with their heads up on extended necks. A heart wrenching howl came up from their mother and all of the others joined in. Peter half turned back to join them and then, remembering his mother's instructions, reluctantly led us away from the clearing, away from the den and away from his family pack.

*

Ardolf Mingan, the werewolf, awoke with a jolt. They had all been sitting, waiting for news from the Commodore regarding the diesel submarine. Ard had fallen asleep after telling his story and, apart from the odd hypnic jerk and occasional snores he had remained unmoved for ninety minutes. Now he was wide awake.

'My vixen calls me,' cried Ard. 'She needs me and so does my Queen, the Lady Aradel. I must go and help them.'

'How can you do that?' asked Joshua, who was sitting next to the werewolf.

'I must go to the bridge and pass through to Faerie,' replied the werewolf.

'Then I shall take you to the fairy bridge as we originally planned,' said Dr. Joseph Burns. 'If they stop me you will be in your uniform and they are looking for the Scott family, not for you.'

'We must go right away,' the werewolf was already at the door as he said this. 'Speed is essential.'

- Chapter 20 -

In the light of the twin moons Peter led us south via a difficult but passable route. Lady Aradel did not know the path we were taking and I, of course, had no clue. As the forest thinned it became clear that Parsifal X had ringed the wood with troops. We looked down the slopes into the top of a valley. Lady Aradel and Peter had better eyesight than me and could see considerable detail whilst I was just about able to discern the movement of soldiers.

'The enemy's forces are impressive,' said Aradel after staring for some time. 'I have made a rough count of just the soldiers I can see. There are about three thousand just below us and roughly similar numbers visible to the south west and south east. Since the forest covers many, many square miles we have to assume that he has mobilised an army that numbers in the hundreds of thousands.'

'Are they all men?' I asked, curious about what we would be facing.

'Some men, mercenaries from the East. But no, there are many different humanoids and other creatures,' she replied.

The young werewolf, in his lupine form, growled softly to Lady Aradel but I was unable to catch the meaning.

'Peter has pointed out that along with the usual cyclops, goblins, trolls and hobgoblins there are several wyverns, a harpy or two and possibly a few griffins,' Aradel explained.

'I don't really know what they are,' I admitted self-consciously.

Aradel looked round to me, her eyes widening. 'No, I don't suppose you do,' she smiled wryly and continued. 'Wyverns are not much to worry about. They are small dragons but..'

'He's mobilised dragons?' I was alarmed.

'Small stunted things. Nothing to worry about. Look,' she pointed down the slope to a creature moving down in the valley. 'You can see one.'

I looked down at the so-called stunted dragon. It was more than three times as large as the men who were directing it. It had huge jaws and I was convinced that I saw fire belching from its mouth. If this was a stunted dragon what were the real things like?

'Wyverns can hardly fly at all,' added Aradel scornfully. 'That they can be herded by those men with pikes proves that they are no real danger... and look.'

I peered in the direction she pointed.

'That is a harpy!'

The harpy turned out to be an ugly winged bird-woman. Perhaps it was one of those that I had seen flying overhead when I first reached the cottage in Skye?

Peter growled again.

'He's asked me to tell you about the griffins,' said Aradel, still peering down into the valley. 'Yes, I can see one now. Look over there.'

I looked in the direction that she was pointing. I saw a monstrous beast with the body, tail and back legs of a huge lion, the head and wings of an eagle and raptor's talons on its front legs. It seemed to be directing operations around it and was herding what appeared to be hairy elephants.

'It looks formidable. Is it an intelligent beast?' I asked.

'Highly intelligent and considered by some as the king of the beasts,' she sniffed at the idea. 'Nowhere near as impressive as a true dragon but definitely dangerous. One of the few creatures that can best a werewolf in a straight fight.'

Peter growled a reply and Lady Aradel qualified what she had said. 'No. Peter is right. They couldn't beat a werewolf in a fair fight but they rarely fight fairly.'

The young werewolf growled again and led us back into the woods.

'Peter says that he knows a cave leading to a tunnel which could possibly take us under the hostile forces. It depends on whether or not they have found the entrance which is deep in the valley,' translated Aradel and Peter growled a reply.

Lady Aradel listened and then translated once more.

'He tells me that the entrance is well hidden but it is close to the back of their encampment. We should go there straight away as we may be discovered any minute.'

The sounds of soldiers working their way through the undergrowth were progressively getting closer. They were right ... we could not afford to delay.

*

Celestia howled and barked her orders to the other four werewolves. The wood elves had already been alerted and the haunting tones of their cries echoed through the woods. Shorter and slimmer than the high elves, their cousins, the wood elves were reputed to be descended from a satyr/elf interbreeding a short time after the separation of realities. They had pointed ears like the high elves and small horns on their foreheads. Renowned for their woodworking skills and their mental powers, they had a strong hatred of any form of slavery and an equally strong love of the forests. Every tree in the forest had an individual name and the elves were able to communicate with them.

As the alarm spread more wolves and werewolves joined the throng and all the forest creatures that were capable of putting up a fight joined in a long line against the oppressors.

Parsifal X had mobilised a huge army. Part of this army had been drafted in from neighbouring areas but a huge part came from caverns deep in the planet's crust where X had sequestered them in a form of suspended animation, maintained by magical incantations and Parsifal's continuing draw of power from the centre of the dying sun. This half-existence was not a happy one. The creatures were aware of the passage of time but could do nothing except wait. Many had gone completely mad longing for the day of action and were now being herded along like animals by their companions. The remainder wanted to show how resourceful, how courageous and how strong they were in order that they would be kept alive on the surface and not returned to the purgatory of a half-life or just snuffed out when their usefulness had ended.

They marched into the forest, thousands upon thousands. Under the direction of hobgoblins and griffins the giant mammoths tore down trees and established broad roads through the woods. Trees that had stood for millennia were ripped from the soil and crashed to the ground. Beautiful avenues of tall, slender elm, copses of ash, spreading oak trees and majestic pines all fell to the invaders. The larger and more perfect logs were being carried back to make giant siege machines for storming the castles in the fairy and elf kingdoms

The forest dwellers fought the malicious army at the front of this onslaught but were no match for the sheer numbers and constantly fell back. As they moved forwards the soldiers carefully burnt all the undergrowth and smaller trees. Total devastation moved through the forest.

Near the back of the advancing forces Parsifal X was sitting in a carriage being pulled along by a team of six legged horses. He had the ability to float through the air under his own volition or to manifest himself wherever he wished but he had become used to this particular humanoid incorporation and enjoyed the physical sensations that went with it. In his pure energy form he found that his desires became dry, aesthetic and somewhat tedious. He had become addicted to the visceral sensations of a body, the admiring attention of men and women, the envy, the spite, the glory of combat and even the pain of loss. Most of all he enjoyed the satisfaction of sadism and cruelty. So he stayed in the bodily form as much as possible. He was directing operations at an easily maintained distance from which he could see the progression of battle. He could tell it was going well. The forest area was being rapidly diminished and the wood elves were falling like chaff in a threshing mill. He had not yet caught James Scott or the meddling elf, Lady Aradel, but it would not be long. They could not escape his encroaching grasp. Of that he was convinced

*

'I'll take you to the fairy bridge,' said the good doctor to the werewolf. 'Perhaps if they stop us your soldier's uniform will get us through.' Dr. Burns was no longer as self assured as he had been. The raid by the military police had dented his confidence in a way that dealing with a military government whilst caring for hundreds of crush injuries and exposure victims had not. Everybody up until now had been respectful to him but today he had been hit in the face... something that had not happened to him since playing rugby at school

'Probably better if he went in his wolf form. You could pretend that he is your guard dog,' suggested Mary. There was a slight growl from Ard.

'Yes,' added Mary. 'I know that you hate being called a dog but we have to get you there, OK?'

'You are right,' replied the werewolf, sanguinely. 'I was allowing old prejudices to colour my instant reaction. If we are going to do it we should go all the way. I'll need a collar, a lead and a stupid dog name. Shane or Rover would do fine.'

Ard transmogrified into his lupine form and the doctor rummaged in the garage to find a collar from his old, long dead, German Shepherd Dog. A new hole had to be made near the end of the leather due to the thickness of Ard's enormously powerful neck. A lead was also discovered and attached to the collar.

'I think Ivan would do as a name. It sounds powerful enough,' suggested the doctor, Ard barked his consent. '...And we better practice a few tricks. Sitting on command, rolling over to have your tummy tickled and begging for a biscuit.'

Ard growled in reply. Mary translated.

'He is happy to sit and to roll over but he will not beg.'

'Two out of three will do fine,' laughed the doctor. 'Come on Ivan. We've got to get to that fairy bridge.'

*

I followed Peter and Aradel as they silently moved through the forest edge, keeping always away from the soldiers. When I was a child I had enjoyed outdoor games that involved creeping up on a base or listening for others doing the same. I had always been proud of my ability to move quietly but now I found that I sounded like an elephant. Every twig that broke put my mind into panic and I was afraid that I would betray our position. Eventually Lady Aradel picked up my thoughts and replied.

It is in your mind, Lord James, you need to believe that you are moving silently and then you will be.

From then on I found that I could indeed move noiselessly.

There were no guards at the entrance to the cave and we hurried inside. I have never liked confined spaces. I am a man for the open air or large airy rooms and even elevators make me feel uneasy. Crawling through loft spaces in my job as an electrician had reduced my level of unease but I never enjoyed it. Nothing had prepared me for the tunnel we now entered.

The entrance cave was fine enough, I had to dip my head to avoid hitting the roof but initially there was light from outside. The tunnel was off to one side of the cave behind a rock and in complete darkness. As in the forest the night before Lady Aradel did not appear to have any difficulty with the darkness. Peter the werewolf was not worried at all. In his wolf form he was happy to go anywhere just using his nose as a guide.

I was a twenty-seventh generation descendant of an elf and my eyesight may be better than most human beings but not by much. After some time of blindly feeling around with my hands Lady Aradel once more took pity on me and whispered a few words of incantation. Hovering in front of me appeared a steady, glowing light that showed me the entrance to the tunnel.

'Fireflies?' I asked.

'You are right,' replied Aradel quietly. 'You are learning. I invited them to join us and now they will guide you through the tunnel.'

I got down on to all fours and put my head into an entrance that was no bigger than the one into the werewolf's den the previous night. This time there was no welcoming room on the other side. The tunnel continued into the rock for an indeterminable distance and I was going to be lucky if I could crawl through it ... just a few yards on I could see that I would be obliged to wriggle through on my stomach under a giant slab of rock. Above this countless tons of rock were pressing down and it would only need a small, directed shudder of the already unstable planetary crust and the whole caboodle would collapse, crushing Peter, Lady Aradel and myself. I was not feeling happy.

- Chapter 21 -

The most direct route to the fairy bridge was back through town and out the other side. This would have entailed passing through two road blocks, something Dr. Burns would happily have done the day before but which he now realised posed a definite threat. So he slipped the car out of the garage with Ard in the back, lying on a rug, and he turned northwards to Staffin. They would be taking the much longer coastal route around the Trotternish peninsula before reaching the bridge at the southern part of the Waternish.

Very soon the road became single track. Despite the devastation that the earthquake had wrought on the human habitation the scenery was still spectacularly beautiful. On the left they could see huge cliffs and the jutting finger of the Old Man of Storr. They passed a fallen road sign which had pointed to the right to the Kilt Rock and its waterfall. As they drove Joseph contemplated what had been happening. Here they were in a still beautiful world but cataclysmic events had destroyed whole cities and killed millions, if not billions of people. They drove through Staffin where most of the house, white painted with grey roofs, appeared intact. A little further North, they rattled over a cattle grid and had to stop at a checkpoint.

At the barrier soldiers came out from their shelter to question him. Dr. Burns leapt out and opened the back of the vehicle. He took the lead and attached it to the werewolf's collar. Ard jumped down onto the ground and Joseph closed the 4 by 4. By this time a couple of soldiers had arrived cradling rifles in their arms.

'There is a two mile restriction on travel,' barked the soldier, a non-commissioned officer. 'This road is closed and nobody is permitted to travel along it so explain why you are here.'

'There's a problem with the road is there?' asked Joseph. 'Damn, that's a nuisance.'

'There's no problem with the road. Did you not hear me?' barked the officious man. 'Nobody is permitted to travel along it.'

'Well I'm the local doctor and I think you'll find that I am the exception that proves the rule,' replied Joseph with a smile, ruffling in his pocket. Ard meanwhile had cocked his leg and urinated close to the soldier's foot.

The soldier backed away swearing at the werewolf.

'Bloody dogs, always peeing everywhere.'

Joseph brought out a letter signed by the local commanding officer stating that Dr Burns, the bearer of the letter, had permission to travel on medical business.

The NCO studied the letter suspiciously.

'Tell me how I know that you are the doctor and that you haven't stolen this from someone?'

'I've got my credit cards and driving licence on me,' replied Joseph, still smiling.

He turned to Ard who was straining at his leash.

'Sit, that's a good boy.' Ard sat down and Joseph patted him on his chest. 'Good dog. That's a good doggie.'

Ard wagged his tail vigorously.

'I hate bloody dogs,' said the soldier. 'That's a huge one. What sort is he?'

'Wolfhound,' answered Joseph. 'He's as good as gold. Very well trained. Soppy really, loves his tummy being tickled.'

The doctor patted Ard.

'Come on Ivan,' he said. 'Roll on your back!'

Ard the werewolf instantly rolled onto his back and Joseph tickled his abdomen. The soldier sniffed disdainfully, glancing at the driving licence as he did so.

'This is just the paper licence. Don't you have photo ID?'

'Not on me,' replied Dr. Burns cursing himself for not bringing his passport.... but then who would have thought you would need your passport to drive beyond Staffin? 'Have you got any locals with you, they'd recognise me.'

'There's Mackenzie,' admitted the second soldier.

The NCO looked at him angrily, annoyed with himself for not thinking of the man.

'Fetch him from the tent,' ordered the NCO. 'The lazy bugger's just drinking his coffee.'

Mackenzie was pulled from the tent and Joseph instantly recognised one of his patients.

'Hello Hamish,' he asked. 'How are the haemorrhoids?'

'Och, hi doc,' said the islander. 'You mean my piles? Not good.'

'Well, cut down on the drinking,' replied Dr. Burns. 'It will help you in all manner of ways.'

'I take it that this is the local doctor and his dog?' asked the NCO, scowling as he did so.

'Of course it is,' replied the soldier. 'Can't you tell?'

'Well we're supposed to be on the lookout for a family and a werewolf going towards Dunvegan,' said the NCO defensively. 'And why is the doctor this far out?'

'Ask him,' replied the local soldier. 'He's had to visit people all over Skye due to the emergency. Anyway I'm going back to drink my coffee. I'm on my break.'

The islander went back into the shelter of the tent muttering as he did so about Sassanachs coming up to the Highlands and Islands and bossing them about. Telling them to look for mythical monsters, for god's sake.

'So why are you here doc?' asked the NCO, irritated now at the islander and not at Joseph. 'If you don't mind telling me.'

'That's no trouble. I've been seeing patients in Staffin and there is a sick mother in Uig that I must see. There are people with crush injuries all over the island who I have been treating. There wasn't sufficient space in the hospital for all of the casualties.'

'Well you can go through but drive carefully,' the soldier lifted the barrier as he said this and Joseph letting Ard back into the car, jumped into the driver's seat and drove on North.

*

I crawled through the tunnel in the rock, worried all the time that I might hit my head. Aradel and Peter were having no trouble with this but I remembered attending lectures about caving and that one of the safety factors they had always stressed was the need for a good helmet. My only safety feature was an Elven sword which got in the way rather than helped.

The tunnel led on for hundreds of yards and by the time we were nearing the end of it my knees were raw and I had received several blows on the head. The tunnel opened into a cave and I emerged delighted to be able to stand up. Peter changed into his human form and explored further up the cave. He rapidly returned.

'The soldiers are using this cave as a store. They obviously don't know about the tunnel but we can't easily get past them,' Peter reported.

Out of the frying pan into the fire, I told myself.

'It is time for an illusion or two,' said Lady Aradel. 'Peter, would you mind being a rat?'

'A rat?' Peter was startled. 'I'm used to being humanoid or wolf but a rat would be strange.'

'Could you imagine being a rat?'

'I could imagine it. A snivelling little squeaking creature that hides in the corners. Yea. I could imagine it.'

In an instant the werewolf had turned into a brown rat. He squeaked in alarm.

'Don't worry, Peter. It is only temporary,' she looked at me and waved her hands again. Both of us took the rat forms that we had used in the Port of the King.

In these shapes the three of us crept out of the cave, past the stores and the myriads of diverse soldiers. We had almost got away when a hobgoblin exclaimed in his guttural voice.

'There are rats here. They're after our stores. Kill them.'

The soldiers reeled round and started chasing us. We ran as fast as rat's legs could move, zig-zagging to avoid the soldiers' boots and the nail-laden clubs that hammered down.

Beyond the camp we changed back into our usual forms and I leant up against a rock to catch my breath, amazed that we had got away with it. I heard a shuffling noise to my left and turned my head to look.

'Well, well. What do we have here?' a captain in charge of a platoon of soldiers was standing staring at us. 'An elf, a human and a small werewolf, if I'm not mistaken. Truss them up and take them to our leader. He will be most delighted to know that we've found them.'

A group of a dozen or more human soldiers advanced towards us, swords and muskets in their hands.

Damn, I thought pulling my Elven sword from its scabbard, totally outnumbered but we had better put up a fight.

*

The doctor's car was nearly at the fairy bridge before they encountered further obstruction. They had driven through the small fishing village of Uig with no problems at all, around the sheltered bay, passed two brochs, hillside forts and numerous waterfalls. They joined the main road and bypassed Edinbane. The Edinbane to Dunvegan road did not go over the fairy bridge any more but instead sported a much newer bridge from the 1960s. Dr. Burns stopped the people-mover a mile before this bridge and then walked quietly along the road with Ard on the lead and with his medical bag in the other hand. They could see from the main road the old track to the fairy bridge and it was bristling with soldiers. The bridge itself was ringed with razor wire. The good doctor walked up to the nearest soldier, showed him the letter from the commanding officer, said that he had been called to see a sick soldier and asked which way he should go.

'I have no idea,' replied the soldier. 'But there are some weird looking creatures down that way. Perhaps one of them is sick?' So saying the man let Joseph and his "dog" through the makeshift barrier and went back to a desultory read of an old paperback novel.

They walked down towards the bridge which was a small humpbacked stone construction with the passage over it blocked to vehicles by large boulders strategically placed in the way.

Ard had earlier told the doctor that he needed to go under the bridge by the river because the window to faerie was beneath the arch. Unfortunately there was a gaggle of army personnel at the site and they appeared to be surrounding another individual. When they boldly walked up close Joseph gasped with amazement. The individual was a huge cyclops.

Joseph's involuntary noise drew attention to the pair. A gimlet eyed sergeant turned his attention on the doctor and his companion.

'What in the blazes are you doing here?' he asked Joseph.

'Doctor Burns reporting,' replied Joseph. 'I hear that you have a sick man?' he presented his papers to the sergeant as he said this, purposely letting go of Ard as he did so.

Seizing the moment Ard jumped at the shimmering portal.

'Stop that dog,' shouted Joseph, as planned. 'Ivan, come back at once.'

However, the werewolf had disappeared from normal reality.

'You'll not get him back now,' remarked the sergeant. 'We've lost several troopers through there.'

'But he's a very valuable dog,' said Joseph, still playing the part.

'Bad luck,' replied the sergeant. 'And I don't think that we do have any sick soldiers.'

'So I've lost my dog and wasted my time,' Joseph complained and then indicated towards the cyclops. 'But what is that creature?'

'I'm told that it is the result of medical experimentation,' answered the sergeant. 'But apart from that I have no idea. All I can say is to keep away from it... it has an evil temper.'

'So I should leave?'

'You shouldn't have come here in the first place.'

Joseph made a show of some annoyance to give the act verisimilitude and then turned heel and walked smartly away. As he walked he felt very exposed turning his back on the army and the monstrous cyclops. It took all of his considerable nerve to walk away without constantly turning back to watch the guards.

*

Celestia and her four werewolf offspring stood shoulder to shoulder with the wood elves. This was the last stand and they all knew it. They had retreated to the middle of the wood, right to the very clearing that led to the huge tree and the werewolf's den.

Leading the attack were several huge cyclops, hundreds of pikemen and a battalion of hobgoblins. Right behind them, urged on by the griffins were the wyverns, harpies and mammoths. At the back came Parsifal X in his luxurious carriage surrounded by his own select guard of cyclopean monsters.

The small remaining group of elves and werewolves took down thousands of hobgoblins and most of the cyclops but eventually they were defeated by the sheer weight of numbers. The final wood elf, already badly injured, cried "Gurth gothrim Tel'Quessir," which translated as Death to the foes of the elves. He then promptly died from a last pike thrust.

The five werewolves were surrounded on all sides. Growling

and snarling they continued to jump at the pikemen despite multiple wounds but they could go no further. From far back in the battle lines Parsifal X's carriage was dragged to the front. The six legged horses reared with fright at the sight of the snarling werewolves but the cyclops pulled on their reins and got them under control.

Parsifal X climbed out of the carriage, flicked some dust of his suit and smelt the air. 'Lucifer was right. Lady Aradel and James Scott were here until just a very short time ago. They have fled like the cowards they are. But you, my pretty ones, cannot flee any further.'

The largest werewolf growled in a menacing deep-throated way.

'No,' replied X. 'You will not have a chance to be avenged and I don't expect to get any sensible information from a semi-sentient being such as yourself.'

X barked an order at his guards and several of the griffins were brought to the front where they proudly strutted backwards and forwards.

'I've often wanted to see a fight between a griffin and a werewolf,' remarked Parsifal X. 'This should be fun.'

A large griffin leapt forward at the smallest werewolf but the lycanthrope, though tired, moved with deceptive speed and bit directly into the griffin's neck. The creature thrashed around and then expired. The largest griffin saw this and in a furious response pounced on the small werewolf from behind and ripped it to pieces, one mythical creature killing another. Celestia howled and jumped forward meeting the largest griffin in mid air. They thrashed and whirled so quickly that the action could not easily be followed. After several minutes of this lightning action the werewolf was clearly winning. Parsifal X muttered a few words and a nimbus of mauve light corruscated down both his arms and stretched out to meet over Celestia's snapping head. The werewolf went limp and the griffin used its talons and beak to rip her to shreds.

Two more werewolves were quickly despatched. The last one, the largest of the cubs, continued to fight but was eventually held down by scores of hobgoblins. As they were about to kill him he transformed into a tall, naked boy and wriggled free. X muttered a few more words and his magic held the werewolf immobilised.

'What is your name, werewolf? I presume you have a name?' asked X.

'My name is Arth,' replied the weakened werewolf.

'How fitting,' smiled Parsifal. 'Arth son of Ard, the so-called king of the werewolves. You are his firstborn and his heir.'

'I curse you, Parsifal X. You love to play the part of a human,' Arth gasped for breath.

'Go on,' encouraged X. 'I'm intrigued to hear the hollow threats you are making with your last few breaths. Do go on,'

'I know what it is to be both human and a beast. But you play at being human,' sighed Arth, in obvious pain.

'Yes...and?'

'And you , X, will for ever be stuck between and betwixt, human and not human, in this world and not in this world,' the werewolf had a far-seeing look in its eyes as if viewing a different reality of future events. 'I can see your fate and I can see mine. Mine is better.'

Arth, heir to the kingdom of werewolves, expelled his last breath and died.

'That was fun!' exclaimed Parsifal X, rubbing his hands together with glee. 'Now we will find Lady Aradel and the annoying man, Scott.'

*

Totally outnumbered, thought Lady Aradel, laughing telepathically. *There are only fifteen of them and there are three of us. They don't stand a chance.*

I looked at her in amazement.

Well, a fighting elf and a werewolf can easily take eight or even ten men each, explained Aradel talking directly to my mind. *Peter and I will share the fourteen and you can have the captain. Is that a deal?*

I nodded and prepared to fight the leader of the platoon but before I could move Peter, in his wolf form, let out a dreadful howl and leapt at the soldiers knocking over as many as ten or more like so many skittles.

'Stop,' cried Aradel as Peter flew into a fury. 'What has happened?'

'My mother and my siblings have all died,' cried Peter, speaking English with some great difficulty even though he was in his wolf form.

I parried a thrust from the captain just as Peter said this and my sword fight with the leader was on. I could tell that I was a slightly better swordsman but that he was stronger than me. Aradel was still talking to Peter and I was worried that I might not last long enough against this powerful opponent.

Suddenly she waved her hands in the air and a beautiful soothing green light bathed the fighting group. Peter, myself and all the soldiers stopped dead in our tracks, paralysed by the magic.

Why didn't she do this before? I wondered. *If she could halt them like this why did she not just do it?*

Because the drain of magical energy draws attention to me on the magical plane, came the telepathic reply. *And we wanted to creep past unnoticed. But I feel these soldiers are important and I am certain that they should not be killed.*

- Chapter 22 -

'What do you bring me?' asked Parsifal X. 'A log?'
Some of his guards were indeed dragging a large log which had been split in two. On one face of the log's interior, words were burnt into the wood. As they watched fire still burnt on the lower part and new words formed.

Parsifal read the message in the smoking runes

> *Thank you for the dwarf souls.*
> *I enjoyed them. They had an unusual nutty flavour.*
> *But remember......I prefer virgins*
> *Until I take your soul*
> *Yours*
> *Lucifer*

'Seer!' screamed Parsifal and the little gnome popped out from its hiding place.

'Yes, sire.'

'What does this message mean?'

'It means he prefers virgins,' replied the gnome.

'Virgin dwarves?'

'Presumably.'

'But we can hardly tell the difference between male and female dwarves let alone discern whether or not they are virgins.'

'No sire. We can't.'

'Then how can Lucifer know?'

'Presumably it is something to do with the flavour of their souls.'

Parsifal was mulling over this exchange when he detected a

flutter on the magical plane. Somebody had used powerful magic to the South of the destroyed forest. He looked in that direction with his augmented perception but the flash of magic had died down.

Presumably a griffin, he thought to himself. *They are the only creatures round here to* use such energies.

Then he went back to pondering the message from Lucifer.

*

Ard leapt through the window between realities into the very surprised arms of a huge cyclops. The guard dropped the werewolf to the ground in disbelief and Ard sprang away in a series of huge bounds. The other soldiers guarding the fairy bridge were primed to prevent any person or creature trying to reach the bridge from the fairy kingdom and were also taken by surprise. Ard was well out of their reach before they could respond.

'Should we follow the creature?' one asked of his superior officer.

'I shall find out from the other side what that was,' the cyclops replied and stepped through the shimmering link.

He returned a few minutes later looking bedraggled and with his rudimentary uniform torn. The guards on the other side had assumed that he was the enemy.

'Took me a long time to convince them that I should be there,' he told his soldiers. 'I had to squash a few heads but eventually I was told that a dog belonging to a medicine man had got loose and run through the reality window. The doctor had already gone so I got no more information.'

'That's not much use,' muttered one of the larger soldiers and wished he had not done so when a huge cyclopean fist landed in his face.

The cyclops, pulling the soldier towards him, growled....

'You do better, pretty boy.'.... And threw him into the link under the fairy bridge.

A few moments later he also returned all battered and bruised.

'Anybody else want the same treatment?' growled the cyclops but there were no takers.

*

Ard ran like the wind, bounding over obstacles, leaping high into the air to clear chasms, jumping from boulder to boulder. He knew already that he was too late for his vixen but he was not sure about his cubs. He had a feeling that some were still living and were in grave danger. The only hope was to mobilise forces from the fairy kingdom, from the dwarves and from his own kinsmen, the werewolves who owed him liegedom and fealty.

Every few miles he sat and howled his message and the werewolves, wolves, dogs and foxes replied. The werewolves would pass the message to the dwarves and elves. He would, himself, have to talk to the fairies and he knew that the fairy ambassador was the one to convince.

He found her in a fairy castle deep in the fairy kingdom but of all the creatures he had called she was the only one who refused to help.

'We have helped Lady Aradel and Lord James Scott. We can do no more. We are bound by the word of the Oberon and Titania. We cannot answer your call.'

Ard, now in his human form, looked at the beautiful, if slightly rotund, fairy figure in disappointment.

'You do realise what is at stake, old bean?' asked Ard. 'This is not just about my own family. This is about the continuing existence of both realities.'

'I understand that,' replied the fairy. 'Nevertheless we must obey the king and queen unless we have a higher or prior calling.'

'And they are still missing?'

'Yes, Oberon and Titania are still lost in time.'

Ard reflected on this for a moment and then tried to convince the ambassador once more.

'I believe that Parsifal X has already wiped out my Celestia and all of the wood elves. He has destroyed the forest. In the real world he has created earthquakes, tsunamis and terror.'

'This I know and that is why we indirectly helped Lady Aradel by allowing her passage through our kingdom. I am very sorry about your loss.'

'If we all acted together the might of all the fairy folk plus the high elves, the dwarves and other magical folk may be enough to defeat Parsifal X.'

'And yet we have never acted together in that way. The peace agreement that King Oberon agreed with Parsifal X has endured for three centuries. He has left us alone and in return we give him a nodding fealty. A peppercorn rent.'

'But now the human world will die and....'

'.....We have no reason to care about the humans. They have done nothing for us,' replied the ambassador. 'We did not help the high elf queen because she is humanoid but because she is not human.'

'....And when the human world dies, so will ours.'

'Why should that be?' queried the fairy ambassador.

'Because we are balanced with the human world. We are intricately linked as a reflection of that reality.'

'I've heard that argument before,' replied the ambassador. 'And I see some sense in it. However, it remains true that we cannot act unless there is a prior calling, a pact that was agreed before Oberon and Parsifal's accord.'

'So you will not help us?'

'No, we cannot,' replied the fairy ambassador, sadly. 'I fear that you are right in all that you say but we are tied by the agreement. We could not act directly against X even if we wanted to.'

*

Lady Aradel released her magical hold on Peter and myself. Peter was still shivering with fury but had turned back into his human form. She then released the captain sufficiently that he was able to speak.

'Where are you from?' she asked the soldier but he did not reply. 'I'll ask you again and then if you do not answer I will use magic to force a reply. That may damage your mind. It is after all, a simple question. Where are you from?'

Judging that the answer was harmless the soldier spoke. 'We are from the Eastern mainland. We are mercenaries hired by Parsifal X to suppress your uprising.'

'There has been no uprising,' replied Aradel. 'Have you been paid at all by X?'

'Not as yet. We will be paid at the end of the action.'

'You have been misinformed,' said Lady Aradel. 'Let me show you what has happened,'

This is going to take some time, I thought and looked round to see if there were further troops who could see our little gathering and attack us. Luckily we were a fair distance away from the main force and they were all moving away in a northward direction.

Not as long as you expect, replied Aradel waving her hands and muttering. In the air in front of us there was an immediate coalescing of dust and light which then focussed as a picture of two worlds colliding, tsunamis, earthquakes, hurricanes, millions of people killed. This quickly changed to an image of the forest, quiet and peaceful... then destroyed by the forces of Parsifal X.

'And let me show you your own future if you continue to work for X,' said Lady Aradel.

The images faded and were replaced by pictures of the mercenary troop lining up to be paid outside Parsifal X's palace. The soldiers filed in one by one and were each cut down by a cyclopean guard who threw the bodies into a pit. X sat to one side laughing.

The captain was shaken by the revelation.

'But that future may not be real,' he said in a slightly hoarse voice. 'You can predict it but it does not have to happen.'

'That is correct,' said Lady Aradel. 'But if you and the other mercenaries continue to work for X that will be your future. You have three potential choices. Stay with X and die, desert and go back home and die or convince your comrades-in-arms to join our side .... in which case you may have a chance of a glorious death but also a chance of life. And so may both the worlds of reality.'

The captain said nothing for several minutes then replied.

'You have us in your power and could kill us right now.....'

Aradel nodded.

'.....Therefore,' continued the captain. 'There can be no reason for you to let us go unless you are telling the truth and we are needed to help save the worlds.'

'So you will help us?'

'Yes,' agreed the captain. 'And I speak for all my men.'

Aradel waved her hands again and the small band of soldiers were all free. One instantly grabbed a musket and held it to the head of the elf.

'I've caught one, captain,' he cried. 'Shall I shoot her?'

The captain shook his head. 'No, no, don't do that,' he ordered. 'Let her go. I have a lot to tell you and these people need our help.'

I relaxed. If the captain had been going to betray us, that would have been the moment but, for now, we were safe.

*

'There is another one, your highness,' cried a cyclopean guard, his one eye swivelling with alarm in the centre of his forehead.

'Another what?' asked Parsifal X, irritated by the lack of specificity.

'Another message, sire,' groaned the cyclops. 'A message from Lucifer.'

'Bring it to me,' ordered the so-called supreme ruler of the faerie reality.

'I can't do that, boss,' grunted the guard as he tried to obey his commander. 'It's written on a rock and it won't move.'

Parisfal X levitated himself from the carriage and floated over to the exposed bedrock. There, in letters each a metre high, etched or even melted into the rock, was a short note.

> *You missed them!*
> *Until I take your soul*
> *Yours*
> *Lucifer*

'"You missed them",' read Parsifal. 'What does he mean? Who have I missed. Seer, seer. Where are you when I need you?'

The gnome appeared from behind Parsifal's seat on the carriage.

'I'm here,' said the soothsayer. 'And I expect he means the elf and the human.'

'We can't have missed them,' replied Parsifal. 'We have the whole forest surrounded. Surely our troops will have caught them somewhere?'

'Can you see them, sire?'

Parsifal expanded his consciousness. He could not see the fugitives. He expanded his reach further still ..... nothing.

'I cannot see them but they must be hiding within the ruins of the forest. I could smell them and they were not far away,' said Parsifal X.

'I can take a peek into the future and see whether you will have caught them,' suggested the gnome.

'Do it,' ordered the fire demigod and the gnome responded by throwing some old bones in the air and watching the way that they fell.

'You don't have them, sire. They are escaping to the south.'

'No!' Parsifal X, blasted the rock face with his anger. The rock melted and the message disappeared. 'No, no, no!'

*

Dr. Burns reached his car with no alarm being raised and drove away from the fairy bridge. Taking the more direct route back to Portree, he was stopped at a checkpoint just outside town. When they realised who it was they waved him through. He drove on towards his home, through the last checkpoint and back to his house.

The Commodore of the nuclear submarine had returned to the house.

'The diesel submarine is moored in the next bay,' the naval officer informed the waiting group. 'We will take you wherever you need to go.'

'What about your orders from Brigadier Blenkinsop?' asked Mary.

'Blinkers has gone completely mad and my admiral, before he was relieved of his post, told me to do whatever I liked!' replied the man, a little sorely. 'Besides, I am a Commodore and that is equal in rank to Blinkers!'

Mary, Sienna and the boys picked up their meagre belongings and followed the commodore and Hannah, the navigator, out of the door. They thanked Joseph and Charlotte and walked down the steep front path onto the road. The two naval officers were moving at quite a pace and the family had to walk very quickly to keep up.

A mile further up the road in a northward direction the commodore took an unmade path down to the seashore. The submarine could be seen a little way out beyond the rocks. A moderately sized rigid inflatable dinghy was moored on the stony shore and a rating was sitting in it, patiently waiting.

The party all climbed into the dinghy and the rating started the outboard motor. The boat moved quickly towards the submarine where several seamen helped the family aboard the vessel.

'Is a submarine a boat or a ship?' asked Joshua as he waited in the dinghy whilst his mother and grandmother were climbing into the sub.

'We call them boats for historical reasons but technically they are ships,' answered Hannah.

'So what is the difference between a boat and a ship?' he pursued the subject.

'Boats go on ships .... lifeboats, dinghies etcetera,' replied Hannah. 'So boats are launched from ships. Submarines are no longer launched from ships but the first ones were launched that way.'

'A bit confusing,' said Joshua. 'So they are ships really?'

'Yes but submariners only ever call them boats or simply submarines,' added Hannah. 'Mind you there is an old saying in the submarine community There are just two types of ships .... submarines and targets.'

'Let's hope that we don't end up as targets,' said Joshua.

'Agreed!' exclaimed Hannah as they climbed aboard.

- Chapter 23 -

'So how can we help you, Lady Aradel?' asked the commander of the mercenary troops from the East. 'You have freed us when you had us enslaved. You have warned us of Parsifal X's plans. How can we now assist you in return?

'There will have to be an uprising against X,' replied Aradel. 'You can create a diversion to aid us now but more important is your role when the uprising comes.'

'OK,' replied the captain. 'And what is that role?'

'I am the rightful ruler of the Western lands,' replied Aradel, 'The Queen of the Elves and leader of the opposition to Parsifal's rule.'

'Yes ma'am,' replied the captain respectfully.

'I do not want a war with the Eastern mainland,' Aradel said carefully. 'You may not be able to get the men of the East to rise to our aid but it is very important that they do not rise against us. If they do we may all perish, East and West.'

'So what do you specifically want me to do?'

'After you have escaped from the diversion you will create you must make your way back to the East and tell the leaders in that land that X's rule must come to an end. If that does not happen you will all be enslaved by him ... every one of you. Tell them that the cry to battle will come and they must choose whom they will serve .... the powers of good or the forces of evil.'

The mercenary captain saluted. 'Yes ma'am. You have my word and my honour. It will be done. But first, how will we create a diversion?'

'Go West and then Northwards round the remains of the forest and when you reach the more Northern part burn this talisman in a hot bonfire,' she handed him a small black object as she said this. 'Leave it burning and move rapidly East back to your own lands avoiding any fighting.'

'Yes ma'am,' the captain saluted.

'And as a token of my goodwill I give you this ring,' she handed a large, ornate gold and ruby ring to the captain. 'This will pay for you and the platoon's services.'

The captain saluted again and the soldiers melted into the shrubbery, moving westward towards the Western mountain range and we headed due South. The night was over and the sun was coming up in the East.

What will the day hold? I wondered. *Can Lady Aradel predict our future as she had the soldiers?*

It doesn't quite work like that, replied Aradel. *It is always easier to predict someone else's future. It is a matter of perspective. However our major seer has warned us that you and your family are crucial to our success and that helping you must be our main concern.*

Great, I replied telepathically but deep in side all I wanted to do was go home to Bristol, put my feet up, have a cup of tea and watch Match of the Day with my boys.

*

'I didn't think the British Navy had any diesel-electric submarines,' said Mary when they were all inside the boat. 'I was told that they only had nuclear subs.'

'You are right ma'am,' replied the Commodore. 'But we were on joint exercises with the Indian navy when the disaster struck. This is really an Indian navy sub.'

'So where are the Indian submariners?' asked Mary, looking around. 'I can't see any.'

'I'm sorry to say that there was only a small skeleton crew on board when the tsunami struck. The rest of the crew were on shore leave and after the wave we could only account for a few of them. The submarine took the wave well. I was the superior officer of the fleet in this area and the junior officer who had been left in charge of the boat immediately handed me command.'

'When the emergency is over?' prompted Mary.

'When it is over we will give it back,' added the Commodore. 'In the meantime we will show you to your bunks. It will be crowded but this is a nice submarine made by Navantia. It's almost new.'

'It's bigger than I expected,' Sienna added. 'I thought that diesel submarines were very small.'

'Yes they were but this is a Scorpene class submarine and measures 66.4 meters by 6.2 meters. Big by diesel standards but a lot smaller than our nuclear subs.'

'But they're not working?'

'No, you are right. The nuclear submarines are still not working.'

*

Lady Aradel, Peter the werewolf and I walked on down through the valley and then up and over the next ridge. In the South I could see the impressive volcanic mountain range. It did not look any closer than when I had first seen it.

Stretched out in front of me was wild moorland on which I could see only the very occasional tree and no discernible animal life. Peter had remained in his human form since we left the platoon of soldiers and he now stopped walking to talk to us.

'This is where we must part company,' said the young werewolf in a serious and very adult tone for his age. 'I have done what my mother asked me to do. My father has returned to this land and has called me so I needs must go. All I can do now is wish you good luck and adieu!'

On the last few words he transformed back into the wolf form I had first encountered and the adieu echoed off into the hillside as a wolf cry.

'Goodbye little Peter,' I said quietly to the wind as the werewolf bounded off into the distance. 'Good luck and I hope that I can see you again sometime in better circumstances.'

'I believe that you will,' said Lady Aradel, patting me on the back.

'But you don't know?' I asked.

'No,' she agreed. 'I don't know.'

*

'I shall move us all south immediately,' said the fire demi-god. 'I don't know where they are going but we can rest assured they cannot cross the moorland swamp quickly, if at all, and they will inevitably be stopped by the Southern Mountain Range.'

'Mmmm, mutter, mmm,' went the seer.

'Speak up,' ordered Parsifal X sand then he looked more closely at the gnome and laughed. 'Oh, I forgot. I cut out your tongue again. Here ....' He waved his hand ... 'Have it back again until you annoy me once more.'

'Thank you sire. I shall endeavour never to annoy you again, ever, sire,' replied the diminutive, bewhiskered gnome. 'And you may like to look at what is happening to the north before you move south precipitously. If the fugitives are trapped by the swamp and the mountains there really is no hurry....but to the North things are hotting up.'

Parsifal X stretched his consciousness in a northerly direction and immediately observed the gathering army of werewolves, high elves, nymphs, satyrs, dwarves and a few freemen. He could see that Ard, the king of the werewolves, was creating the alliance.

'What do they think they are doing?' asked X. 'They can't have the audacity to rise against me. I hold the power of the Earth at my beck and call.' He immediately let out a tremor that shook the gathering army. Though some were alarmed it was clear that the majority had decided that they had to fight even though it might be hopeless.

Parsifal X reluctantly decided that he would have to redeploy his forces. This would take a considerable length of time. He had no more troops in reserve suspended animation and he could not magically move the huge army he had without draining more power than he wanted to expend. They would have to be moved by the usual mechanical means and that meant days of work, a long chain of command and a difficult logistic problem of back-up and supplies.

He had intended to use his army quickly and then feed half the army to the other half. It was a ploy he had utilised successfully in the past but it looked as though he would need all of his forces to fight this gathering army. That would definitely be the case if the fairies had joined the opposition.

He spread his perception again. They had not done so! He could not see a single fairy in the gathering army. The most powerful of his opposition, except of course the dragons whose minds were always on other things. The fairies combined were greater than the high elves when they put their peculiar collective insect minds to it. They were not there!

This is going to be easy, he thought. *But I will still need to use nearly all my army. I will leave a small contingent here to ensure that Aradel and Scott do not turn back on themselves and I shall personally supervise the destruction of this ragtag collection. And I shall particularly enjoy killing the werewolf king in the same way that I killed the werewolf queen. This will be fun.*

*

I stepped out in a relatively happy mood. Just cross over the moorlands, avoid the dragons and we're home and dry.

It will not be that easy, replied Lady Aradel in my mind. *The swamps have not been crossed on foot for several hundred years and we will not be able to circumvent the dragons.*

'Then we're doomed,' I answered out loud.

'Not entirely,' said Aradel. 'The swamps can be crossed. It has been done before but they are riddled with traps and illusions.'

'And the dragons?'

'We will have to meet them and speak to them. We cannot fight them. Dragons are far too powerful. However, I do have a strategy for dealing with them.'

'Which is?'

'Which is something I wished to avoid and have been avoiding for some time.'

'?'

'I will tell you when we get there and not before.'

*

The hatch closed with an ominous clang. The boys were extremely excited about going in a submarine. Sienna was not so sanguine.

Oh god, she thought. *What if we meet that sea monster? Could it damage this sub? How could we get out if it happened when we were submerged?*

As if he was reading her mind in the same way that her mother could, the Commodore looked over at Sienna.

'Submarines very rarely sink if that's what you are worrying about but we do have escape suits with an all in one hood so you can continue to breathe. There are enough for all of you.'

'Thank you,' replied Sienna. 'That's a relief.'

'I must leave you now and direct operations. It is time that we got underway.'

*

To the East of Parsifal X's encampment he detected a movement in the magical plane. It was unmistakably Lady Aradel's magical signature. She was actively using magic and moving in a westward direction.

That makes more sense than going South, thought X. *Aradel will be travelling to her cousins, the High Elves of the West. I will send my most powerful commanders to cut her off and bring her and the man, Scott, back to me in iron chains. That will prevent her using any more magic against me. I will tolerate no more rebellion.*

*

I stepped boldly out onto a patch of verdant green pasture before Lady Aradel could give me any warning. My foot sank into a deep bog and within minutes I was up to my neck in slimy, smelly mud. One of the things we always worried about as children was what you should do if you found yourself in quicksand or a sucking bog and as I sank I remembered some advice I had read at the time. The provenance of the advice was not particularly encouraging ....it had been in a weekly comic. However, here I was rapidly sinking and the comic was the only help I had unless Aradel could do something. The advice had been "Don't struggle, pretend it is just thick water and swim out of it."

I made some gentle breaststroke movements with my arms and a frog-legged action with my lower limbs. To my surprise it worked and I was able to get into a horizontal position. I 'swam' round painfully slowly to Aradel, who was standing absolutely still on a grassy tussock. I eventually managed to get a grip on some of the stronger vegetation and haul my exhausted body out of the mud. I lay still panting, cold and filthy from my neck down to my feet.

'So it is not a moor it is a bog,' I sighed.

'Which is why it has only been crossed on foot just the once,' she replied in a despairing voice. 'I hoped that you might be able to pass straight over it.'

'Why should I be able to do that if you can't?' I queried.

'The person who crossed it was a human being like yourself,' explained Lady Aradel.

'And he didn't use magic?'

'No,' answered Aradel. 'There is something about the swamp that negates magic. Which is useful if you want to hide, as we do.'

'But not so good if you want to go over it, as we also do,' I surmised out loud.

'So what we are doing is doomed as you said earlier. I have led you astray and I am no more worthy to be the Queen of the Elves.'

To my horror the rat/elf lay down on the tussock and cried as if her heart was breaking. The beautiful young girl, who was actually thousands of years old, had been so cheerful despite all the adversity we had encountered but now she was sobbing so hard that I felt my own heart would break too.

This really is the most desperate place, I thought despondently. Then a further thought was tipping on the edge of my consciousness. *What was that half thought? No, it had gone, this really is a bad, bad place. The black dog of depression has caught me at last.*

'Wait,' I cried. 'What was the name of the person who made it across?'

'His name was Christian,' replied Lady Aradel. 'But it won't help you to know.'

I disagreed. 'It might well. When did he cross the bog and did he tell you how?'

'He did it in 1678 under your dating scheme. He claimed that he was directed by someone in your World called Bunyan but I think that is a swelling that humans get on their toes.'

'No. He was right,' I actually laughed, right there in that terrible place. 'This is the Slough of Despond. It is supposed to make you miserable due to the weight of your sins.'

'So why are you now happy?' she asked.

'Once you know what you are up against you have won half the battle,' I replied. 'It's not quite so bad as I thought it might be. I've been enmired in worse committee meetings than this bog. I don't suppose that John Bunyan had to sit through management meetings and political correctness awareness days.'

'I don't know what those are, Lord James.'

'Let's hope you never have to,' I replied. 'We'll find a way through this. Never fear!'

- Chapter 24 -

Several hours later my boast that we would find a way through was beginning to haunt me. How could we find a safe route through the swamp? I had tried putting sticks down into the mud to no avail. I had thrown stones in to try to determine a solid route and again it did not work.

One such stone, a fair sized lump, had almost been my undoing. I threw the boulder into a part that appeared solid and it did not sink. Emboldened by the boulder's non-sinking nature, I stepped out onto the stone and immediately sank until my head was below the murky water level. For a moment I panicked and I was certain I was going to die but my survival instincts kicked in once again and I swam to the surface of the muddy mire and hauled myself out, even more filthy and dripping with mud. I was, quite naturally, loath to repeat that particular experiment.

It took me a considerable length of time to start examining the problem logically. I had been so long in the faerie reality that I had stopped thinking like a scientist but now I needed to. I sat down to consider all the possibilities. Unfortunately my stomach was rumbling due to lack of food and I was exhausted ... we had only succeeded in snatching two hours sleep in the night before, due to Parsifal X's army of ill-begotten creatures attacking us.

In the end I gave up for a while and asked Lady Aradel how her diversion worked.

'It's a simple phantom spell,' she replied. 'Magically noisy and quite disturbing on the thaumaturgical plane.'

'Tell me more,' I demanded, hoping that the diversion from our present problem might allow my subconscious to find a solution.

'The smoke from the piece of charcoal is under an illusion that it is a person. It tries to shape itself into an individual but is blown by the wind and eventually dissipates,' Aradel explained. 'The wind is blowing to the West at present so I knew that it would carry the smoke over the Western mountain range.'

'And Parsifal would follow it?' I queried.

'I hope so. The spell I used made the smoke look just like me.'

I obviously looked a little sceptical for she continued her explanation.

'You must have seen clouds in your own world.'

I nodded the affirmative.

'Sometimes they look like people or things... they might look like mountains or trees?'

Again I agreed.

'This is similar ... a noisy spell like a firecracker to draw the attention and then the smoke makes a cloud that happens to look like me,' she spread her hands as she finished this and added. 'See, it's simple.'

I pondered her answer for a while but could not see any angle that would help us in our current predicament. Eventually I decided to ask again about the one person who had crossed the Slough of Despond.

'This Christian guy, did you know him well?'

'I walked with him for a while but he wasn't the sort of person who you could easily get to know well.'

'Why was that?' I asked, curious about the character I had read about as a child.

'He didn't think that I was a suitable companion for him on his pilgrimage,' Aradel replied with a somewhat petulant toss of her fine head of hair.

Aradel had not fallen into the bog. She still looked beautiful and clean and, apart from an air of despondency brought on by our current impasse, exactly the same eighteen year old girl that

I had first taken her for when she transmogrified from the fat rat illusion.

'Why was that?' I asked, wondering whether she had tried to climb into bed with him and knowing that Christian would certainly not have approved of that behaviour.

'I was not fixed on following the same difficult path as he was. He called me names that he made up to insult me .....Lady Feigning, Mistress Fairweather, Queen Two-Tongues. That sort of thing.'

I nodded that I had got the drift and she continued.

'He had names for everybody and few were complimentary.'

'What did he think of Parsifal X?'

'He called him the Great Deceiver, I believe. It amused X enormously.'

'Was Parsifal as evil in those days?' I asked this since it seemed strange that Lady Aradel should know that Parsifal X had been amused by Christian.

'He was becoming so. We had a truce at that time and he had not usurped all the legitimate rulers. However, as he tapped more power from the planet's core and eventually also from the sun he became more corrupt and malevolent.'

'Absolute power corrupts absolutely.'

'Lord Acton, the historian, 1887,' Aradel shot back at me.

'Really?' this time I was surprised. 'I thought it was William Pitt the Elder.'

'No. Pitt said "Unlimited power is apt to corrupt the minds of those who possess it",' Aradel corrected me. 'He said that to your House of Lords in 1770.'

She really is good with her quotations, I thought. *Which makes it that much stranger that she does not know more about Bunyan.*

She did not read my mind which may have been due to the swamp's damping effect on magic. I asked her to continue describing Christian's pilgrimage and she readily did so.

'If we came to a choice of routes he would always take the hardest. He would clamber over the rock that I walked round. We would meet on the other side but I got impatient waiting for him. It was as if he had to take the narrowest, hardest and most direct route to his goal with some form of internal guidance that he suspected I did not possess.'

'Our ex-prime minister Brown would have called that a moral compass,' I interjected.

'Why?' asked Aradel. 'Did he go on a pilgrimage?'

'He thought he had saved the world,' I replied, laughing at the painful memory. As I did so a recurring half-thought came into my mind. A clue to our problem. What was it that Aradel or I had just said that was jogging my sub-conscious?

*

The diverse army of werewolves, dwarves and elves led by Ard attacked the exposed rump of Parsifal's forces before he could wheel them round to a defensive position. Despite the much greater numbers and enormous power of Parsifal's vast army the lack of logistic back up hampered them and the sudden order to turn round served to confuse. The battle went well for Ard, at least initially, but the final outcome would be inevitable once Parsifal's best commanders returned from chasing Lady Aradel.

With her in chains and James Scott once more hanging on my wall the opposition will melt away, thought Parsifal. *And I will be able to concentrate on the amalgamation of realities.*

Parsifal had heard word from his generals that they were still following a very obvious trail left by Lady Aradel.

'She is becoming careless and I will catch her soon! Ha,ha,ha!' Parsifal's laughter echoed over the battlefield

*

'Wasn't there some sort of scandal about the Scorpene submarines?' Mary asked the Commodore as he was leaving them in the tiny cabin to which they had been assigned.

'Malaysian not Indian navy,' replied the Navy Chief. 'I'll invite you to the control room as soon as we are well underway.'

'Not to the bridge?' asked Joshua. 'I thought the captain always went to the bridge.'

'Not on a sub,' replied the Commodore a little impatiently. 'The bridge on a submarine is just a small exposed platform on the sail. The sail is what you might incorrectly call the conning tower, which contains periscopes etcetera. Unusually we attached a sail to our sail on the nuclear submarine when it stopped functioning. Immediately below what you hitherto called the conning tower, is the control room. Righto.' He paused at the doorway. 'See you there later.'

The Commodore gave a friendly wave and disappeared, shutting the door behind him.

'What have we got ourselves into now?' asked Sienna rhetorically.

'A diesel-electric submarine, daughter,' replied her mother, choosing to answer the question semantically.

'And another big adventure, Mum!' added Samuel.

Sienna groaned. *I can do without Famous Five adventures and Secret Seven shenanigans* she thought to herself.

Cheer up, daughter, replied her mother with her new found gift of telepathy. *We could be worse off.*

Yes, thought Sienna. *In the belly of a real sea monster, I suppose.*

Might still happen, thought Mary and laughed out loud.

*

'So what did you say can be used to dampen magical powers?' I asked.

'I'm not sure that I did say but the most obvious thing is Iron,' replied Lady Aradel. 'Which is why Parsifal likes to clamp his prisoners in iron chains... or at least make them think they are in iron chains.'

Then it came to me.

'A compass!' I exclaimed. 'A magnetic compass. Do you possess one?'

'I don't even know what one is,' she replied.

'It is a small magnetic needle that points the way. I said that Gordon Brown had a moral compass. Perhaps Christian had a magnetic one.'

'What does magnetic mean?'

'You must know,' I said, frustrated by this astonishing lack of knowledge on Aradel's part, 'Two pieces of iron either attracting or repelling each other.'

She still looked confused.

'A lodestone,' I added. 'They used to be called lodestones.'

Aradel brightened. 'Yes, I do know what you mean. Peculiar pieces of iron ore that have bizarre effects on magic because they are magical themselves.'

'No,' I replied. 'The attraction and repulsion is just due to magnetic forces. The electromagnetic force is simply one of the four fundamental forces of nature.'

'In your reality. As magic is in our own.'

'Your Arch Chancellor said when we were in the tavern "magic is just science that is not understood",' I added. 'So perhaps magic is a fifth force here in Faerie or a combination of unknown forces.'

'How does this help us get across the swamp, Lord James?' asked Lady Aradel.

'We find a lodestone and use it to guide us over the despond,' I replied.

'But this planet has no specific lodestone direction,' replied Lady Aradel. 'So how will that work?'

'The planet has no magnetic field? Is that right ?........Because if so it is very interesting but does make it difficult to use a compass.'

I had been pacing around on our small piece of dry, solid

land. I sat down once again to piece all the facts together.

*

'My navigator tells me that you are an adviser to the Navy on engineering. Are you really an adviser?' the Commodore asked Mary as he led her to the control room. The submarine had been underway for several hours.

'To be completely honest I am not,' Mary replied. 'It seemed the best thing to say at the time since the soldiers invading our beach were very officious.'

'And yet you do know a lot about submarines. Hannah told me that you had a good explanation for the nuclear reactor not working.'

'Yes,' Mary answered. 'It is due to a shift in the fundamental physical constants. My daughter and son-in-law know more about these things than I do. I simply read their minds.'

'Yes, I see,' said the Commodore thinking .. *She really is a weird, cranky old witch.*

'Yes I am,' agreed Mary.

'Sorry, yes you are what?' the Commodore was confused.

'Just as you thought... I really am a weird, cranky old witch,' and then she projected the thought to the Commodore that he was a rather attractive mature man.

The Commodore went bright red with embarrassment to the tips of his wavy red hair and beard.

'I, I didn't mean to insult you,' he stammered. 'But you clearly can read minds.'

'Ever since the disaster,' replied Mary.

'And where is your son-in-law?' asked the Commodore.

'He is in the Faerie world, presently lost to us,' Mary said. 'He's with the fairies.'

'Do you mean he has dementia?'

'No, he really is in another world.'

'And I have to believe that?'

'You've seen the werewolf...'
'....But that's in this world.'
'And he came from the Faerie world. I know that James Scott, my son-in-law, would have said that it is in another set of dimensions. The werewolf told us that the two worlds are colliding and that the metaphysical impact is the root cause of our problems.'

'And you really do have to meet up with James Scott?'
'We do, to save the planet.'
'This is so odd, so peculiar.... but we will do what we can.' As he said that a spasm of pain shot across his face and the Commodore shifted his position.

'Are you alright?' asked Mary, concerned about the man.
The Commodore pulled himself together and stood upright.

'Yes ma'am. Just a slight problem but I'm OK. Don't worry about me. We will get you to the Isle of Man and the fairy bridge.'

Another spasm shot across his face and this time it lasted longer than before.

*

'What do you mean you can't find her?' Parsifal X was furious with his generals and his latest beautiful suit was suffering because of his rage.

Smoke was rising from his shoes and from his shirt cuffs. The back of his suit jacket was going brown and the combustion would be bursting through any minute.

'How can it be that you can't find her? You told me that her trail was blazoned across the sky. I saw it myself.'

He looked round for the gnome.

'Where is that diminutive soothsayer? That foretelling gnome, where is he?'

'Here, sire!' exclaimed the gnome peeping out from his habitual place in a nook behind the throne.

'Why can't they find Lady Aradel? Tell me!'

'Because she does not want to be found, sire,' replied the gnome.

'But how can she be so obviously careless, blazing a trail and then disappear?'

'Perhaps she used a diversionary spell, your honour, your highness, sire.'

'What sort of spell?'

'Well,' the gnome though for a moment. 'I would use a golem but I doubt that she has the capacity to do that now. Perhaps she used a phantom spell.'

'She used a golem when she freed James Scott from my prison.'

'Yes sire, but she was able to prepare for that. Now she is on the run it is unlikely that she could do something so solid, so expensive and so time consuming.'

'And a phantom spell?'

'A little smoke and pyrotechnics and we follow the cloud.'

'I believe you are right. But where is she now?'

'I have no idea. Can you not find her with your enhanced perception?'

'No, No, NO!' cried Parsifal, bursting into flames and destroying another of his best suits.

- Chapter 25 -

'Magnetic monopoles!' I exclaimed. 'That is the answer.'
Lady Aradel looked at me as if I had gone mad.
I was prancing around our little island of solidity with glee shouting "monopoles, monopoles, monopoles." All feelings of despair had completely left me although I could see that they had not fled from Aradel.

'What is a monopole?' she finally shouted this at me.
'It is a hypothetical particle in theoretical physics that has only one magnetic pole. An isolated magnetic pole.' I sat down exhausted.

Aradel looked confused but I continued.
'You see magnets always have a north and south pole. The north pole attracts the south and vice versa. But a south pole repels another south pole, a north pole repels another north pole.'

'So unlike poles attract and like poles repel,' surmised Lady Aradel.

'Quite right.'
'But if a magnet always has a north and a south pole you can't have an isolated magnetic pole. Monopoles don't exist.'

'But theoretically they do. They may just be too massive for us to make them and too rare for us to find them,' I explained. 'That, of course, is in my Universe. Here they are common.'

'Common?'
'Sure. I just threw a boulder into the mire. When I picked the thing up and hefted it into the swamp the stone was very heavy so it should have sank but it didn't. When I stood on it the thing went down and I almost drowned. But if it is a monopole it would hover above other monopoles.'

'I still don't understand.'

'Put it this way ... the iron magic made it float and we can use it to find our way through.'

'That I do understand. But can we find another stone like it?'

'We don't need to,' I replied. 'When I came to the surface the thing shot out of the water and landed beside me. I'm sitting on it right now.'

*

Mary was still in the control room watching operations and had been for some considerable time. The rest of the family were sleeping on their tiny bunk beds. Mary had not gone back to the small cabin assigned to her because she was worried about the Commodore. She had spotted that he periodically had a very pained expression on his face as if fighting an internal battle. He noticed that she was watching at one point and looked as if he was going to say something, changing his mind only at the last moment. She could not read what he had been thinking which also seemed strange as she had established considerable rapport with him only a couple of hours previously.

As she watched him a pinging noise started to emanate from the sonar machine and a scan picture was emerging.

'Sir, I have a bogey following us.'

The sonar operator was speaking clearly and precisely but he was obviously alarmed.

'What do you think it is, officer?' asked the Commodore. 'What does it look like on the high resolution sonar?'

'It is about thirty meters long and streamlined, sir.'

'Yes, but what do you think it is, a torpedo? Another submarine?'

'Too slow for a torpedo and too streamlined for a sub,' the sonar operator was a little reluctant to continue.... 'I would say that it is most likely to be the sea monster from Loch Portree, sir.'

'And it's catching us?'

'Yes sir. It is swimming at about twenty knots and we are only doing fifteen.'

'Navigator!' the Commodore called Hannah to him. 'You saw this sea monster. Would you say that it posed a threat to our submarine?'

'Definitely sir,' Hannah replied.

'It is overhauling us. Should we turn and fight or surface and try to out race it?'

'I would suggest that we surface and get away as quickly as possible. That monster is capable of biting through our metal skin and I have no idea whether our torpedoes will harm it. It made very short work of our rowing boats.'

'Then we surface and scarper..... Helm!'

'Yessir,'

'Take her up and put on the diesel engines. I know we will be visible but it is better to be seen than to be swallowed.'

'Yessir!'

*

I picked up the lodestone and smacked it down onto a granite outcrop. It broke into pieces and, sure enough, when I put the pieces together and then let go, they flew apart. This would not have happened with a normal magnet .... if I had put two like poles together one would have twisted round and the unlike poles would have attracted each other.

I took a relatively light piece of the lodestone and asked Lady Aradel if she had any string.

'Only in my dress,' she replied and unhesitatingly pulled a piece of gold thread out for me. This created a small gap in her décolletage allowing me to see the delightful flesh of her cleavage. I shook my head and concentrated on the job in hand.

I tied the strong gold thread around the lodestone and held the end of the string. The stone hovered over the other heavier pieces of monopole.

'OK,' I told Lady Aradel. 'My theory is this. Monopole magnetic forces interfere with magic forces in some way negating them. This causes magical folk such as yourself and myself, as I am part elf, to become insubstantial and sink rapidly through swamp that might otherwise just reach to our ankles.'

'Yes, Lord James.'

'It also takes away part of our life force making us feel low and depressed. Hence the Slough of Despond. OK so far?'

'Yes.'

'If I take this stone and swing it around, wherever it hovers or is deflected there are significant deposits of monopole lodestone under the surface. That is the path to avoid whether it looks solid or not. So we go where the lodestone does not deflect. We will then just have to be careful as we would going through any normal swamp .... tread only on the grassy tussocks and not on the wettest muddy bits. Should be a doddle.'

'OK, Lord James,' agreed Lady Aradel, Queen of the Elves. I could see that she did not really believe me but I knew that it was our best bet.

*

Night had fallen in Faerie and Parsifal X had to concentrate on the battle. As far as X was concerned the ragtag rebel army led by Ard the werewolf was doing far too well. X directed his most fearsome generals to do a pincer movement cutting round both sides of the advancing rebel forces. The group that moved West came close to the mercenaries who were now helping Lady Aradel but missed them in the dark. Peter the werewolf also bounded past the pincer edge in his lupine form and joined up with his father's forces.

Peter raced to the command centre which was just behind the front line. He changed back into his human shape and presented himself to his father.

'Peter,' howled Ard in delight. 'You are alive!' The werewolf father and son hugged each other.

'I am, Father,' replied Peter. 'But I am much afraid that Mother and my siblings are not.'

He then explained as quickly as he could exactly what had been happening to him and what he had learnt about Parsifal's forces, the numbers, the pincer movement and the mercenaries who were now on Ard and Aradel's side.

Ard listened to all of it with growing concern.

'The numbers of Parsifal's army are many more than I thought. We cannot defeat them by just fighting.'

'No Father,' replied Peter. 'But they have no supply chain. I heard the mercenaries talking about this. If we staged a strategic retreat, removing all supplies as we go, they will run out of food and they will also run out of ammunition for their muskets. They will fall on each other like the monsters they are.'

Ard looked at his son in amazement.

'You have grown up very quickly, son,' he said. 'I am proud of you for your heroic efforts and for thinking what to a werewolf would normally be unthinkable. We will retreat and starve Parsifal X's army. The idea is sound and the strategy good.... and if we are able to meet up with the mercenaries and help them .... then all the better.'

*

I set off following the path directed by lack of deflection of the magnet. It certainly took faith ... normally with a compass you followed whichever point of the compass you chose and the compass unwaveringly pointed North. We were following an absence of movement. Any deflection or hovering and we avoided the route. I had no idea whether there still was a safe passage through the swamp to the foothills of the Southern Mountain range but it was our only hope. I was a drowning man clutching at monopoles rather than straws.

Lady Aradel followed exactly in my footsteps. Once or twice

we went astray but luckily never both at the same time. I went in up to my waist at one point having mistaken a deflection as a simple swing of the pendulum. Aradel pulled me out with surprising strength. She sank in twice but each time only to her knees and I was able to haul her out.

We started off at dusk and then initially kept moving onwards in the light of the twin moons but eventually we were too exhausted. We found a slightly larger solid island in the middle of the Slough of Despond and settled down to a night of disturbing dreams, waking minutes of regret and half-conscious reflection on our sins, real and imagined. We did this huddled together to keep warm.

*

'We are winning the war, sire,' announced one of Parsifal's trusted generals. 'The rebel force is pulling back.'

'Follow them and exterminate every last one except the werewolf king,' ordered Parsifal X. 'I want to kill him myself. Slowly!'

The thought of inflicting a painful death on the werewolf cheered X considerably.

*

'Fall back in a disciplined way as planned,' commanded Ardolf Mingan, the werewolf king and field marshall of the rebel army.

A hasty conference with the leaders of the high elves and the arch chancellor of the dwarves had examined Peter's remarkable proposal and accepted its validity. They would retreat back making sure that X's army had no supplies. They would create numerous ambushes as they went. Parsifal X would expect that they were retreating in confusion. They would lay a few simple spells to reinforce that belief whilst actually doing everything according to a careful plan.

The rebels had not yet discovered the friendly mercenary force led by the captain. However, when they did they knew that their leader would be able to identify himself by showing them the ring that Aradel had given him.

*

The submarine rose gently to the surface. The captain climbed up into the sail and threw open the hatch. About one hundred feet behind them was the plesiosaur and it was still gaining on them. The diesel engines fired up and the submarine started to gather speed. The sea monster was still catching them but not so quickly. The powerful engine throbbed and the sub responded. Now they were running at full speed and the monster was only just keeping up.

The pursuit continued for a further thirty minutes and then, abruptly, the monster stopped and turned and could be seen vanishing back towards the North.

'What is our top speed?' asked Mary when the Commodore returned inside.

'Just over twenty knots on the surface and considerably less below,' answered the Commodore. 'It will take us another twenty four hours to reach the Isle of Man going at full speed on the surface.'

'And if we submerge again?'

'More than twice as long because we would be relying on the batteries and there is greater fluid resistance or drag.'

As the commander of the submarine said this another spasm went through his face. He grimaced horribly and then controlled himself. The internal mental battle was continuing and Mary was worried that the Commodore might not be winning whatever fight he was in.

*

I awoke feeling mentally refreshed despite the bad dreams that had assailed me. Lady Aradel had not fared so well. She was asleep but shaking with fear. The lack of efficacy of magic was affecting her much more than me .... it was draining her both mentally and physically. I shook her awake and she sat up in shock. This subsided when she saw me and realised she was relatively safe on our small solid island but the memory of her nightmares were still haunting her.

The morning in the swamp was dismal. It had become foggy and only a little light filtered through but we had to get out of the morass as fast as possible. I was worried that if we did not do so by noon, with the lack of food, water and magic, Aradel may not be strong enough to continue. We had to push on and fight our way through.

I looked round for the lodestone. I had tethered it to a rock but it had worked its way loose ... it had gone! There were no other lodestones on our little island and I had left all the other pieces of that rock at the edge of the swamp.

Aradel saw my frantic search, could see the problem and immediately began to despair. She knelt down in the wet grass and produced a keening sound, a wail of anguish. Then, glory be, I saw the monopole. It was hovering over a patch of swamp with the tail of golden thread hanging below it.

Damn it, I thought, *without that lodestone we are doomed. I'm going after it.*

I started to walk into the swamp towards the lodestone and immediately sank to my waist and then down to my chest. I threw myself forward and swam over to the hovering stone. I reached the position without difficulty but the stone was several feet above the swamp and I could not catch the string.

Eventually one herculean jump and much pushing down with my hands pulled me up out of the mire and I was able to grab the golden thread..... but down, down, down I went as gravity took hold of me and the monopoles made me insubstantial. I slipped much further into the filth than I had done on my two previous complete immersions. This time I was ready for it and I had taken a large breath. I held tightly onto the lodestone, kicked for the surface and broke water just as my lungs felt like bursting. I gasped for air and made for the small island .... our refuge in the mire of desperation.

Lady Aradel was still curled up in a foetal ball, moaning to the damp grass. I touched her lightly on the shoulder.

'I've got the lodestone, Princess,' I said in a jovial mood.

She looked at me in stark amazement. 'I was convinced that the swamp had got you,' she said. 'I was already grieving for you!'

'They don't call me Scott of the Swamp for nothing,' I replied.

'Do they call you that?' asked Aradel.

'Well, no they don't,' I admitted, shaking the filth from my body 'But they might from now on!'

- Chapter 26 -

The journey in the submarine began to feel interminable even though the vessel was moving at its top speed on the surface. Mary spent as much time as she could in the Control Room watching the Commodore. She was worried about the spasms affecting the submarine's commander. On two occasions she saw him slap his thighs as you might when swatting a fly. On several other occasions he appeared to be having difficulty in controlling his limbs and there was just one instant when she thought that his eyes glowed unnaturally but which could have been a trick of the light.

He continued to direct the boat impeccably and night fell with the sub still making progress towards the Isle of Man moving quickly on the surface of the sea. The family, Mary included, all went to sleep in their little cabin but the Commodore did not go to bed... despite protestations from the crew, he stayed in the Control Room. The spasms were coming more frequently and at three in the morning Hannah called Mary, Sienna and the boys urgently from their room.

'Come quickly to the Control Room. The Commodore is in a bad way.'

They all ran the short distance to the small control room shaking the confusion of sleep from their minds. Mary, in particular, found that she kept thinking about her dreams of unending swamps and timeless murky depths and had to fight hard to fully wake up.

The Commodore was standing in the middle of the room with a strange, tortured expression on the once-handsome face. His red hair was writhing independently and the man was talking, or more correctly arguing, with himself. Then one factor gained control and he pressed two red buttons on the console. A flare shot up from the submarine.

'We have put out a radio distress call,' said the radio operator. 'Did you intend to do that, sir.'

'Of course I did, fool,' cried the Commodore, his face twisted in fury. 'I have put it out on all channels!'

'But I thought we were maintaining radio silence since we did not want people to know where we are...' complained the operator.

'I need to send a radio message as well as the distress call and flare,' said the commander of the boat. 'Let me use the communications console.'

The radio operator reluctantly stood to one side and the Commodore took over the position. His fingers flew vanishingly fast over the console composing a note stating that the family of James Scott were aboard the vessel and they needed to be taken off the submarine as soon as possible and taken to the headquarters of Brigadier Blenkinsop. He then sent this by all means available... radio, text, and email .

'Quickly fetch me a fire extinguisher,' demanded Mary.

'Whatever for?' asked one of the naval officers.

'Don't question her, just obey,' ordered Hannah.

'What is happening that you need this?' asked the sailor, passing the extinguisher to Mary.

'It's not what is happening that is worrying me but what is about to happen,' she enigmatically replied.

*

The swamp was getting worse. The fog had not lifted and we were weakening. On several occasions I could have sworn that I saw a skull floating in the mire and once I was certain that something large, green and slimy slid in a silent, crocodilian manner into the water in front of me.

Lady Aradel had weakened considerably and at midday she sat down but could not rise. I picked her up gently and put her over my shoulder in a fireman's lift. She was astonishingly light and initially I did not notice the weight at all. However, by mid-afternoon I was desperate. I was hungry, my throat was parched and her weight, although so slight, was becoming too great to bear. The fog had risen but there was still low cloud and it was unnaturally dark.

The stench of the evil place was worsening. I did not want to spend another night in the swamp, I was convinced that we would not survive it so I was moving as quickly as possible. In my haste I stumbled slightly and almost dropped Lady Aradel into the bog. She did not stir from her unconscious state and I was not sure whether she was alive or dead. Staggering I held onto her and pulled her back from the filth but not before a ghostly skeletal hand came up from the mire to grab her slim ankle in a tight grip. I was then in a tug of war with the skeleton. A second hand and a third pulled at her legs. I took my sword and hammered the bones with the hilt and eventually they loosened and the elf was free. From then on I could hear ghostly voices in my head imploring me "Join us, Join us, Join us."

The chorus of an ancient English song came back to me again and again:

> *Down among the dead men,*
> *Down among the dead men,*
> *Down, down, down, down,*
> *Down among the dead men let him lie*

I pushed through some particularly troublesomely thick reeds and deep dark mist. In a clearing I saw a feast. Tall, beautiful, brightly clothed men and women were eating and drinking whilst others were dancing.

'Come join our merry band,' cried a particularly good looking lady, holding out her hand to me.

Perhaps I've reached our goal and it's the end of the swamp, I thought.

But the lodestone was swinging wildly and I hesitated.

'If you don't want to join us, leave your friend,' said another, this time a tall Elven man. 'She is a burden on you and she belongs with us.'

I looked closer and realised that they were all elves, not exactly human. They had pointed ears and an unnatural beauty. Perhaps she does belong here, I thought, perhaps the whole point of this quest is to bring the Queen to this party?

Then I imagined my mother-in-law's acerbic voice in my head.

Just like you, James, to get the poor girl into this and think of abandoning her.

What? I replied to my own imagination.

Well, it's obviously an illusion. Can't you see the bones?

I peered with my eyes half closed at the beckoning hands. They were indeed skeletal.

'Join us, join us!' they implored.

'No thank you,' I replied, staggering back from the brink with the deadweight of Lady Aradel straining my back. 'I don't think I will.'

Instantly their manner changed and the skeletal hands tried to grab at my ragged dirty clothes. I moved away from the mists and the thicket and, on looking back, could only see skeletons pulling viciously at each other and then disappearing down into the sulphurous depths.

Well done Mary, I thought.

The imagined voice or memory of my mother-in-law had served me well. I pressed on, trying to sing Bunyan's famous hymn to cheer me as I toiled but found that I could only recall two lines and these kept repeating.

He who would valiant be 'gainst all disaster.
Let him in constancy follow the Master

Then the previous song combined with Bunyan's in my exhausted mind.

He who would valiant be
Down among the dead men,
Down among the dead men.

Fighting overwhelming weariness I reached a small hillock with great difficulty and gingerly placed my burden on the driest part. She opened her eyes and looked at me blankly before stirring slightly.

'No need to move,' I said to her gently, relieved that she was still alive. 'I'm just resting for a moment so you should do so too.'

I climbed onto the highest part of the hillock and looked out. For the first time I could discern a difference in the view. In the South I could just about see the looming dark mountains which were the volcanoes... the abode of the dragons. Much closer I was able to make out that the swamp sloped down into a valley.

On the other side of a small river, above a diminutive cliff, I saw green pastures and the sun was playing on fields of waving corn. I thought I could see people moving in the fields. Was it a mirage, another illusion? I kept looking and the scene did not waver. The conditions were not right for a mirage and not inviting enough for an illusion. I concluded that it was reality. We were reaching the end of the swamp.

'Time to move,' I said to Lady Aradel. I picked her up again with some grunting and heaving and continued our pilgrimage with the Queen of the Elves lying like a sack across my shoulders.

*

Parsifal X was furious. 'Why are we losing the fight?' he asked the generals.

'We are gaining ground,' replied one of X's commanders. He had been elected as the spokesperson for all of them…. a position that he had desperately tried to get out of.

'But when we get there they have vanished and they keep ambushing us,' X stated. 'We don't need to gain ground. We need to kill werewolves, destroy dwarves and eliminate elves. It should be simple.'

'But sire,' the spokesperson continued. 'They are elusive. They are moving back into territory which they know better than we do.'

'And what is happening to our troops?'

'We are not losing many compared with our numbers but they are becoming hungry and want to rest.'

'Rest? REST?' Parsifal was smoking again. 'They can rest when the job is completed. They can rest permanently!'

*

The submarine came to a complete halt at the Commodore's angry command. He climbed up and opened a hatch before anybody could prevent him. The sea was choppy and copious cold salt spray flew over the commanding officer soaking him. He pulled the hatch down again and ran over to the operator.

'Cancel the distress signal,' he ordered in a much more normal voice. 'And get ready to dive.'

'Yes sir!' exclaimed the relieved man at the helm. However, before he could respond to the orders the Commodore had changed again. His face became more agitated and he started to writhe in pain.

'Do not dive!' he exclaimed in a very loud, harsh voice. 'Keep the distress signal running.'

'Sir,' asked Hannah, the most senior of the officers in the Control Room apart from the Commodore. 'Do you want us to dive or do you not?'

The commander of the boat turned to look at Hannah and as he did so his feet started to smoulder, then his thighs burst into flame. Sea water rose from his wet clothes in clouds of steam as the conflagration spread to his body and arms. Mary brought up the fire extinguisher and let loose with its contents. The jet of cold CO_2 gas shot over the burning man, extinguishing the flames and causing icicles to form on his limbs. He sank to the ground with a sigh.

'Thank you Mary, I should have thought of that myself,' said the Commodore. 'I think you've caught the bugger but I fear it is too late. I'm burnt up inside and I won't last long.'

Hannah and Mary undid his still smoldering jacket in order to render first aid. They jumped back in horror for the man's body was just a mass of black charcoal.

'I think the fire monster got into me when the Red Cap died,' the Commodore whispered. 'I've been fighting him ever since. He has been trying to control my mind but I have fought hard.' The naval officer rested for a moment and then, in his weakening whisper resumed his dying message.

'I fear that I may have betrayed you by calling the distress signal. That was the fire monster in charge when I failed to hold him down. You must defeat him. He may have succeeded in getting into my mind but I could also read some of his intentions. Parsifal X is his name.'

The damaged commander of the submarine paused, turned to look at Sienna then spoke again.

'Sienna, he has not caught your husband and it is all still worth fighting for. X has agreed a pact with a creature he calls the Lord of the Far Realm. This creature sounds suspiciously like the Devil but I cannot be sure. Never believed in Satan until now but there you have it. You must all try to convince the authorities that they should not work with Parsifal X or the Lord of the Far

Realm.'

The Commodore coughed and a copious amount of bright red blood spurted from his mouth. He gasped for breath and carried on.

'Lastly, and perhaps most importantly, Blinkers Blenkinsop is completely controlled by the fire monster. He is in a totally delusional state and does whatever X tells him to. Blinkers always was weak minded.'

The Commodore lay on the floor of the Control Room gasping and tried to speak again.

'I'm sorry Mary. I would like to have known you better.'

He let out a last cough and his whole body jerked into a spasm and then fell limp. His eyes rolled up in his head so that only the whites were showing.

'He's died,' said Mary.

'Quick,' cried Hannah. 'We must try to resuscitate him.'

She pressed down hard on his chest with both of her hands and to her horror the charcoal fell apart onto the floor. The fire had consumed the Commodore.

Mary carefully sprayed each piece and even sprayed a small ember that had fallen onto Hannah's uniformed arm.

*

'No, no, NO!' cried Parsifal. 'The pain, The pain. The unbearable agony! They've destroyed another of my avatars! Whoever did this will regret it. They shall all die a miserable and painful death, their skin flayed and burnt over a hot griddle whilst their guts simmer in a cauldron of boiling oil. I shall remove their brains with a straw and ......'

'Sire,' cried the general's spokesperson. 'The hobgoblins are eating the mammoths.'

'No great loss,' replied Parsifal X, pleased to be distracted from his personal loss. 'The mammoths were only a liability.

Anything else?'

'Well.....' the general wondered what else he should tell X. 'The cyclops have eaten the wyverns.'

'More of a problem but lets not worry. What about the Trolls?'

'They're busy eating everything, sire, even the larger billy goats.'

'We had billy goats in our army?'

'No sire.'

'Then why did you tell me that, you fool?' Parsifal had heard more than he wanted to hear.

He permitted a streak of orange and red flame to burst from his fingertips and incinerate the general where he stood. Feeling better for having let out his feelings, X sat down again on his mobile throne. Deep underneath in a small niche the gnome shook with fear. Things were not going exactly to plan and he did not really want to be around if it all went wrong. No sir!

*

We gradually threaded our way out of the last part of the swamp. I was truly relieved to be away from the Slough of Despond. As we reached solid ground Lady Aradel regained some of her strength and was able to hobble along, holding on whilst I took a lot of her weight on my arm.

We reached the crystal flowing river.

'Is it safe to drink?' I asked Aradel.

'If you don't drink too much and don't fall in, then the answer is yes,' she replied.

I reflected that she was definitely getting better.

I am came the reply.

I bent down and cupped some of the water to my lips and Aradel did likewise. It was the most beautiful, cool refreshing drink I had ever had. We both stood up and I looked out over the river. It was considerably wider than I had initially imagined.

'Is it possible to swim across?' I asked Aradel.

'It used to be possible to wade across but over the last three hundred years it has become much deeper and there are now poisonous snakes on the far side,' she responded.

'So how can it be crossed at all?' I asked.

'You can use the ferry,' she answered.

'There's a ferry?'

'And a ferryman,' replied Aradel. 'Christian called it the ferry boat of Vain Hope but the ferryman is usually called Charon.'

'Wait a minute,' I cried. 'What is this river called?'

'It is the River Jordan,' replied Aradel. 'You seem surprised?'

'I am not just surprised I am amazed,' I countered. 'Charon is the ferryman for the River Styx not the River Jordan.'

'Well now,' she replied and pointed with her finger. 'It is the Jordan from this side and over there is the Promised Land. From the other side it is either called the Styx or the Acheron and this side is Hades or Hell. Take your pick.'

'Can we ride in the ferry?' I asked.

'If you can pay the price,' she replied. 'Charon always demands payment or he will not take you. Then you would have to wander the banks for a hundred years.'

'What does he take as payment?'

'He likes a silver coin such as a Greek Obol.'

'I have a few so-called silver coins in my pocket but they are all worthless cupro-nickel,' I replied.

I had not thrown away the coins even though they were useless here. They and my mobile phone had remained in my inner pocket throughout the time I had been in the faerie world..... the coins were worthless and the phone did not work but they were a tangible contact with my own reality which I was loathe to lose.

'I have several silver coins,' explained Lady Aradel. 'But it has to be something made of rare precious metal that you have personally carried across the swamp and that you value.'

So we had come all this way and I was stymied by a lack of precious metals! The last year that they had minted coins containing silver in the UK was 1946 and we had changed over to decimal coins in 1971. None of our coins contained silver!

Then I remembered the phone. I knew that the motherboard of the phone was plated in gold, all the connectors were also gold plated. The ceramic capacitors would undoubtedly contain palladium.

'Does it have to be in the form of a coin?' I queried.

'No, a ring would do. Basically it must be precious metal. Any shape.'

I did not wear rings. I had broken my finger when wearing my wedding ring and they had only managed to remove the ring by cutting it off and I had never put a ring back on my hand since then. So it would have to be the phone.

'There are precious metals in this phone,' I told Lady Aradel, showing it to her. She stared at the object.

'What is it?' she asked.

'It is a mobile phone,' I replied. 'A cell phone. A communication device. It contains gold and palladium.'

'Oh,' she replied. 'I understand. I saw telephones when I was last in your world. Big black machines connected to each other by wires. You keep them in large red boxes which have little panes of glass all around.'

I sighed.

So we did I thought. *But they are becoming rare.*

'This is what they look like now?' she asked.

'Yes, and if it was working I could show you all the apps on it,' I said and thought vividly and nostalgically of the games, the camera, the music, the texts, the emails and all the other applications.

Aradel read my thoughts. 'It does all that?' she said, amazed.

'It is a wondrous magic wand.'

'No, it's just science that you don't understand,' I retorted and could not help laughing.

'What is funny Lord James?' asked Aradel.

'My science is magic to you and vice versa!' I exclaimed, still laughing. 'But would this be sufficient payment for Charon?'

'Undoubtedly so,' replied Lady Aradel. 'That is a high payment indeed.'

- Chapter 27 -

'Recommence radio silence and prepare to dive,' Hannah ordered.

'Aye, aye, captain,' said the junior officer at the helm.

'Probably too late, ma'am,' interjected the sonar operator. Nobody had been watching the sonar machines whilst the Commodore was dying but now they all turned to look at the consoles. Even to a novice it was clear that something huge was very close to the submarine.

The radio crackled into life. 'This is the USS Albert A Gore calling. We are responding to your Mayday. Repeat, we are responding to your Mayday.'

'That's an aircraft carrier, ma'am,' said the sonar operator.

'I know,' replied Hannah. 'Nimitz class. What's it doing here? It's based in San Diego.'

'If we receive no response we will board your vessel,' came the message from the radio. 'This is the USS Albert A Gore calling. We are responding to your Mayday. Repeat, we are responding to your Mayday.'

'OK,' said Hannah to the communications operator. 'Tell them that there is no emergency.'

The communications officer immediately fired off the reply but from above them they heard the clang of metal on metal. The noise resounded throughout the submarine.

'They are already on the submarine, ma'am,' said the helmsman.

'They are our allies and we can't submerge with our so-called friends marching around on the top of our boat,' reasoned Hannah. 'It would cause a nasty international incident. Especially if they really are here in response to our call. So we better let them in.'

She climbed up the steep metal ladder that the Commodore had so recently ascended and swung open the hatch.

'Hello boys,' she said with a smile. 'Thank you for coming.'

*

A rowing boat drifted slowly towards us on the bank of the River Jordan. A figure stood up at the back of the boat holding a long pole but he rarely dipped it into the crystal water .... the vessel appeared to be moving under its own volition.

As the ferry came closer I could see the figure more clearly. The ferryman was a slightly stooped person wearing long black gowns and a deep hood. I could not see his face.

'Lady Aradel,' I said looking at the ominous apparition moving towards us over the water.

'Yes,' she answered.

'Have I died? Is this some kind of strange afterlife?'

'For some, maybe. But for you ....no.'

Before she could explain further, and I certainly wanted an explanation, the boat had reached our shore.

'Who calls Charon?' came a sepulchral voice. 'And can you pay the fare?'

'We are two pilgrims who kindly request passage to the other side,' replied Lady Aradel in her sweet melodic voice.

'But do you have the fare?' repeated Charon. 'If you do not have the fare you will not pass.'

'We have the fare,' I replied and Charon turned to look at me.

'A mortal!' he exclaimed. 'A live mortal that has crossed the Slough of Despond, the eternal swamp of Hades. That is unusual.'

The ferryman became almost animated compared with his previous slow movement.

'If you have the fare,' said Charon. 'I will be delighted to take you and Lady Aradel across to Camp side.'

I looked at Aradel. 'He knows who you are?'

'I've been here before,' she replied passing a silver coin to Charon. He examined the coin and nodded slightly, then helped her aboard the craft.

'I have no silver coin,' I started to say and Charon held up a hand as if to stop me stepping aboard. 'But I do have something else that contains gold and palladium.' I held out my mobile phone to the ferryman. He looked at it quizzically for a moment and then responded.

'That is a very nice cell-phone,' he intoned in a voice from the grave. 'Do you not have something of lower value?'

'I've got some cupronickel UK coinage,' I replied. 'But no other precious metals. I have to be honest. The batteries have died on that phone and it is not functioning. It has been in and out of the swamp several times.'

'Well, it is more than sufficient payment and I'm sure it will work for me,' the ferryman actually seemed pleased with the phone.

He took it from my hand and pressed the "on" switch. The machine lit up and the display said "slide to unlock". This he did and he asked me for the passcode.

'5,5,5,5,' I replied.

Charon entered the code and he had all the apps on display. He went straight to the Game Center.

'Do you have Tetris?' asked Charon in the same sepulchral voice but with a hint of excitement.

'Sure, it's in the game center somewhere,' I answered.

'Great,' said the usually lugubrious ferryman. 'Thanatos and I have been playing this game and he keeps beating me. Now I can get some practice.'

Charon looked lovingly at the smart phone lying in his bony hand.

'This is worth at least four trips on the ferryboat. I do not give change but if you ever return here there are three free trips waiting for you.'

Whilst we had been talking the boat had moved out with no obvious input from Charon. We were now in the middle of the river..... it felt chilly and wide so I hoped that the old spiritual hymn was right and that there would be milk and honey on the other side. The waters of the crystal flowing river had slaked my thirst and now I was able to really feel the hunger pangs from eating nothing for the last forty-eight hours.

Deep River, my home is over Jordan
Deep River, I want to cross over into camp ground

Charon had the music playing from the phone, spreading out like ethereal hands reaching to infinity.

*

Hannah was the first to step onto the aircraft carrier from the launch that had taken her and the family off the submarine. The US naval officers had been most insistent that Mary, Sienna, Joshua and Samuel came with them to the USS Albert A Gore but Hannah, as the highest level officer on board the submarine had persuaded the officers that she should accompany them. They were taken straight to the fleet commander, Rear Admiral Ulysses Hannibal Jackson.

'Hi, I'm Ulysses Jackson, ma'am,' he introduced himself first to Hannah and then nodded to the family. 'I'm sorry to drag you off your submarine but we have received specific instructions to find your vessel and we have been searching for any wreckage for well over a month.'

'A month?' Hannah was utterly astonished. 'But we have only been to sea for less than two days.'

'What date do you think it is?' asked the admiral.

'April 15th,' she replied instantly.

'You went missing on April 14th. It is now June 7th, ma'am.'

'I don't see how that is possible,' replied Hannah. 'We did not have enough supplies to keep us going for that length of time.'

'And we only got one night's sleep on board the sub,' put in Joshua.

'And yet it is June the seventh,' stated the fleet commander. 'You have lost seven weeks. Has anything strange happened to you?'

'Anything strange? You can bet your life it has,' replied Hannah and started to tell the admiral about the werewolf, the sea monster and now the conflagration of the Commodore.

Whilst she had been talking several white clad sailors had gathered behind her. At a wave of the hand of the fleet commander one stepped forward and injected her in the thigh. Hannah slumped to the floor unconscious.

'Why did you do that?' cried Sienna. 'She was telling the truth. We were all there.'

'Well ma'am,' replied the rear admiral politely. 'We have received strict instructions from our chiefs to treat you all with the greatest of care. They have been told by your own emergency government, led by Brigadier Blenkinsop, that a form of infective insanity has spread to some submariners and that they would ramble on about monsters and werewolves. Things that obviously do not exist.'

'But they do exist, we've seen them,' shouted Samuel.

'He's right,' agreed Joshua, more sullenly. 'And you just assaulted our friend Hannah.'

'OK,' said the fleet commander holding up his hands. 'I don't want to have you all sedated. If you agree to come with me quietly we will provide you with food and comfortable bunks until your own people get here. Which will be soon.'

He waved his hands dismissively and the white clad navy

personnel led the family away.

*

'The rebel army has all retreated into the fairy kingdom,' said one of Parsifal X's generals warily.

'Then follow them and kill them,' replied X.

'The fairy ambassador would like to speak to you before you do that,' replied the general.

Parsifal X pondered for a moment. *I had better see the ambassador. The fairies are powerful and I would not like to break our agreement right at this moment.*

The fairy ambassador floated into the room, her gossamer thin wings gently buzzing in iridescent colour.

'We will not permit you to enter our kingdom with your ill-disciplined forces, Lord Parsifal,' she said. 'It would be a direct breach of our pact and construed by most as the commencement of hostilities.'

'No, no. We have no intention of doing that,' said Parsifal X smoothly. 'Of course I will keep to the pact, our terms of understanding are explicit. I will tell my generals to move the army back from the frontier and you in turn will continue to honour our agreement?'

'That is so,' trilled the fairy. 'We are bound by our oath.'

'Would you like some nectar?' suggested Parsifal X.

'That would be most convivial,' agreed the fairy taking a sip from the proffered drink.

*

I looked over Jordan and what did I see?
Coming for to carry me home

As we reached the other side of the Jordan I was aware of a change in nature of the water. Previously it had been a beautiful crystal-clear flowing river and now it was muddy and slow, the dark stygian depths of legend. Peering into this sludge I could see long snakes or possibly eels writhing around, mouths open, biting intemperately at each other. Fog gathered in miasmic tendrils over the surface and the smell reminded me of the Slough of Despond from which we had so recently escaped. What strange feature of the flow kept one side clear and clean and the other so filthy and dark?

From this side I could understand why it was called the River Styx so I was glad when the ferry boat tied up on a wooden jetty and Charon helped first Lady Aradel and then myself onto the boarding. I turned to wave goodbye to Charon but he had already disappeared into the mists.

The shore was a short shingle beach leading to a continuous cliff that stretched off to the horizon in both directions. Now that I was close to it I could tell that there was only one way up this outcrop ... a narrow gap between two higher promontories. A steep path wound up through this gap and at the top I could see a gatehouse, and a statue. Beyond this I could just make out the tops of two distinctly different buildings, the nature of which I could not discern.

However, before we climbed that path we came across a party of people on the beach having a glorious picnic from several large trestle tables. There was food and drink in huge abundance but the guest were all dressed in black suits, white shirts and black ties. They were partaking riotously of the food and talking to each other very loudly.

'What is going on here?' I asked Aradel quietly as we came up close to the party.

'It is a funeral wake,' replied the Queen of the Elves.

'Who has died?' I inquired.

'He has,' answered Aradel, pointing to a small, morose man who was sitting on his own, dressed more colourfully than all the rest.

'He doesn't look very dead to me,' I countered. 'He looks

quite healthy.'

'Nevertheless, he has died. That is why they are all ignoring him,' Aradel retorted.

'Do you think he'll let us eat some of the food?' I asked 'I'm completely famished.'

'I don't expect he'll mind,' replied the elf. 'He'll be amazed that you can see him. None of the others can.'

I went straight up to the unconvincingly dead man and spoke to him. He jumped up with a start.

'Gracious me. You gave me a start,' he stared at me. 'Do I know you?'

'I don't think so,' I answered. 'But I was wondering whether we could eat any of your food.'

'Go ahead,' said the man. 'Mind you, you are in a bit of a mess. How did you get so muddy?'

'We've just come across the River Jordan,' I replied. 'It is very muddy indeed on the other side.'

'So that's the Jordan, is it?' asked the dead man. 'I was beginning to think that it was the River Styx and that Charon would be coming for me. I'm of Greek origin you know.'

I confessed that I did not know that he was Greek. He looked me up and down again.

'Are you sure that it is the Jordan and not the Styx?' he paused and continued, somewhat hesitantly. 'You see, I have not been very well recently and I thought that I might have died. Then I thought that I was being stupid ... "Cogito ergo sum, I think therefore I am" does rather imply that I am still alive.'

Rene' Descarte 1637 .... I could feel Lady Aradel project this information into my mind.

'My companion has just told me that indeed you have died,' I responded to the sad dead man rather bluntly.

The fellow's face surprised me by brightening at this news.

'There,' he cried. 'I told them I was ill but they said I was a hypochondriac.'

He then became morose again as he continued to speak.

'But it's not a great one to be right over, is it?'

I had to agree that it was not and he once more started to talk.

'I had a bad attack of indigestion, at least that's what the doctor said I had. Then it got worse and I don't remember anything else till I woke up here at this strange party and nobody would talk to me.'

I commiserated with him and told him that I too had landed in the reality unexpectedly.

'What's it like over there?' he asked, pointing over the river.

'I think you'd do better going that way,' I suggested, pointing to the cliff and the cliff path.

'I can't see anything that way, just blackness, nothing else,' said the man.

'But you can see the river?'

'Oh yes. But what is it like on the other side?'

'It's like Hades. Boggy, wet and smelly,' I answered.

'Of course it is,' he answered. 'You'd expect it to be like that but is there any way through?'

I remembered the lodestone which I still had in my pocket, attached to the gold thread that came from Lady Aradel's dress. I took the stone from my pocket and gave it to the man.

'Here,' I said. 'Take this. It might just help. Do not tread anywhere that this is deflected from. Hold it in front of you on the string. You are OK if it is pulling to the ground but don't go where it is hovering.'

He looked reluctantly at the stone before taking it.

'This will help,' I added. 'Believe me. You can get through but you must have faith.'

'And where will I get to if I do get through?' he asked reasonably enough.

'You just might get to the highlands of the elves or the kingdom of the fairies. It is very beautiful beyond the swamps.'

The man looked at me strangely and handed the lodestone back to me.

'Thank you all the same,' he said. 'But I think I'll take my chances without the stone.'

'Do you have a coin for Charon?' I asked.

'I have a silver thruppence that I found in my Christmas Pudding when I was a child,' he said with glee. 'I have kept it in my wallet ever since, for this very eventuality.'

I nodded and then asked again about the food.

'Sure, go ahead,' said the dead man. 'But avoid the crab meat. I think it's off.'

He then looked at the two of us again. 'Who did you say your companion is?' he asked.

'Let me present Lady Aradel, Queen of the Elves,' I bowed slightly as I said this.

'Funny,' he remarked. 'This being dead is making me see things. She looks like a beautiful girl and a huge beast, one at the same time.'

He shook his head and then stared at us again.

'It's double vision. I must keep off the bottle.' He then laughed. 'Silly me. It's too late to worry about that!'

Lady Aradel shrugged her shoulders dismissively and we walked over to the tables to help ourselves to a variety of foodstuffs. The party goers ignored us completely.

*

The ship was enormous and very new. Mary, Sienna and the two children were taken to a four-bed cabin and locked in. Hannah was removed to a secure area in the hospital section. After an hour on their own two US naval officers brought food to the family on a tray. Mary stared hard at the more senior of the two men and spoke in her most authoritative tone.

'I would like to see the rear admiral right away, young man. Make it so.'

The man flinched as if hit by a mental sledge hammer.

'Certainly ma'am. Come with me,' he replied, ignoring his companion who tried to point out that they had strict instructions to keep the Scott family in their cabin.

The seaman led Mary through numerous corridors and via an elevator to the flag bridge. This was one level down from the captain's bridge, the ship's command center, but was still high up in the tower or "island".

The man walked as if in a mesmeric daze, not stopping to ask permission to enter the flag bridge which was clearly a breach of protocol. His companion, running along behind them, apologised the best he could. The older seaman led Mary up to the rear admiral who was sitting at a desk on his own. He looked at the procession with some surprise.

'You have imprisoned us without cause and with no justification,' said Mary staring into the rear admiral's eyes. 'I need to tell you some important facts before Brigadier Blenkinsop's men get here. Firstly, there is no infective insanity. We have all seen and experienced that which we say we have. There is no mass hysteria and no madness. Secondly, you must question all of the submariners in order to establish the truth. This you will do. Thirdly, you have indeed assaulted Hannah. When you hand us over to Blenkinsop do not hand her over.... they are not expecting her. Sit her down and listen to her story.... and lastly you must arrange to meet my son-in-law, James Scott, on the Isle of Man. He will arrive sometime before the summer solstice and will need to get to Stonehenge by sunrise on that day. Is that understood?'

'Yes, ma'am,' replied the rear admiral meekly.

'When I count to three you will come out of this hypnotic trance and will then put into action what I have said believing it to be your own ideas,' she paused then added. 'One, two , three.'

The commanding officer of the fleet blinked and then looked at Mary as if seeing her for the first time.

'Ma'am, I asked the security officers to confine you to a cabin. What are you doing here?'

'I asked them to bring me here,' Mary replied quietly. 'I would just like you to think carefully about your actions. I believe that Brigadier Blenkinsop is being directed by somebody else and that you must avoid the same happening to you.'

The rear admiral laughed.

'My dear good lady, you do not need to worry about me. I'm sure I am made of sterner stuff than that. Perhaps you would permit me to direct the security to take you back to your cabin?'

He said the latter part in a semi-sarcastic tone but after she had been led meekly from the room he sat alone at his desk and scratched his head.

Perhaps he had been a little too abrupt with the submarine's officer? Lieutenant Hannah Lee had not been mentioned in the orders from his superiors, they only mentioned the Scott family. Perhaps when Blenkinsop's men arrived he would purposely neglect to mention her? In any case it would be interesting to hear in more detail what she had to say .

These and other thoughts started to fly through his head and he resolved to put them all into action.

*

PARSIFAL
You must be at Stonehenge
With the innocents
at Dawn on the Summer Solstice
Till I eat your soul
Yours
Lucifer

'Where did you find this creature?' asked Parsifal X. He was staring at another message from the Lord of the Far Realm but this time it was tattooed on the back of a dead cyclops.

The guard had been killed in an ambush just before the rebels retreated into the fairy kingdom. The cyclopean guard's shirt had been ripped from his back by another guard who wished to purloin it. The body would then have been eaten but for the message that they had found tattooed on its back. The corpse had been dragged to the feet of the Faerie world's overlord.

This Lucifer is beginning to annoy me, thought Parsifal X, but being at Stonehenge must become my priority. Where exactly is Stonehenge?

'Where exactly is Stonehenge, gnome?' screamed Parsifal. The gnome jumped out of his hiding place, white beard sweeping the floor in his haste.

'It is in the South of England, sire, your highness. In the real world, sire. In the complicated reality with which you are attempting to merge this realm. It is a designated World Heritage Site.'

'Can you direct us there, open a gate to it or something?'

'Certainly, sire, with your assistance, yes!' replied the gnome.

The fire demigod sat back on his throne, much placated.

*

We did not overeat. We both realised that eating a large amount when you have been fasting is a most dangerous thing to do. I did, however, find a large bag and place some of the food and a bottle of beer into it. At no time did the roistering carousers notice us at all.

We walked over to the narrow path that wound up the cliff. The ascension was very difficult but we eventually reached the gatehouse and the statue.

The massive carving appeared to be made of white marble. It had the haunches and body of a lion, the wings of an eagle and the face of a woman. It was clearly a sphinx but not the benign sort I had seen in Egypt. It had a more malevolent look but, like the Cairo version, it certainly looked inscrutable.

As we went to pass the statue it sprang to life and blocked our passage.

'Halt. Who goes there?' it demanded.

'Lady Aradel and Lord James Scott,' I retorted.

'Lady Aradel can pass but Lord James must answer my riddles,' the animated statue stated.

'And if I don't get them right?' I prompted.

'Then I shall eat you.'

To back up this reply the sculpted monstrosity opened its mouth revealing rows of sharp, white marble teeth.

Lady Aradel looked at me quizzically. 'Do you think you can do it?' she asked. 'If you can't we may be able to find another way round.'

The sphinx slowly turned its huge head and stared at Aradel.

'There is no other way through. You know that.'

'Don't worry,' I said. 'I'll have a go but I would like to know the rules first.'

'That is fair,' thrummed the statue. 'You must answer two out of the three riddles correctly. You can have three attempts at each riddle. I will tell you the answers before I eat you so that you can regret your lack of ability as you die.'

Phew, I thought. *Perhaps Lady Aradel can help me telepathically.*

No cheating, the sphinx put the command into my head in answer to my thought.

'OK,' I said. 'There's no point hanging around. Fire away.'

With a bit of luck, I thought, *it will be that hoary old number about legs. What has four legs in the morning, two at midday and three in the evening?*

The sphinx answered telepathically.

Everybody knows that one now. The answer is man.....baby, adult and old age. No, I have something new for you.

'Here is the first riddle,' the sphinx spoke out loud. 'Who put the frivolity into murder?'

'Who put the frivolity into murder?' I repeated. 'That's a question rather than a riddle.'

'No,' replied the statue. 'It is a riddle.'

'OK,' I replied. 'Is it Parsifal X.'

The sphinx laughed with a deep, hollow, reverberating sound that made my ears ring.

'That is not correct but I can see why you might think that way. Lord Parsifal X does find killing people amusing.'

'Then I have no idea,' I said. 'But at a guess Adolf Hitler?'

'Wrong!'

Perhaps it means an author, I thought.

'Agatha Christie,' I suggested.

'Wrong,' responded the sphinx. 'The answer is "Whosoever put the laugh into slaughter".'

I sat back on a nearby boulder.

That's just repeating the same thing in other words.' I protested.

'No,' replied the sphinx. 'It is the answer to the riddle and now I shall ask the second. You must get this right by at least your third attempt. The riddle is.....' the sphinx paused for effect. '..... Who put the monster into evolution?'

'Charles Darwin,' I answered instantly.

'Wrong!'

'Alfred Russell Wallace.'

'Wrong. You have only one more attempt and then I shall eat you.'

The sphinx started grinding its teeth in a most disturbing way.

'I won't answer until you stop grinding your teeth,' I complained. 'It is unfair. It is putting me off.'

'Sorry,' replied the sphinx, rather chagrined. 'I like to be scrupulously fair. I didn't even realise I was doing it. This is the first time I have used these particular riddles and I was enjoying myself. I'll give you some extra time.'

Riddle, riddle, riddle, I thought, *what is the difference between a riddle and a question? A riddle has a trick in it but it must still be logical in a peculiar sort of way. Let's think of one. OK. What is the longest word in the English language?... The answer to the question is "antidisestablishmentarianism" if technical and coined words are excluded. But the answer to the riddle is "smiles" because there is a mile between the two letters S.*

I sat back and thought for a few more moments. Unfortunately the sphinx was becoming restless.

'You promised me extra time,' I pointed out. 'And you've started grinding your teeth again.'

'Sorry, sorry. I forgot,' said the animated sculpture. 'Would you like me to repeat the riddle?'

'Yes please,' I said, sweating with anxiety.

'The riddle number two is .....Who put the monster into evolution?'

The trick in my longest word riddle is in the wordplay, I thought. *The word "mile" is hidden in the word smiles. Could there be something similar in riddle number two? Is there a word hidden in the answer to riddle number one.....yes there is.. it's easy...the letters L,A,U,G,H are in the middle of slaughter. So what I have to do is find a word that means evolution and look for a hidden word.*

The sphinx was moving towards me with its jaws wide open, teeth and claws exposed.

'Ogre in progress!' I shouted quickly as it came right up to me snapping its jaws. 'The answer is "Whosoever put the ogre into progress".'

The sphinx stopped moving and looked at me contemplatively.

'Very good, little human. That is correct. The third riddle is

...Who made honesty tedious?'

For the question several correct possible answers sprang to mind.... various religious leaders for example and the occasional politician, perhaps George Washington? But I could only see one correct answer to the riddle.

'Whosoever put the rut into truth,' I cried out with glee.

The sphinx looked momentarily angry and then actually smiled the famous inscrutable smile.

'I find that I am pleased you have passed the examination. The riddles did test you and you were not found wanting. I was not hungry anyway......I just ate a complete coach load. The driver had gone to sleep at the wheel. They did not get a single answer right. It was poor sport.' I waited and the sphinx did not move out of the way.

'May we pass please?' I enquired politely.

'Oh yes, certainly. You don't have any new riddles do you?'

I told the monstrous sculpture the longest word riddle. The deep, hollow, reverberating laugh rang out again.

'I like that one. To whom should I credit the authorship?'

'Beano 1959,' I replied instantly.

- Chapter 28 -

'If you could persuade him to let Hannah go why didn't you make him let us go too?' argued Sienna. 'We're all locked in this cabin waiting for Blenkinsop's henchmen. How has that improved things?'

'It doesn't work like that,' countered Mary to her daughter. 'I searched in his mind and could only make him do things that he was half-wondering about anyway. You've got to understand that this telepathy thing is a bit hit and miss.'

'You managed to make the seaman take you to see the dratted rear admiral, for God's sake,' replied Sienna, still frustrated by their incarceration.

'His mind was feeble compared with the admiral's,' answered Mary and then added. 'Besides I have a distinct feeling that we have to go with Blenkinsop's army and see this thing through to the end.'

'So you're seeing the future now, mother?' queried Sienna disbelieving.

'Not exactly but some patterns are emerging,' Mary replied. 'Things have changed everywhere and the whole of reality is unstable. For some reason I can feel these things.'

'If anything happens to the boys because you didn't set us free when you could have done I'll never forgive you,' argued Sienna, bitterly.

'I'm just your mother, Sienna,' Mary reminded her daughter. 'I'm not bloody Superwoman.'

'And you're their grandmother. Don't forget that!' countered Sienna.

Joshua and Samuel sat on their bunks with their hands over

their ears. They both hated to hear their mother and grandmother arguing and found that the best thing to do was to ignore it.

*

'Good news, sire, your great highness,' announced one of Parsifal's generals.

'Yes?' chimed X in his most melodious voice.

'The Scott family, including the two male innocents, has been found and Blenkinsop's army will have them in their control very soon.'

'That is good news, thank you. Take a minor promotion,' so saying Parsifal X waved his hand and the general's uniform altered slightly, sporting an extra star. The general marched off delighted.

*

In front of us the path diverged. In the gloom of dusk one road, broad and shiny, led to a warm, welcoming tavern. Golden light spilled out from the leaded windows and a large open fire was burning merrily in its grate. There were crowds of people inside drinking and eating merrily. Sounds of laughter and song came in billows from the open doors in a very inviting manner. The sign swinging outside showed a stylized painting of the tavern balanced on the edge of a cliff and had the words "The Inn at the Very End of the World" emblazoned upon it.

The other path was narrow and uneven and the building was of an austere ecclesiastical design. There were narrow windows and a short steeple. Two wooden doors led to hard wooden pews. The sign outside stated "Church of the Promised Land.'

'We should take the narrow path that leads to salvation like Christian did if we are to follow in his footsteps,' suggested Lady Aradel, who by this time had fully recovered her strength and felt like taking the lead again.

'Then this is where we part,' I replied, wearily. 'I'm going to the happy place where they are singing and laughing. I believe that music is good for the soul and that laughter is the best medicine.'

'But is it wise?' asked Aradel.

'It's predictable that we should take the hardest route because we have done so each time so far,' I answered. 'And whenever I have made a "wise" decision here the result has been less than satisfactory. Thus I say we should be unpredictable and go to the pub rather than the church.'

Aradel laughed. 'I agree. I was just testing your resolve. Let's go to the pub.'

*

Whumph, Whumph, Whumph, Whumph. The din of the helicopter blades was enough to deafen Mary, Sienna and the boys as they sat in the military helicopter, handcuffed together and manacled to their seats. The inside of the machine was completely spartan. The seats were made of metal and had a very thin foam cushion. The family all faced backwards. The walls of the helicopter were unlined metal. Brigadier Blenkinsop's men were sat on similar metal seats facing towards the family.

The soldiers had not tried to question them and had given no indication as to why they were so important but they had gleaned from the few conversations they had overheard that they were en route to Tidworth Army Base. They also gathered that it was about three hundred and fifty miles and the flight would take about two hours.

Sienna was still annoyed with her mother but had realised that she could personally do nothing about the situation at present. Mary had convinced her that she had been acting from the best of intentions. It was, however, the boys that Sienna was most worried about. Why were the armed forces so interested in her boys? It was inexplicable.

*

Parsifal X had discontinued any hostilities with the rebel forces. Most of them had retreated into the Fairy Kingdom but

X had been harrying the remaining few. This activity had also ceased. X was preparing for his major invasion of the real world and this was now taking up all his faculties. He no longer believed that James Scott was important.. as far as he could tell the most significant factor was Scott's two sons. Perhaps they were the Enigma Key?

He would sacrifice the boys to the Lord of the Far Realm and the Far Lord, in return, would stabilise the worlds. Parsifal X believed that he, X, would then reign supreme over both existences until the yellow sun of the real world ran out of energy. By that time, perhaps four or five billion years, X reckoned he would have learnt how to control the energy of the cosmos including all the galactic centre black holes. When he had used up the energy of the entire universe, then, and only then, Lucifer could have his soul. Which, of course, X was convinced did not exist.

For now he had to concentrate on the considerable logistics of moving his forces over to the real world.

*

Inside the Inn at the Very End of the World there were hordes of people making merry. The area around the fire was dominated by a big bunch of rugby players who would strip off whilst intermittently bursting into song

> *Haul 'em down!*
> *You Zulu warrior!*
> *Haul 'em down!*
> *You Zulu chief!*
> *Chief! Chief!*

I was attracted to a particular bunch of characters at the other end of the room. Some of them were acting out parts from a play to the applause of the onlookers.

'They're thespians,' murmured a bald headed, bearded man in the audience.

I asked him if he knew anything about them.

'I prefer musicians but this lot are OK.' He turned and looked at the rugby players at the other end of the room. 'Better than that crowd down there. Nothing they like more than a punch up. I'll be out of here before they start.'

He picked up his pint of ale purposefully as I asked him whether he was a musician himself.

'Sort of.'

'What do you mean by that?' I asked.

'What do you call those people who hang around with musicians?' asked the man in reply to my question.

'Groupies?' I answered.

'Nope,' replied the bearded man with the challenged head follicles. 'They're called drummers. I'm a drummer.'

I looked more closely at him. He was wearing a hoodie top, jeans, waist belt with leg loops, had ropes around his left shoulder and on his feet were peculiar trainers. The man saw my enquiring glance and laughed.

'No, I wasn't playing the drums when I came here. I was climbing the gorge and the earthquake struck. I was dislodged, fell and arrived here.... with all my equipment.'

'You came from the real world?' I asked.

'Sure. That's right,' he answered . 'I realised straight away that this place wasn't quite right. I should have been in hospital if anywhere.'

'Where did you arrive?' I queried.

'Down by that smelly river amongst a whole load of freeloaders,' he replied pointing down over the cliff.

'And you came up here?'

'Well, I watched the people going over with the weird boatman and I did not fancy the look of that. The land on the other side is particularly inhospitable. I then sat looking carefully in the other directions. It took me a long time to be able to see that there was anything there except blackness but in the end I saw the cliff and the path up from it.'

'And you came up and beat the sphinx at his game?'

The man laughed again. 'No hope of that. I was never any good at riddles. No. I climbed up.'

At that even Lady Aradel, who had been listening half-heartedly, jumped with amazement.

'You came up the sheer cliff face?' I asked. 'It's several hundred feet high.'

'No big deal with the right gear,' said the rock climber/drummer. 'I've done far worse. I did not fancy the River Styx and Hades so I climbed up. The church looked dead so I came in here. I've been here quite a while.'

He had finished his drink and he glanced down the bar at the rugby players. 'Look, the rugger lads will start a fight any minute. There is a quieter bar upstairs...we could all three of us go up there and have another pint and you could tell me what has been happening to you. From the look of you I believe you could do with a rest and a clean up.'

I looked down at my clothing, all muddy and torn and over at Lady Aradel. She had a natural radiance which was shining through but her clothes were now also in a terrible state. We hadn't just been through the wars we had been through hell so it was really no surprise.

'You're on,' I said with a grin and he led the way through the throng.

*

Mary, Sienna and the boys were led to a barracks at Tidworth Base and locked in. On the wall was a plaque naming the particular barracks as Assaye. It explained that the barracks were all named after British Army battles in India and Afghanistan and that Assaye had been fought in 1803 in Western India between the Maratha Confederacy and the British East India Company.

After they had been locked into a small room in the barracks

Sienna and the boys looked round to see if there was anything that they could use to get free. The room had clearly been made secure just before they arrived as there were signs that the small windows had been screwed permanently shut very recently. There were five beds, each of about two feet across, six feet six inches long and made of a hard synthetic material. On these were very thin foam mattresses covered in a protective plastic layer. One small blanket and one meagre foam pillow were allocated to each bed. There were five cheap chairs and a formica table. One small toilet cubicle was attached to the room with rudimentary washing facilities but no bath or shower. In comparison the cabin in the aircraft carrier was the height of luxury.

'You are wasting your time,' announced Mary as the others carefully examined the room. 'We can't get free and we will not be let out of here until the night before the summer solstice.'

'How do you know that Grandma?' asked Joshua.

'I can't really say, Josh,' said Mary. 'But I do know.'

'What will happen next, Granny?' asked Sam, his eyes wide with intrigue.

'We will be taken to Stonehenge on Salisbury Plain and the fire god will try to sacrifice you to the devil,' replied Mary.

'Will he do it?' asked Sam, even more agog.

'I don't think so but it becomes difficult to see,' said Mary. 'I believe that with the help of you father we will be able to stop him.'

Sienna jumped up and down with frustration.

'Mum,' she cried. 'How can you tell the children such dreadful things? That was an awful thing to say.'

'No point lying to children,' replied Mary. 'They can always tell when you are lying. Forewarned is forearmed. If I tell them now we all have a better chance than if I don't.'

Sienna shook her head. Her mother was acting so strangely and she was not sure how much more of this she could take without cracking up completely.

*

'The Scott family are ready for you,' said the general to Parsifal X. 'They have been placed in captivity near Salisbury.'

'Good, good. That is good news indeed,' replied X. 'They led us a merry chase but now we have them. I will give Blenkinsop a job to do. It will keep him out of mischief. How are the troop movements going?'

'We have moved twenty thousand cyclops, five thousand hobgoblins and a platoon of griffins through already. A flight of harpies are about to go and we are wavering over the mammoths.'

'Why are you wavering over the mammoths? What is the problem?'

'They require a large amount of thaumaturgical energy and we are already draining your power significantly. Our latest estimates are that our sun will die in just two hundred years unless there is stabilisation before then. The movement of troops has brought this forward by at least ninety years,' said Parsifal's five star general.

'Scrap the mammoths then,' agreed Parsifal. 'And no more plesiosaurs. They are difficult to control and we only use them for shock value.'

The gnome, hidden in the throne, quivered as he heard the reports. The plans he had helped to formulate had better work or everyone in Faerie was doomed.

*

We sat down upstairs with the bald climber.

'Call me Chris,' he announced as we sank into the comfortable leather chairs, the sort you might usually find in a gentleman's club.

Under the table he had stowed away all the rest of the climbing gear.

He's got the full kit, I thought. *Enough for an assault on Everest.*

'So tell me what has happened to you two,' he quizzed us.

I introduced Lady Aradel and myself and then went through the whole story from the moment I had fallen down an Alice in Wonderland hole to the final trumping of the Sphinx.

'Well done, mate, with that Sphinx creature,' Chris said. 'Smug monster. He sets all the questions and decides which answers he likes or doesn't like. I watched him for quite a while before I decided my only hope was to climb. So well done.'

'Tell me what is going on here,' I asked. 'Have you found out anything useful?'

'You are the first people I have met that I think are truly alive,' he said. 'Even the landlord, Good Will, seems allegorical. The barmaid is called Mercy....'

'...But what happens?' I interrupted him.

'It's like the film Groundhog Day where Bill Murray plays the part of a weatherman who repeats the day over and over again. Every day since I have been here if you go down the staircase we came up you will find the rugby players singing bawdy songs, the actors playing their pieces. This goes on for hours until a fight breaks out between the rugby lads and one of the actors gets hit on the head accidentally. Then the landlord breaks it up, everybody apologises and one of the rugby lads pays for drinks all round. They go on drinking after last orders and don't leave until one o'clock. They're all in here again tomorrow.'

'Where do they go to?' I was intrigued by the story.

'I don't really know,' replied Chris. 'I followed some of them one night but it got very dark and I lost them. They were back again the next day.'

'All of them?'

'Not necessarily all. There is a very slow turnover. Some come and others go, one or two at a time.'

'What do you do each night?'

'I've taken a room on this floor. En suite, the lot. They do a good breakfast too.'

'How do you pay for it?' asked Lady Aradel, presumably mindful of our encounter with Charon.

'That's another strange thing,' replied Chris in a puzzled tone. 'I paid for a night's lodging, bed and breakfast, the first night I was here and ever since then whenever I ask the landlord he tells me that I have already paid.'

'Anything else that you would call odd?' I asked, keen to discover all the relevant details.

'Yes, one more thing. The Landlord and the Vicar of the Church of the Promised Land are one and the same person.'

'Really?' I raised my eyebrows. 'Now that is odd.'

'Yes,' replied Chris. 'I followed him one day and after breakfast he went into his office and emerged carrying a bag. I followed him outside and he walked behind the tree and instantly emerged on the other side dressed as a priest. Cassocks the lot. He walked into the church and took a whole service with only three people in there... himself, myself and the organist. He even shook my hand when I came out. I thanked him for his sermon ..... he didn't seem to recognise me but he does when I am over here.'

I sat and pondered the story then a point struck me about something Chris had said earlier on in the conversation.

'You said that going down that staircase takes you to the scene we left,' I pointed to two more staircases. 'What happens if you go down that one or that one?'

'The first takes you to a hall the size of this entire building with a ceiling thatched with golden shields. It's full of Vikings. The other leads down to a room full Greek heroes.'

'Valhalla and Elysium,' said Lady Aradel. 'The glorious slain Vikings meet in Valhalla and the righteous Greeks in Elysium.'

'I reckon you are right there,' agreed Chris. 'However, whether it is Valhalla or not I've been trying to find a way out of here ever since I arrived. I keep finding I'm back again. It is mighty confusing.'

'We'll find a way out,' I said confidently. 'If we can find a way through Hades itself I don't suppose Valhalla can be much of a problem.'

'I'll tag along too,' said Chris. 'But first we must find a clean set of clothes for both of you and then a good bed for the night.'

'Tomorrow we should leave at first light,' suggested Aradel.

'After breakfast,' added Chris.

'Naturally after breakfast,' agreed the Queen of the Elves.

- Chapter 29 -

For one week Mary, Sienna and the boys were kept in the locked barracks, fed just twice a day by armed guards who came in three at a time, two watching the man who passed the food to Sienna to share out. The family's main problem was boredom, relieved only by a white-coated man taking blood from them on just one occasion. Sienna kept everybody going by inventing word games, trying to see who could count the fastest, getting them to sing old songs and teaching them new ones. Mary joined in initially but as time passed she became more depressed.

Outside just after dawn each day they could hear squaddies marching up and down, either being shouted at by a sergeant or singing marching songs. The sergeant would shout one line and the rest would respond.

Way hey rock and roll, Way hey rock and roll,
A little bit of rhythm and soul, A little bit of rhythm and soul,
Early in the morning, Early in the morning

The family could not look out but they could imagine the scene with the young recruits or, since the martial law declaration, conscripted soldiers. They would initially be all out of step but after a short time of drilling they would get in line or face the Sergeant Major's wrath.

On the seventh day a sergeant came to see the family straight after the first meal of the day.

'All right,' he shouted at them as if they were recruits. 'Look lively. You have a very important guest.'

Following behind, flanked by numerous monstrously big

SAS men, came Brigadier Spencer Blenkinsop. The man looked a little confused but the soldiers all acted towards him very deferentially.

'I've come to ask you a very big favour,' said the leader of the emergency government of the United Kingdom to the family 'Will you please sit down and listen to me?'

'Come in,' said Mary pleasantly enough. 'I have been expecting you. Come and sit down and we will listen to your proposals.'

'Thank you dear lady,' the Brigadier looked round owlishly and then asked the accompanying soldiers. 'You don't know where my secretary is, do you? She should be recording this.'

*

Chris the drummer took Lady Aradel and myself to meet the landlord, Good Will. The man was a jolly, plump, red-faced individual. It was difficult to imagine him as a vicar because he looked so perfect for the role he had. Chris explained that we were new there and asked if the inn had any spare room and also if they had new clothes that Aradel and I could buy. The publican was happy to oblige on all scores and Aradel gave him a silver piece. The man expressed himself as being more than happy and hastened off.

When he returned he brought with him a change of clothes for both Aradel and myself. They fitted us perfectly both in size and style. He then showed us to our rooms. The rooms were adjoining and had a communicating door between them. Feeling exhausted we bade goodnight to Chris and agreed to meet over breakfast.

Lady Aradel and I went to our separate rooms and I climbed into a really comfortable feather bed and went fast asleep. At some time in the night Lady Aradel must have joined me for when I opened my eyes she was cuddled up close to me. I smiled and went back to sleep. We had come through hell and reached

Valhalla. Tomorrow was another day.

I just hoped that it did not keep turning out to be exactly the same "another day".

*

'We need your voluntary assistance in our fight to control the problems brought about by the emergency,' said Blenkinsop.

'How can it be voluntary when you are keeping us locked up?' asked Sienna.

'We are simply protecting you,' lied the brigadier.

'How can we possibly be of help to the Government?' queried Sienna. 'Joshua and Samuel are just children and we are two ladies who have nothing to do with Government policy.'

'It is because you have become famous,' replied Blenkinsop. 'We have been looking for you for some time and your names have been in all the newspapers. Now we have you here safe and secure we would like you to sign a little form saying that you have not been maltreated. That's all. Just a little form.'

The man pulled out four sheets of dark coloured paper with white printing on it. Sienna read the notes which each stated that in line with the Geneva convention the family had not been maltreated in any way and had not been subjected to torture. There was a separate sheet for each of them with their names individually at the top.

'It's just a PR exercise, dear folk,' said the Brigadier. 'Nothing more than that but it would be very helpful. Don't you want to help us?'

Sienna looked at the text carefully but could see nothing outrageously wrong with it. She passed it to Mary, who had not said a word since welcoming the Brigadier to their barrack room. Mary examined the papers and then held them up against the light.

'Deary me, Blinkers,' she said. 'Did you really think you would get away with this?'

Mary called Sienna over to see what had become apparent when the paper was transilluminated. In dark letters were the words "I sell my soul to the devil" and underneath was the space for their signatures.

'Written with our blood I presume?' suggested Mary. 'And some in the ink of the pen, perhaps? Clumsy attempt at best, Brigadier.'

The Brigadier looked genuinely alarmed and disturbed. He turned to the nearest soldier and asked.

'How did that get onto these papers? Is this some kind of prank? I need my secretary, does anyone know where she is?'

There was a slight kerfuffle amongst the SAS men and one was sent off to find the secretary. Eventually he returned with a buxom girl in a short skirt. She led Blinkers Blenkinsop away and as he went they could hear him muttering to her about being made to look a fool. The secretary was stroking his hand and calming him down.

*

I don't normally eat a full English breakfast but on this occasion I did. I reckoned that it was probably the only chance I would get to eat the first meal of the day in Valhalla.... that was if we got out of there, otherwise I could be doing it every day.

I swallowed down the fried bacon, two poached eggs, sausage, baked beans, fried tomato and toast, washed it down with two cups of coffee and sat back replete. Only the absence of my family was making me feel at all sad and I felt that I could almost stay there happily.

How long I would have sat in that state I do not know but I found myself being shaken by Lady Aradel and Chris. I sat up, shaking myself mentally.

'God, man,' said Chris. 'You've stayed absolutely still all morning. We couldn't shift you.'

I looked at him without blinking and replied.

'But I know how to get out of here. I've worked it out .'

Chris and Aradel, in unison, asked me how.

'OK,' I said. 'Let us suppose that this place is controlled by somebody or something.'

'Sure,' said Chris.

'Who or what could that be?' I asked.

'No idea,' replied the drummer/rock climber.

'You do, you do,' I said. 'Think!'

'The sphinx?' suggested Aradel.

'Of course,' I replied. 'The sphinx made it seem as if we had passed all the tests but this is simply another. So it is a type of riddle. Wordplay must be involved and we must get the wording right.'

'So what do you suggest?' asked Chris.

'I thought we could ask Good Will to give us Mercy so that we could get out of here and back on our route, now that we have had a good breakfast.... oh yes, and compliments to the chef.'

I said this loudly and the landlord appeared with his barmaid. She immediately led us down the stairs and showed us a low door in the wall at the back of the courtyard.

'I walked past here every day,' said Chris as we walked through. 'And there was no door. No door at all.'

'They are masters of illusion here,' I said. 'They must be. They even fooled Lady Aradel, and she is the Queen of the Elves.'

*

'Can't that idiot do anything right?' screamed Parsifal X. 'It was such a simple thing. A few signatures.'

He sat on his throne and fumed for a few moments until he found his waistcoat was glowing and then calmed down in order to save his clothing. The little gnome was scurrying around trying to attract his attention but X continued to fume.

'I don't know why the Lord of the Far Realm wanted the Scotts to sign the things anyway. It would hardly have been legal if they couldn't read it.'

The gnome laughed and muttered something and Parsifal felt obliged to respond

'Yes, yes. You are correct. What do I care about legality? I am the ruler of a world,' X looked almost human as he said it. 'But what use could a tricked signature be?'

The gnome muttered again and Parsifal repeated it out loud to no-one in particular except the gnome and himself.

'Every day people are made to sign things they can't read. True. Print too small to read. Terms and conditions which would take a week to peruse,' X nodded his head in agreement. He was in a more reflective mood than usual. He shook himself out of the reverie and then said scathingly. 'No, I still think it is foolishness. We need to stabilise realities, amalgamate whole galaxies... not play silly games. Writing in blood? It's so primitive.'

The gnome muttered again.

'You think that it would have been acceptable by law?' said X. 'They are that gullible? Well, that does give me some good ideas for business ventures once I control the real world. Yes, that's pleasing. Maybe I'm picking up management ideas from this Lucifer character.'

The gnome muttered something again.

'You believe that management in the real world has always taken lessons from Lucifer? That's good. I like it.'

The thought cheered Parsifal X considerably and the gnome scurried back into his hiding place. X looked at his waistcoat... good, it was still intact, a beautiful garment from the Queen's couturier, made only for him. Normally the couturier made clothes only for female members of royal families .... but for Parsifal they had made particularly good waistcoats.

*

We passed through the door and in front of us I could see paths leading off in several directions.

'I will go a short way with you to make sure that you are on the correct route,' said the barmaid called Mercy.

'Thank you,' Chris and I spoke almost together. Lady Aradel just nodded her appreciation and gave a half smile. She looked radiant today but in a distant, inhuman way. She was certainly more aloof than the girl who had cuddled up to me in the night ... the thought seemed impossible in the cold light of day.

We walked towards the Southern Mountain Range which now loomed over us in gigantic proportion, blotting out a good part of the sky. When we were well on our way Mercy bade us farewell and was gone. Just like that.... disappeared.

'What was that all about?' asked Chris. We walked along at a brisk pace as we talked.

'The way I figure it is that the inn and the church are all part of a construct controlled by the sphinx,' I replied. 'It is some kind of entry requirement for this part of the world, the foothills of the dragon's abode.'

'But the riddle of the landlord and barmaid was so simple compared with the clever wordplay of the sphinx,' protested Chris.

'The difficulty was in even realising that you were inside another riddle. The sphinx did not eat you if you just stayed there... it acted fair. You could stay there for ever if you wished.'

'So where did the people go who moved on?' asked Chris.

'Some of them may have worked out the riddle. Others, perhaps, went back down to the shore and over the River Styx,' I guessed.

'You said that Lady Aradel did not have to answer a riddle. Why was that?' asked Chris.

I turned to the Elven queen. 'You said that you had been here before, didn't you?'

She looked at me distractedly and then appeared to be replaying the conversation in her head.

'Yes,' she replied in a small distant voice. 'Oh yes. I lived here.'

She was then silent for a short time. She was obviously finding it hard to put into words whatever it was she had to say.

'When we make friends,' she started. 'We imagine the friendship will last for ever.'

I nodded and she continued, rather haltingly.

'But people change, situations alter.'

We walked on and she did not say anything more for a while, Chris dropped back a bit as he could tell that Aradel and I were having a more personal conversation. I mused on what she was trying to say and then replied.

'Lady Aradel,' I said. 'I know that although you do not look it you are very many years older than I am and that you may live for many more years. I will grow older at a much greater rate. Is that what is worrying you?'

Aradel stopped on the track, almost causing me to bump into her.

'Not exactly,' she answered quietly. 'Really I was trying to say that if we change we should still remain friends. We may not be lovers but I would like us to still be friends. Good friends.'

'Of course we will remain friends,' I took her in my arms and kissed her on her forehead. 'In my real world I am married to a beautiful lady who is much like you to look at and I miss her. When I return to that world you and I will have to be friends at a distance. Perhaps we will be able to meet occasionally?'

'Even if I change a lot we will still be friends?'

'Of course,' I said.

We walked on, quickening our pace. We were in the foothills now and I could make out movement in the distance...large creatures much like the wyverns I had seen around the forest. Lady Aradel was quiet as if there was something else she wanted to tell me but could not quite put into words.

- Chapter 30 -

After Brigadier Blenkinsop's visit the atmosphere at the Tidworth Army Base changed for the worse. The soldiers bringing the food did so very abruptly and even had a look of fear in their eyes. The noises from outside had changed. The marching songs could still be heard occasionally in the distance but the sounds from nearby had changed to grunting animal-like babel and guttural words.

One of the soldiers bringing the food looked as if he wanted to say something. Finally, when he returned on his own to remove the tray of empty plates and cups, the man took the family into his confidence.

'I'm not allowed to speak to you but I've got to,' he said.

'Go on,' said Mary.

'They say that you are organisers of the resistance movement against Brigadier Blenkinsop. Is that true?'

'I wouldn't put it quite like that but essentially the answer is yes, we do oppose his policies' replied Mary, worried that they might have wired the man to get a confession of sorts recorded so that Blinkers could use it against the family.

'Well, I want to get you out of here so that you can rejoin the opposition,' said the soldier.

'Has something happened to make you feel like this?' asked Sienna. Joshua and Samuel were also listening intently to the man.

'Several things,' he continued. 'Firstly, they clamped down very heavily on a protest march that started on the Isle of Skye. It was another Battle of the Braes. Unarmed men have been beaten and jailed without a jury trial.'

'You know about the crofters' fight of 1882?' asked Sienna, surprised that an English soldier should have even been aware of the fight against land clearances in the Highlands and Islands.

'Oh, aye,' said the man. 'My mother's from Skye although my dad is from Liverpool.... and my name is Malcolm, but they call me Callum!'

'What else has happened?' asked Mary.

'Since the Skye incident your names have appeared in the newspapers, such as they are,' said Callum and his voice now dropped to a whisper. 'But the thing that is making this urgent is that they are importing some very weird soldiers to this base... some of them don't even appear to be human!'

*

The path led up and over a hillock and I could now see the wyverns up close. They were about fifteen to eighteen feet in length from head to tail, dragon's head, reptilian body and a barbed tail. Some were yellow, some green and some a mixture of the two. I thought I saw one in the distance that was red but I could not be sure as it disappeared behind a copse of trees. The wyverns were being herded by humanoid creatures that looked as if they were half human and half goat.

'Those are the wyverns,' I said, pointing. 'But what are the creatures herding them?'

'They are satyrs or fauns depending on whether you like Greek or Roman names,' replied Aradel, rather distantly. 'And don't call them creatures to their face. They are easily offended. They are also highly intelligent, very gentle and live a carefree life like children. '

'One of them is playing a pipe,' remarked Chris.

'They are very musical,' replied Aradel.

*

'It's June 17th now,' said Callum. 'I want to get you out of here before the 21st, the Summer Solstice. Something big is happening then and it is going to include you four.'

'Do you have any idea what is going to occur on that day?' asked Sienna.

'I don't but I heard one of the top brass talking about Stonehenge. I expect that there will be a lot of civilians there on the twenty-first. Some of them are likely to protest against old Blinkers and I think that it will be a lot worse than Skye.'

'You said that some of the troops aren't human. What are they?' asked Joshua. Both boys had been waiting with bated breath to hear more news about the alien troops.

'I think they are genetic experiments,' said the soldier. 'They are all huge and look like monsters. A lot of them have only one eye in the middle of their foreheads.'

'Cyclops!' said Mary. 'I once saw a still-born baby cyclops pickled in a jar.'

'Mother,' exclaimed Sienna. 'You shouldn't say such things. You know there is no such thing as a cyclops.'

'They don't usually survive in this world as they have brain defects,' replied Mary. 'But they do exist and who knows what might occur in another reality. Anyway Doctor Burns said he saw one near the fairy bridge in Skye.'

'Whether they exist or not they're marching up and down outside this very barracks,' said Callum. 'And they're not the worst. There are some with almost no head, some that are a nasty greeny-grey colour like fairy-tale goblins and some huge ones which I heard someone say were trolls.'

The soldier looked round and dropped his voice to a very quiet whisper.

'They've sent some of the biggest, ugliest ones up to Scotland to deal with the revolt.'

'So the Skye protest led to a revolt?' surmised Sienna.

'Didn't I say that? No?' asked Callum. 'Well after they imprisoned the local doctor, who was leading the protest, they beat up a whole load of Skye folk. The revolt spread to their relatives on the mainland and now the Highlands and Islands have declared independence from Scotland and from the UK.'

All the family simultaneously and independently started to ask for more information. The soldier flapped his arms to quieten them down.

'Shhh! Shh!' he shushed. 'Keep the noise down. I'm not supposed to be here. Anyway...... I figured that you would be better off freed and back up in Scotland fighting Blinkers than a hostage here in Tidworth.'

'What do you intend doing?' asked Mary.

'We're breaking you out. There's a bunch of us with relatives and friends in Scotland. If there's to be a civil war you have to take sides.'

*

'The wyverns are like cattle,' explained Lady Aradel. 'They are herbivores kept for their milk. They look fierce but they are relatively harmless if handled correctly.'

'Are they actually dragons?' I asked. 'What are the real dragons like?'

'Wyverns are dragon-like but they are not true dragons. A real golden dragon is a magnificent beast with an IQ in the thousands, a life expectancy in the thousands of years and enormous magical power,' she looked into the distance, refusing to look me in the eye as she talked. 'A real dragon can fly round the world in minutes, teleport through space, breathe plasma rather than fire whilst at the same time solving complex problems in tensor calculus and multi-dimensions.'

We had reached the base of an enormous cliff and, looking up, could just see a natural cave with a large wooden door at the entrance.

'You'll be able to see one soon if we are able to gain entrance up there,' remarked Lady Aradel, pointing with one delicate finger.

The entrance and its massive door had to be at least two or three hundred feet up the sheer cliff...and I had never rock climbed in my life.

*

'I can't tell whether this is the right thing or the wrong thing to do,' declared Mary.

The small cadre of rebelling soldiers had arranged to break the family out of the camp as soon as it was dark. Mary and Sienna had been weighing the pros and cons of the exploit ever since the soldier, Callum, had first suggested the escape plan.

'In which case we go,' argued Sienna. 'We've got to think of the children first and this is the only sensible opportunity to do that since we were taken off the submarine. Except, of course, when you hypnotised the rear admiral.'

'Don't start that again,' countered Mary and then more resignedly added. 'But you're right. We must think of the children first. What do they say about it?'

'We should go,' agreed Joshua immediately.

'Yeah, get out of here,' said Samuel.

'That's yes, get out of here,' corrected Sienna, pedantically.

'Then we're all agreed,' Joshua concluded, purposely misinterpreting his mother's statement.

*

We were half way up the cliff face. Chris had reconnoitered a short way and to start with it had not been too bad. At least the footholds were clearly strong enough to take my weight. Chris was leading, putting the pitons into rocks or cracks to take the rope. We only had the one harness and Chris had given it to me as it was clear that I was the weakest climber.

Lady Aradel had amazed both of us by showing that she was an astonishing free climber. The rope was not long enough for one of us to stay on the ground as the anchor but Lady Aradel was ably bringing up the rear.

Which left me as the strawberry jam with jelly legs between two pieces of firm bread. This was relatively OK until we reached the chimney, as Chris called it. Actually it was just a vertical crack between two rock faces. There were no footholds and no handholds. We had to put our backs against one wall and brace ourselves putting our feet against the other. Chris had decided that this was the only way ... otherwise it was a "handholds only" overhang and we all knew that I could not do that.

The problem was getting from the one wall over to the other with my feet. I had done this in a narrow passageway we had in our house when I was a child. Then it was easy because there was no hundred foot drop below me..... now, as I gingerly put my feet across, trying to hide the wobble in my legs brought on by fear, I lost my tenuous grip on the near side and fell. The rope went taut but the pitons did not hold. Chris was being dragged down as well.

Lady Aradel below me instantly waved her free hand and a mesh of glimmering green light spread across and caught me. With a superhuman effort she was able to put me back into the rock chimney and I started to move up again. Chris was able to re-establish his position bridging the chimney.

'That will have signaled our position to Parsifal like a beacon,' grunted Aradel from below. 'So now we have to hurry more than ever.'

Knowing that Aradel could catch me if I fell gave me considerable confidence. The slightly reduced gravity compared with Earth also assisted me and I had no further mishap. We eventually reached the platform and I sank down exhausted.

'You did well, mate, apart from the one wobbly,' said Chris.

'Once Aradel had saved me it was the knowledge that she could catch me if I fell that gave me the confidence. It was a doddle knowing that,' I told him.

Aradel looked at me rather distantly.

'Oh no,' she said. 'I couldn't have done it a second time. You have no idea how much magical energy is required to lift somebody like that and in my present form my magic is strictly limited. It will take hours for me to fully recover.'

I looked at her, wondering exactly what she meant and then thanked them both profusely for looking after me.

I took a few moments more to catch my breath and then shakily looked over the edge.

'But I couldn't possibly go back down again by this route.'

'You won't have to,' replied Aradel, even more distantly than before.

*

'A flash of deep magic!' cried Parsifal X, looking round wildly. 'They have not left this reality. They have reached the dragon's lair. Curses, damn, blast.'

His beautiful waistcoat went up in smoke. He only had five more of them left and he knew that the couturier had died during the collision of realities. He would be able to replace them but they wouldn't be exactly the same. He, Parsifal X, would know that they were not made by the Queen's own costumier.

*

The sun went down at 21.30 and the family waited for the signal. Callum had come past earlier and left the doors to the room and barracks unlocked so Mary, Sienna, Joshua and Samuel quietly crept out of their place of imprisonment as soon as they heard the owl hoot.

The rebelling soldiers had decided that there was no way they could get the family past the checkpoint and had, instead, cut a gap through the perimeter fence. This was not a high security fence as there had never been a necessity for such measures. It had been a work of just a few moments to snip through the chain links and this had been done in broad daylight under cover of a maintenance crew van.

The family now had to look for a faint blinking light which would only show for a few seconds.... there it was over to the left. They made their way gingerly towards it passing nobody as they went, then under the fence and into the waiting car.

Callum was in the driving seat and he had already opened the doors. He had removed the internal light so that there would be no giveaway light seepage. He drove off without the headlights on. A couple of miles down the lane they were to meet their pals and from then on it would be a dramatic rush by road, up the country to Scotland. They had no access to aircraft or other transport so this was the only way they could do it.

Mary had major reservations but did not air them. At least it had gone well so far.

*

The door to the dragon's cave stood in front of us. A huge, dark, wooden structure with a lock of a type I had never seen before. It was highly intricate and apparently worked bolts on three levels. The hinges on the door were massive and made of bronze.

Chris rattled the door.

'That's it then, it's locked. What do we do now? Knock and wait?'

'No,' replied Lady Aradel, Queen of the Elves, speaking in an ever more distant voice.

I had never seen her looking more beautiful but it was now in an ice-queen manner, pale and unapproachable. Although she still had the same smooth, beautiful skin and glossy hair, I never would have mistaken her for a teenager if I had seen her like this originally. There was a silvery-gold shimmer about her form like moonlight on an almost still lake or stars shining through space from a distant galaxy, or perhaps the Milky Way at midnight in the summer when the weather is clear. Now she looked as if she was timeless and could have been alive for thousands of years. I began to feel slightly afraid of her, this inhuman elf queen, my little fat rat.

'No,' she repeated. 'I have the key.'

She took from within her clothing a small golden key. Where she had kept it I had no idea as I had not seen it before and she had changed her clothes, shape, appearance. But she had it. The key slid into the lock and Lady Aradel, Queen of the Elves opened the door into the Dragon's chamber.

*

The car sped off down the quiet lane. Mary sat in the front passenger seat, belt securely clipped in place. Sienna sat with a boy on each side of her. Samuel had hidden his head up against her side and she had her arm round him. Joshua was trying to put on a brave face but it was clear that he was afraid so she was also holding onto him tightly.

They drove round a long, blind bend and slammed into a road block. The entire lane was entirely obstructed by army vehicles positioned to stop them and the car collided into the side of an armoured vehicle. The family and Callum were thrown forward by the impact, then held forcibly by their seat belts and pushed back by the explosively expanding airbags. The four doors of the car were wrenched open simultaneously and the occupants roughly pulled out by soldiers wearing red caps.

Callum had fared worse than anybody, the airbag having hit him in the face with considerable impact and he was groggily trying to work out what had happened. Mary, Sienna and the boys were immediately handcuffed to each other and to a huge red-capped soldier who pulled them to one side. An aggressive sergeant pulled Callum away from the group. He spoke to an enormous figure in another armoured car. The family could not hear the question but they could hear the deep, guttural reply.

'Kill the traitor.'

The sergeant protested that it was not the way they did things.

There was an explosion of anger from the monster and it stepped out from the car into the glow of the searchlights that had been switched on immediately after the impact.

'The traitor must die,' said the huge monster, standing in the light and holding a sub-machine gun. 'Put him up against the tree.'

The red caps pulled Callum over to the tree and had barely got out of the way themselves before the monster shot a stream of bullets through his body. Callum slumped to the ground, dead.

'Hey,' shouted Joshua bravely but his voice tailed away as the monster turned round to look at them for the first time.

Staring at them was one enormous eye set in the middle of the creature's forehead. The soldier in charge of the red caps was a cyclops.

*

We stepped inside. The chamber was titanic in size, several hundred feet across and we were looking down into it. The entire mountain was hollow. To the far side there was a deep hole and a red glow emanated from the depths. The light of the cavern, however, was mostly sunlight reflected down through a couple of tunnels and then refracted by the incredible ceiling. This was completely covered in prismatic crystals that looked like diamonds. Some were as big as a human head and one could have been two feet across.

'I suppose it's quartz,' I suggested, my gaze fixed on the display.

'No, your first thought was correct,' replied Lady Aradel. 'They are diamonds brought from a far distant solar system.'

'How can that be?' I asked. 'That would require interstellar transport.'

'Dragons can teleport across the vacuum of space and span the entirety of the galaxy,' replied Aradel, her voice like silver bells. 'They can even cross to other galaxies. They are immortal and they have no fear.'

'How many Golden Dragons are there in these mountains?' I asked very quietly, overawed by the cavern and afraid to speak too loudly.

'There was just the one until recently,' she replied.

'And now?' asked Chris. I was a little afraid to hear the answer to this question.

'Now?' replied Lady Aradel. 'Now there are two.'

*

The family were pushed back into the room they had so recently escaped from.

'Now until the solstice you will have no human contact,' said the sergeant red cap. 'We will put food and water in here on a tray just once a day. You will take it and pass us the previous day's tray in return. If you don't do this you will be severely punished. If you make any fuss, try to escape when the door is opened, shout or make any disturbance you will be severely punished. Is that understood?'

They all agreed that it was and the door was locked again.

'Don't say that you were right!' exclaimed Sienna to her mother.

'I wasn't going to say a thing,' replied Mary. 'I am not able to tell what is going to happen now any more than you can. Perhaps less.'

'Dad is going to come and save us,' piped up Samuel bravely. 'I know he is, you just wait and see.

*

'Where are the dragons?' I asked of Lady Aradel. My eyes were becoming accustomed to the diamond-refracted light and I could now see considerably better but I could not discern anything that resembled large gold wyverns.

'Look down at the floor,' replied Aradel. I stared where she indicated and suddenly realised my mistake. What I had taken to be the floor covered in gold and jewels was the dragon. At least one hundred and fifty feet in total length it was curled up on a bed of hoarded gold, camouflaged against the treasure. Its head was immense and somewhat flat, the eyes closed. The body was long and streamlined down to a barbed tail, similar to the wyverns. There were four huge legs with retractable claws but the wings were surprisingly small.

'Can those wings really support it in flight?' I asked.

'He doesn't rely on his wings to fly,' replied Lady Aradel, distantly. 'He is a magical creature and he uses pure magical force.'

'What is going to happen when he wakes up?' asked Chris, whispering like myself.

'That really depends on his mood,' replied Lady Aradel. 'And whether or not he is pleased to see me.'

*

The sleeping beast stirred. Our whispered conversation was waking him, a sight I was not sure that I wanted to see.

One enormous eye opened and swivelled around, locating us. Then the head turned on the long, powerful sinuous neck and both eyes stared at us. It slowly stood up and looked over to where we perched on a ledge.

He was truly tremendous in size and a deep gold colour that I had never seen before. I realised that this must also be due to refraction of the light through his scales rather than just pigment ..... the same way that bird feathers display such deep, satisfying colours. Each scale was a slightly different gold that shimmered in a way that reminded me, surprisingly, of Lady Aradel.

The dragon opened its mouth and spoke. His voice was not the harsh shriek I had expected or even a bird's tone. It was a beautiful, melodious male voice. The voice of a famous tenor opera singer perhaps ..... a seductive voice such as that heard on an old valve radio.

'Hello Aradel,' said the dragon. 'Welcome home.'

- Chapter 31 -

Do not lose the innocent boys again
Or I will eat your soul
Immediately
Yours, Lucifer

'Did we lose the boys?' asked Parsifal X, combustion starting on his best suit.

'Only temporarily, sire,' said his five star general.

'What does that mean?' screamed the fire demigod, flames bursting from his hair and destroying a particularly jaunty hat.

'The family escaped from the room they were imprisoned in but were recaptured straight away.'

'Why wasn't I told?'

'It was all dealt with so quickly that we spared you the worry of even thinking about it, sire.'

'So how did Lucifer know about it. Do we have an informer in our midst? Is there a traitor?'

Flames were dancing all over his body and any semblance to a human being was now only incidental.

'We executed three traitors from Brigadier Blenkinsop's army, sire. No other traitors were found.'

Parsifal X calmed down. He now needed a completely new set of clothes.

Blenkinsop is becoming more of a liability than an asset, he thought to himself. *When the Stonehenge charade is over I will personally kill the man.... and enjoy it!*

*

'Come down and join me, Aradel,' said the beautiful dragon, his voice filling the entire chamber.

Aradel jumped from our ledge and then climbed down a stone staircase cut into the wall. She looked tiny against the huge bulk of the dragon and I wondered for her safety. What if the huge beast, the glowing worm, accidentally stepped on her?

But in the blink of an eye the situation had changed. Aradel was not at the feet of a fire breathing dragon anymore. Standing next to her was a tall, dark, handsome man. He was clad in golden armour and held a huge broadsword. On his head was a crown set with fabulous rubies. They made a perfect pair.

'I say again, welcome home dear Aradel.'

The king of the dragons, for such he obviously was, held Aradel to him and she strained up to kiss him on his lips.

I felt a pang of jealousy but tried to dismiss it, I had no right to Aradel. We had simply been good friends on a quest. Well, to be honest we had been more than just friends but all good things must come to an end. Now I knew what Lady Aradel had been trying to say to me when she had asked that we be friends even if she changed....but she hadn't changed, she was still the sweet, if more distant and ever more desirable, Aradel.

It wasn't just that, dear Lord James, Lady Aradel's voice was in my mind. *There was more that I could not tell you.*

At that moment there was a lightning flash and an almost simultaneous thunderclap right above the mountain. I looked up and when I looked down again in place of the dragon king and elf queen stood two, yes two, enormous dragons. The first golden dragon had been joined by a slightly smaller, second dragon. This was an even more beautiful silvery-gold creature and I could tell that it incorporated aspects of Lady Aradel.

'Yes, dear heart,' came Aradel's sweet melodious voice, emanating from an enormous fire-breathing dragon. 'Yes, I am a dragon.'

*

'Curses,' cried Parsifal X melodramatically. 'The dragons are awakened. They will keep to their oath, they cannot fight me but I must keep to the letter of the contract on my side. I can, however, do what I like in the real world. We'll see how real it is after I have drained its energy.'

*

'But you told me that you were an elf. How can you be both and elf and a dragon?' I cried in anguish.

'Because I am a magical creature and I am the offspring of a male dragon and female elf,' replied Lady Aradel, Queen of the Elves and of Golden Dragons. 'Part elf, part dragon and zero human.'

I wondered what her dragon friend would make of me.

Was he be annoyed with me? And if the dragons are so powerful why didn't Lady Aradel use that power when we were in trouble? Why did I need to carry her through Hades? Why didn't she teleport us directly here? The questions were multiplying in my mind.

'Your champion and I need to talk,' intoned the Dragon King, clearly reading my thoughts. 'And your rock climbing companion. We should feast and talk while we eat.'

The dragons changed again and were once more humanoid king and queen, resplendent in robes and crowns. The Dragon King disappeared for a couple of minutes and then returned.

Manifesting quietly behind him was a table groaning with a full Sunday roast.... It looked like a shoulder of lamb, roast potatoes, peas, carrots, mince sauce, the whole blinking lot.... and full silver service.

'Is that real?' I asked, my eyebrows raised in amazement.

'Certainly,' replied the Dragon King. 'It came from the Ritz.'

'How did you arrange it so quickly?' I asked. 'It must take a while to prepare but you were only gone an instant.'

'Come and eat and I'll tell you,' laughed the Dragon King.

It didn't look as if he was going to incinerate me on the spot for my dalliances with his somewhat wayward lady friend so Chris and I walked gingerly down the stairs and sat on the plush red velvet chairs by the table and waited whilst Lady Aradel and the Dragon King served us the stupendous meal.

*

'Packets of cereal, milk, bread, butter, cheese and bottled water again,' said Joshua looking at the tray that had been pushed hastily through the doorway. 'I'm really fed up with this food.'

'It's all we're getting,' said Sienna, sharing it out. 'So eat as much as you can and keep your spirits up.'

Sienna looked over at Mary as she said this. Her mother looked really depressed. She was sitting in the corner of the room, on her hard narrow bed with her head in her hands staring blankly into space. Sienna for the first time felt sorry for her mother. It was hard to think of her as an old lady, she had always been so resilient. Now, however, she looked frail and beaten.

Sienna went and sat next to her mother.

'Mum,' she said softly. 'The food is here.'

Mary waved her away.

'I'm busy, Sienna, busy,' she said mysteriously.

*

A thunderclap is hardly sufficient to show my anger, thought Parsifal X. *And it would be unwise to break my pact with the Dragon King quite yet..... and now there is some other entity tickling at my consciousness. What could it be?*

*

I sat stunned by the news that Lady Aradel was part dragon. My mind was not really on the Dragon King's conversation as he explained how he had managed to produce the meal at such short notice

'I discovered a good few hundred years ago that people are prepared to sell you almost anything if you give them well over the going rate,' said the Dragon as he carved the joint. 'Take this meal, for example. You can buy a Sunday lunch at the Ritz for, say, fifty pounds or maybe a little less. I displaced bodily to the Ritz and offered three gold sovereigns per course per person. At two hundred and fifty pounds per coin that is ten times the normal price. So I obtained somebody else's meal as it was about to be taken to them. If they had not played ball I would have teleported to another restaurant. Simple really. They'll get back all the dirty cutlery, tables, etcetera, of course.'

'I got the impression from legend that dragons collected gold so that they could hoard it and sit on it,' I said. 'Have I got that wrong?'

'No, that's basically true. We're like magpies, we like shiny things,' agreed the golden dragon.

'But we can also see a role in using the gold,' explained the silver-gold dragon, alias my friend Aradel.

But I still wondered why had she not used her power when we needed it? I looked at her questioningly.

I could not do so, she replied in my mind. *I had sworn not to use my dragon form until I returned here, to our lair, and used the golden key. Until then I could use only my elven powers.*

'Now we need to talk about what is happening on this world,' said the Dragon King, abruptly changing the subject. 'I've been away for a while, around the various star systems and nebulae. What with relativity, warp factors and near light speed I can't say quite how long ago I went. I returned and slept to gather my strength. How long was it since you left and I went travelling, dear? Six months? A year?'

'Clawfang you have not been taking note. It has been two hundred years,' replied Aradel.

'Now that is a significant period of time. Two hundred you say? How much of that have I been asleep?'

'The last thirty-five years.'

'Has anything important been happening? I noticed that dear old X did a thunderclap. Is he as jolly as ever?'

'No, dear, he isn't. He has even been threatening me.'

'Threatening you? He dares threaten you? LITTLE X DARES THREATEN MY WIFE?' King Clawfang stood up and magical power burst from his hands and he gradually grew into the golden dragon we had seen before.

This time, instead of a sleepy dragon we saw an angry one and my knees knocked together with fear. I've never said that I'm a brave man but there is no doubt that an angry dragon makes me into a coward

'You can't do anything to X because you agreed a pact. You signed an oath,' Aradel pointed out. 'We both signed an oath with him, with the fairies as a co-party. We cannot be oath breakers.'

'But you say he threatens you, Aradel. That must surely be breaking his oath?'

'No Clawfang, if you remember I swore to stay in my elf form until I returned to have your children. My magical power was limited. It was when I was in my elf form that Parsifal X threatened and he has no pact with the elves.'

'But X is a mere elemental. He's not a demigod even if he thinks he is. He can't threaten a high elf and you are Queen of the Elves. You are still Queen of the Elves aren't you?'

'I am still the Queen but X has developed the ability to tap power from the centre of the planet and even from the sun so he is now the supreme ruler.'

'The supreme ruler? I am the supreme ruler. There is none with power like mine. Certainly not a mere elemental. Can he cross time and space? Can he teleport a meal from the Ritz?'

'No dear but he can incinerate a whole forest of wood elves and werewolves.'

'He did that? Why should an elemental, an intelligent fire creature of ascetic nature, do something like that? It is essential that I read all your memories and those of your champion.'

The dragon looked at me and my soul was laid bare. Everything that had happened to me in my life, my schooling, physics, astronomy, electrical business, wife, children, my mother-in-law, the fall into faerie, rat/elf, nights with Aradel, the forest, Slough of Despond, Sphinx, climbing. Everything bar nothing was absorbed by the extraordinary mind of the Golden Dragon. At the same time he was melding his consciousness with Aradel's and I caught a glimpse of the amazing gestalt of the two dragon minds. I wished I had not done so for I found my awareness falling into the infinite complexity of the dragon's multidimensional manifold destiny. It was Aradel who saved me, observing that I was drowning in the sheer intelligence of their minds. She shut off the connection and planted me firmly back into my own self.

I stood there dazed.

'Now I see,' said the Dragon King. 'Parsifal X has spent too long acting the part of a human being. He has incorporated himself and identifies with his own construct. This construct has human emotions that an elemental would never have and X has enjoyed those emotions. They include greed, anger, pride, sadness, love and hate but he has found particular pleasure in the greed, anger, pride and hate. How sad.'

'But can we do anything about him or are we still bound by the pact?' asked Aradel.

'I've been examining that as we talk. We, as dragons, cannot act directly against him unless he violates the agreement or there is another prior agreement that he infringes. If he does that we can act. Until then we can only act through your very adequate champion.'

And that means me, I presumed.

- Chapter 32 -

There, thought Parsifal X. T*here is the gnat that is tickling my consciousness.*

X did a mental flip. Swatted it.
That's better.

*

Mary had a sudden huge convulsion that shook her body like a massive electric shock. She fell off the narrow bed onto the plain concrete floor and lay without breathing in a crumpled heap.

'Granny,' shouted Sam and ran over to her, Sienna and Joshua just behind him.

'Let me get to your Granny, dear,' said Sienna, her nursing experience and first aid classes coming to the fore as she knelt down and felt, unsuccessfully, for a pulse.

'Quick,' Sienna said to Joshua and Sam. 'We must lay her out flat on the hard bed. She's had a cardiac arrest. I shall try resuscitation.'

They lifted the old lady up onto the bed. Sienna gave a first large thump on Mary's chest. Before she could repeat the action Mary sat up with a gasp and caught Sienna's hand.

'One was enough!' Mary exclaimed to Sienna, grudgingly. 'But thank you. You saved my life.'

She pulled herself up and sat gasping for breath as her brain and body started to function.

'I don't think I'll try that again,' she said, shaking her head. 'Far too risky.'

'What, having a cardiac arrest?' asked her daughter, perplexed that her mother thought she could control when it might happen.

'No, no. Reading Parsifal X's mind,' replied Mary. 'I kept

hearing about this monster causing our problems and I thought I could find out more by searching for his mind. It was not difficult to find.'

'How do you search for a mind, Mum?' asked Sienna, still bewildered.

'You saw me,' replied Mary. 'I just sat there and thought about it hard. Then I made contact. His mind is huge, amorphous and shapeless. It pervades much of faerie reality but not all.'

'Did you learn anything from the experience?' asked Sienna.

'Yes Granny,' added Sam eagerly. 'What was it like?'

'It was fascinating, truly fascinating, Samuel,' Mary replied to her grandson. 'And Sienna, of course I learnt something. You can learn something from any experience.'

'You're the first person I've heard say that they learnt something from a cardiac arrest,' countered Sienna.

'Nonsense, daughter, nonsense!' exclaimed Mary. 'What about all those people who see a light at the end of a tunnel? They must be learning something.'

'But what did you learn, Grandma?' asked Joshua. 'What did you discover in the monster's brain?'

'Firstly, he does not have a brain like we do. He likes to look like a human being but he is actually a creature of fire and superheated particles...'

'...That's amazing,' said both of the boys together.

'...And he is trying to take over the whole of this world as well as his own,' Mary continued. 'And your father is somehow trying to stop him.'

Mary was concentrating on the boys as she said this then turned to Sienna.

'Though what your husband thinks he can do I have really no idea!' Mary sniffed as she said this and shook her head.

'Go on, Granny, tell us more!' demanded Sam.

Mary turned back to the boys.

'Parsifal X did not like me searching his mind and he swatted me like a fly,' she whispered conspiratorially.

'How did he do that?' asked Sam, confused, 'He wasn't here.'

'No, but part of my mind was there,' answered Mary. 'He mentally slapped me and I had a convulsion and almost died. Your mother saved me.... No, you all did.'

Then she did something that she very rarely did. She held out her arms and gave them all a hug.

'Well done family. We'll come through this.'

Sienna smiled. Despite all the hardship it was good to see her mother acting like a decent human being.

Mary almost seemed happy, which was really for the first time since her husband, Sienna's kind, generous, overworking father, had died. Then Mary looked over at the table and saw the sparse meal.

'Not cereal, milk, bread, butter, cheese and bottled water again,' she groaned. 'I'll make the caterers of this establishment suffer when I get the chance.'

*

We had almost finished the first course and the Dragon King had returned to his human form. He was the genial host again, serving the dessert with a smile.

'Apple pie or rhubarb crumble?' he asked. 'Or a little of both?'

We ate in silence for a few minutes enjoying the tartness of the rhubarb and the comforting nature of the custard. Then the Dragon King spoke again.

'Thank you, Lord James, for saving the life of my wife on so many occasions.'

'She saved my life and I was only doing what any man would have done' I replied self-deprecatingly.

'Certainly some of the time you were doing what any man would do,' he agreed with a smile and then shook his head. 'But carrying her through Hades. Only Orpheus has tried to carry a lover out of that place before and he failed at the last post. You did very well and have earned my eternal thanks.'

The Dragon King turned to Chris.

'And you my bearded rock climber. You also have been of great assistance. Thank you.'

Bearded! I thought. *Why hasn't my beard grown whilst I have been here?*

'You didn't want it to, replied Aradel, still reading my thoughts. *And here, magically, it obeyed you.*

Beats shaving, I replied in my thoughts and Aradel laughed, her musical, schoolgirl laugh.

'So now we have to work out how we can help you,' stated the Dragon King. 'Aradel and I cannot directly oppose the elemental. Moreover, Aradel will now stay in her dragon enhanced state. She can help you to the edge of this world but no further.'

'With Parsifal X despoiling your world and my own, why can't you just break your oath and oppose him directly?' I asked, just a little irritated by this creature's inability to grasp the importance of direct action on his own part.

'Because we are not human,' replied the King. 'We are products of a magical world in which our oaths genuinely bind us. Unless there is a prior oath which over-rides our avowed agreement we are physically, mentally and fundamentally unable to break our agreement which therefore prevents us from opposing Parsifal's or his agents actions.'

I began to see the problem. 'So what can you do?' I asked.

'That is what Aradel and I are going to spend some time working through,' replied the ancient but so handsome Dragon King.

If I could just get these Dragons and any of their relatives on my side we would be able to overcome Parsifal X, I thought. *They are certainly powerful enough.*

We will be looking closely at all interpretations of our agreement, replied Lady Aradel. *Indeed we shall*

*

'Isn't there anything we can do to help Jimmy?' asked Sienna, bringing up the subject for the one hundredth time since Mary had tapped the mind of the fire elemental, Parsifal X.

It was now the twentieth of June, the eve of the solstice

'I have been searching the minds of our jailers,' said Mary. 'Whilst keeping well clear of Parsifal X in case he swats me again... and staying clear of X is not so easy to do as one might imagine. Pasifal X has little bits of himself called avatars that he secretes in people.'

'That, I presume, is what happened to the engineer on the island, to the red capped soldier in the doctor's house and to the submarine commodore,' surmised Sienna.

'You are right. Initially they can operate as human beings but eventually they are taken over completely. The Commodore fought for the longest ... mostly they are completely converted within a couple of hours,' Mary told them.

'How does that help us?' asked Sienna.

'It doesn't,' Mary retorted. 'I just have to avoid them. But there are human soldiers out there who are sympathetic to our cause and beyond them in the village and further afield there are many civilians who are smarting at the gross nature of this martial law and suspension of democracy.'

'Can you contact them?' asked Joshua.

'I can and I have done,' answered Mary.

'Will they help us Granny?' asked little Samuel.

'If they can. To start with I have confirmed that the soldiers intend taking us to Stonehenge in the middle of the night, tonight,' Mary paused and looked at the eager faces of the two boys, who considered anything their Granny said as being fascinating, and her daughter, Sienna, who considered it to be frightening.

Then she continued.

'I have been putting into the minds of any receptive person the notion that they should turn up tonight at Stonehenge to be ready for sunrise.'

'Any success?' asked Sienna.

'I think so. There are quite a number of people who will be going there anyway but they are mostly new age hippy types. I want a range of people from all walks of life to act as a witness to whatever happens. This is bound to be a momentous moment whether we beat them or they beat us.'

Not if they kill us all, audience included, thought Sienna. *Then there would be nobody left to consider it as momentous.*

*

'Is there anything that happened in your dealings with human beings that could be considered as precedent for breaking our oath?' asked Lady Aradel, directing the question to her husband, the Dragon King.

'No, I came to no agreements that were binding,' said the golden dragon. 'Mind you they tried to bind me physically on two occasions. It happened at Silene in Libya, a guy called George and in Geats some chap called Beowulf.'

'I thought that Saint George killed the dragon,' I blurted this out without thinking but the dragon simply laughed.

'The reports of my death have been greatly exaggerated,' said the Dragon King.

'Mark Twain after his obituary was published in the New York Journal,' interjected Lady Aradel, Queen of the Elves and silver-gold dragon.

'I do wish you didn't always do that, dear,' complained the Dragon King. 'I was probably either on the other side of the galaxy or asleep when he said it. I thought it was original.'

'I'm sorry Clawfang, love,' Lady Aradel put her beautiful arms around her husband who looked quite forlorn. 'I'll try not to do it. It's from playing too much Trivial Pursuit with Kinsman Iron-Builder.'

I had another entirely incorrect pang of jealousy but this was dismissed by the revelation of Aradel's game playing. Trivial Pursuit! That was how she knew all the quotes!

I still have to remember them, spoke Aradel in my mind. *And I have done a lot of research on questions that might turn up.*

'Kinsman Iron-Builder, he's the Dwarf Arch-Chancellor isn't he?' asked Clawfang, the Golden Dragon King. 'How is the old fellow?'

'Still going strong,' replied Aradel. 'Worried about Parsifal X.'

'Yes, yes. I can see that, Quite,' replied Clawfang. 'Now the matter in hand. We will continue to look for ways for the fairy kingdom and ourselves, the dragons, to supercede our agreement with Parsifal. It was never intended that our non-combative pact would allow him to destroy worlds. Quite the opposite.'

'And in the meantime we will get Lord James and Chris to the nearest functional inter-reality gate?' suggested Lady Aradel.

'Yes, yes,' agreed Clawfang, the golden dragon. 'Assuming Chris wants to go back, that is?'

'If I may, your majesty, sir,' agreed Chris, bowing deeply. 'And thank you for the food.'

'It's a pleasure... but don't do all that bowing,' the dragon king actually seemed embarrassed. 'You can call me Cluff if you want. That was always my nickname at school. Cluff the mighty dragon. Something like that.'

'Thank you Cluff,' said Chris. 'And I also want to help fight this monster. What was it you called him? An elemental?'

'That's right,' agreed Clawfang. 'An intelligent entity embodying one of the five elements, earth, water, wind, fire and the aether or quintessence. Strictly speaking the fairies and elves can be considered as elementals but we tend to use the term for those magical beings that have no solid, corporate state. Parsifal is a fire elemental. Or was, until he started meddling with the natural order of this reality.'

'Excuse me Cluff but when do we leave?' I asked this hoping that his invitation to use the sobriquet extended to myself. I really did not want to offend this enormously powerful individual but I did want to know what the plans were. "When", "how" and "where" were the questions. "Why" and "who" I thought I knew the answers to.

Once again the dragon answered the questions in my mind as well as the one I had asked.

'Certainly call me Cluff. I like it. We go immediately, when you are ready. We will take you ourselves, one to each dragon. We will take you to the nearest gate, assuming that we cannot use the fairy bridge that you know in Skye. The nearest functioning gate is...,' Clawfang stopped and explored the reality.... '...In the Isle of Man as Lady Aradel had assumed.'

He turned to his wife.

'You are quite right dear, as always. Are you happy to carry one of the humans?'

'Yes, I'll carry Lord James,' she replied.

'I thought you might,' replied Clawfang with a quiet chuckle.

- Chapter 33 -

'Somebody is stirring up trouble in the populace around the army camp,' said Parsifal's five star general to the fire elemental.

'Who could be doing this?' asked X. 'And how is he doing it?'

'We don't think it is a man,' countered the general. 'We have probed the mind of a protester who has set up a tent right outside the camp perimeter.'

'And what did you find?'

'He knew about the transfer of the family to Stonehenge which is taking place tonight. He could not remember who told him but he thought it was an old woman.'

'The gnat!' exploded Parsifal, burning his new slippers right off his feet.

'The gnat?' queried the general.

'A tiny minded creature had the gall to probe my mind. To explore the complexities of my great intelligence. I swatted it but it sounds as if I did not swat it hard enough. Next time it tries to enter my mind I shall take its entire being and stretch it from here to one of our twin moons. That should teach it not to meddle.'

'Sire, sire!' the little gnome was trying to get his attention.

'What is it you want, tiny speck of foresight?' asked Parsifal.

The gnome scurried out from its place of concealment carrying a small diamond and a magnifying glass. He passed the diamond to Parsifal and the elemental had to minify his perception down to the minute level. Written in tiny flaws in the diamond, now visible to Parsifal, was a message.

*Don't let the old woman stir the populace up too much
We might need them
It would be unfortunate to kill them
They have not yet pledged their souls to me
So prevent any uprising before it occurs
Your soul is mine
Lucifer*

'Damn the impertinence of the Far Lord,' screamed Parsifal X, and then smacked his left cuff with his right hand.

He did not want to lose this shirt. It was made of a very rare white silk and he was certain he could not replace it.

*

I was perched on Aradel's neck just behind her enormous head. I could not resist stroking the silvery gold scales. For some reason this Aradel was still cuddly, even as a dragon.

Oh, thank you, James, thought Aradel, dropping the Lord epithet for the very first time. It was as if she had previously felt obliged to keep to the formal title she bestowed on me because she was worried about being half-dragon. Perhaps she was worried about how I would respond? As I pondered this she replied.

You are right and I love you for not rejecting me.

Reject her? I thought as I stroked her neck. *How could I reject someone so beautiful? Mind you, taking a dragon to bed with me does not sound that inviting.*

You'll not get the chance again, Aradel thought regretfully. *My husband would not let you now I have resumed my dragon nature. But we have our memories.*

She's like a beautiful pet siamese cat, I thought. *Or maybe, considering her intelligence level, I'm the pet and she's the owner.*

What makes you think that you are the owner of a cat? asked Aradel. *Cat's don't have owners they have staff.*

*

'Treble the number of troops around Stonehenge,' said Parsifal X to his five star general.

'But sire, that will serve to bring attention to the place,' replied the soldier.

'Just do it or die,' said X. 'We need to keep the human public away from the stones.'

'When will you be arriving, sire?' asked the general.

'What time is dawn at Stonehenge?'

'About 4.50 am local time, sire.'

'I'll be there at exactly 4.10am. Yes, that will do.'

'Do you think that gives you enough time to prepare, sire?'

'What? For a simple sacrifice of a couple of innocent boys? Of course it does.'

*

The door to the room was flung open and the enormous cyclops who had killed Callum was standing staring at the family with soldiers standing on either side of him toting machine guns.

'We go now to Stonehenge,' the creature spoke in a harsh, deep voice. Although he used English he had great difficulty in forming the words as if it was not only a foreign language to him but also a completely alien way of speaking. 'I take the males.'

'No!' screamed Sienna, flinging herself in front of Joshua and Samuel. 'You must not take my boys. Take me but don't take them. They are completely innocent of anything.'

'That is what we need. The two young male innocents,' croaked the cyclopean monster. 'I will kill the old lady if you try to resist. I will do it slowly and painfully.'

The eye of the cyclops rolled with delight at the thought of killing Mary.

'We all go together or nobody goes,' said Mary in a reserved manner, apparently unworried by the threats.

'Then we all go,' groaned the cyclops, disappointed. 'We all go.'

*

Flying over the mountains and then over the sea was a magical experience in every sense of the word. I had asked why we could not be teleported to our destination but the answer was predictable. The expenditure of magic involved would have highlighted our position like a radio homing device.

So here I was high in the stratosphere of this alternative reality, out in the open but unaffected by the low air pressure.

There is a force field around us maintained by a small expenditure of magical force, explained Aradel, telepathically.

And this keeps the air in? I queried.

Yes and keeps it fresh, she replied.

And why does it now seem as if we are flying between stars and planets? I asked.

The shortest route between two points is not always a straight line when you use more than the normal number of dimensions, came the answer.

So it was an inter-dimensional trip to the next fairy gate perched on the neck of a silvery-gold dragon. I looked over to my right. Chris was riding on Clawfang, the Dragon King and he waved back to me. Clawfang, keeping his head straight forward for least resistance through the dimensions, looked at me reproachfully with a baleful left eye.

The trip was certainly quick. We arrived in a matter of minutes.

'How far was that,' I asked Aradel, speaking out loud as we dropped to the ground.

'Just under two thousand miles,' replied my beautiful Queen of the Elves, Dragon Queen, and one time fat rat.

'But I thought it was only just over the water in the Isle of Man,' I protested.

'That is in your world. As I said before there is not a one-to-one concordance between the worlds. They have spun apart over the thousands of years which is why trying to put them back together by force is causing such dire consequences.'

The time for me to leave the Faerie reality was fast approaching. Whilst I had been here I had spent most of my time trying to get back to my own reality. Now I was close to achieving this I felt reluctant to go. It was likely that I would never be able to step back into this world and I had made friends with Clawfang the golden dragon, Peter the werewolf, Kinsman Iron-Builder the arch chancellor and many others who had helped us on our way. I felt the way that people emigrating in the early days of colonisation must have felt when they knew they could never return home. I *was* going home but the Faerie realm had strangely become more of a home than the real world. It would take some adjustment getting back there. But most of all I knew I would miss Lady Aradel, my amour, my rat, my elf, my dragon. Would I ever see her again? Would we remain friends even though we were apart? Was I her pet animal or was she mine?

The gate was nothing like a fairy bridge from the faerie side. It was a simple wooden door in a low wall. I bade farewell to the two dragons. They changed into their human form and I embraced them both in turn.

We will meet again, Lady Aradel whispered in my mind.

Then I opened the door and we both walked through. I had thought that the family would be there to meet me but a lass in a navy uniform was standing next to the bridge, looking bored.

'Hello,' she said. 'I'm Hannah. I've been waiting for some hours. We've got to move quickly if we are to get to Stonehenge on time.'

- Chapter 34 -

* Stonehenge *

Sienna, Mary, Joshua and Samuel shivered as they sat huddled behind a large standing stone. Guarding them to prevent their escape were at least twenty soldiers and a huge army contingent in tanks and armoured cars which had encircled the ancient monument. Beyond the army encampment tens of thousands of civilians had assembled and were singing protest songs. During the previous day and over the night an enormous crowd had gathered including an eclectic mix of sun-worshippers, latter day druids and revellers. The various rebellious groups against Brigadier Blenkinsop's martial law, egged on by Mary's telepathic prompting had also attracted supporters who had been told that a showdown was in the offing. An unholy alliance had been formed between liberals and conservatives, communists and hard-line monarchists, religious groups and humanists.

Every now and then a great cheer would go up as a leader would stand and, in the moonlight and rather blue illumination of a mechanically generated LED torch, pronounce on the overthrow of the totalitarian, military authority. Then a song would be started ... "We shall overcome, we shall overcome" followed by a spiritual "This world is not my home" and the swelling noise of ten thousand voices would drift over to the family in their captivity.

In reality there was little that the ragtag army could directly do to free the family. The armed forces were there in sufficient force to hold back any attempts to liberate them. It was, however, a telling demonstration of the way in which Blinkers Blenkinsop's grip over the country was weakening.

Everybody was waiting for dawn and the summer solstice sunrise over the Heel Stone ... or, to be more accurate, slightly to one side where, in antiquity, the sun would have shone through a corridor between the heel stone and its once standing partner. The sky was clear and the stars twinkled in glorious profusion.

Sienna looked at her watch. It was just past three thirty and there was more than an hour to go before sunrise. She was feeling very disheartened and frightened. She had so many questions that her mind was in a ferment. Surely they weren't really going to sacrifice her boys? What would be the point? Had they journeyed all this way to simply wait for a hippy festival? She thought of the heartache on the way and the absence of Jimmy. Where was he? According to Ard, the werewolf, and to Mary it was essential that she and the family were here on the Summer solstice. Why? Mary had been convinced that Jimmy would join them. What about Blenkinsop? The army was here but was he with them? If they did try to sacrifice anybody could they be stopped?

At four a.m. the sky was lightening due to the false dawn and, as they looked to the north they could see some swirling green lights. Was it a laser display or some new firework? There was no sound from the direction of the light and Sienna realised that it was the aurora borealis. Over the next five minutes the wavering lights increased in intensity and spread to cover most of the sky. The linear green lights were joined by a diffuse blue and then red glow. The Northern Lights were putting on a greater display than had been seen in southern England ever before.

All the people present were looking up at the lights.

Perhaps now is the time to escape whilst they are all preoccupied? thought Sienna.

I don't think so, replied Mary, telepathically. *We have to watch this.*

She waved her hand to point to the altar stone, a six ton monolith of green Welsh sandstone. The altar stone was being lit up by the aurora borealis and in its flickering light it gave the impression of movement. Then, to the astonishment of all who watched, the stone was flung to one side as if it were a film prop made of polystyrene.

In its place was a throne and sitting on the throne was a beautifully clad man with chiselled features. Around the throne were seven gigantic Cyclops and in the man's hand was a dog leash. On the end of the lead, attached by a collar on his neck, drooling on all fours, was Brigadier Blenkinsop. The army went on to immediate alert, raising their guns. The perfectly clad man waved his hands and their weapons became fiery red-hot, the soldiers instantly dropping them.

'It's almost over,' said Parsifal X. 'The time is nearly on us, the innocents are ready and my colleague from the far realm will make his appearance. Splendid.'

Scuttling round from his niche behind the throne came the little gnome seer. '

You have forgotten the nemesis key and the lock.'

'No I haven't,' replied X, his fiery eyes dancing in the unnatural glow of the aurora. 'I have the answer. I am the key and Stonehenge is the lock. It was easy.'

As the minutes ticked off towards dawn the aurora borealis lit the sky in myriad profusion, green, blue and red now twisting and writhing in long tendrils. In the midst of the ionic display a darkness appeared in the shape of a head. The darkness deepened and terrible features could be picked out in the shades and patterns of black. An enormous horned head and centrally two red, glowing eyes that danced with mischievous evil. Behind and below the head a distorted body started to appear. Fluttering dark shadows, like giant bats, appeared on either side of the gigantic presence and started to fly down towards the henge.

Even Parsifal X looked daunted, if only for a moment, then he stretched up and expanded his own embodiment, draining power from the centre of the Earth. The fire demon burst through his smoking clothes and up, up he went until the fiery red demigod met the black, evil presence.

The two creatures were now standing within Stonehenge, each as much as one hundred feet high, with their feet stood inside the main circle but straddling the inner stones.

The soldiers and the captive family had retreated back to the earth ditch surrounding the site. Even the cyclops guards had pulled back as far as possible. The pitiful figure of the brigadier was unable to move away due to his leash but appeared blissfully unaware of the frightening figures as he grovelled in the dirt.

'We meet as equals,' intoned the fire demon. 'Our wishes will be fulfilled.'

A loud evil noise came from the black figure with the glowing red eyes. 'Equal?' the black mass appeared to shake as if laughing. 'Yes, if you want to believe that. We meet as equals.'

The black creature appeared to be looking round for something. His eyes grew hotter and his appearance more malevolent. 'Where are the innocents? They should be on the altar stone.'

'Ah, yes. That's where I have placed my throne,' replied X. 'But the innocent victims are here.'

'Then move your throne, reinstate the altar and place the children on it. Then we wait for dawn. When they die you will have your wishes. Your realm will blend with this one and I will own your soul.' The black creature's body rolled with evil mirth.

The fire demigod bent down and spoke to the largest of his cowering cyclops and the one-eyed monster heaved itself over to the soldiers in charge of the captive family. Meanwhile the cyclops assigned to Blenkinsop had released him from his leash and was now, tenderly, leading him to safety by one hand. He actually appeared fond of the totally deluded brigadier.

The huge uniocular creature sent to procure the victims grabbed Joshua and Samuel and started to pull them towards the stone ring. Sienna wailed for the cyclops to stop and attempted to prevent the creature from taking the children but she was roughly thrown to the ground. The cyclopean guard strode along with Joshua under his right arm and the small struggling form of Samuel under his left. He placed them on the reinstated stone and securely bound them to it with some rope.

Lucifer and Parsifal X towered over the diminutive figures on the sacrificial stone.

'I'm not worried, Josh,' said Sam to his larger brother, his faith in his father undimmed. 'Dad's on his way here. I can tell that he is coming. Then this lot will be in for some trouble.'

*

I sat next to Hannah and Chris in the helicopter surrounded by American soldiers. Would I get to the place in time? I nervously looked at my watch as we flew in the dark over the sea, then down over Wales, and thence deep into the south of England. The time was ticking away and to my horror I could see the first rays of sunlight. The sun was indeed rising in all its glory in the East. It was only 4.30 a.m. and I had not expected sunrise for another twenty minutes. Lady Aradel had been quite adamant that I must be there as the sun peeped over the Heel Stone and I was too late. Then I relaxed slightly. We were flying quite high and the extra height had given me an early dawn. The sun would, of course, be rising above Salisbury Plain exactly on time.

As we reached the ancient monument I could initially only make out the huge crowds gathering around the site, the inner circle of army encampment and the stone rings. Then I noted with intense surprise the two huge figures standing over the central stone. How had I missed them?

The helicopter hovered over the grass between the outer ring of stones and the ditch and clattered to a landing. I jumped out with my escort and ran to the site of the action.

I could see Joshua and Samuel lying on the altar stone, held there by ropes and two cyclops.

'Hello,' I said. 'Were you expecting me?'

'Who is this?' the deep voice of the black, horned monster enquired. 'Who dares to interrupt us?'

It was clear to me that the two enormous creatures, X and the horned beast, were not going to listen to quiet words so I took a loud hailer from my escort and put it to my lips. I pressed the button on the megaphone and my voice could now equal that of the oversized beasts.

'Jimmy Scott here. I've come to prevent your little game so please release my kids before I am forced to get angry,' I said this having no idea what I would do if they refused, which did seem on the cards. I reckoned that there was no gain to be had by being overawed by them. Not at this late stage in the proceedings.

'Prevent us? Nothing can do that,' cried the horned monster, its eyes blazing with hellfire. 'I will ascend into heaven and exalt my throne above the stars. I shall finish the war and become the Most High.'

He turned towards the altar stone raising a clawed left hand which held a knife blazing with light from the rising sun. What was I to do?

Use the sword. I could hear Lady Aradel's thoughts in my mind.

Although she was still in the Faerie realm the three realities were so close together now that I could almost tangibly feel her presence supporting me. The rays had not yet reached the altar stone and I thrust myself forward, the Elven sword, Morning Star, flashed in my hand. I cut at the heel of the black monster and evil brimstone bubbled from the wound.

The monster staggered at the cut, significantly wounded. No normal sword could have touched the creature but not only had this magical weapon been forged in the faerie kingdom it had been named, centuries before, by the very name of the creature it was cutting. They say that if a bullet has your name on it, it will never miss. Morning Star was not the bland, wishy-washy name that I had considered it to be ... I would have been more circumspect about carrying the faerie weapon if I had known that literally the Elven name meant shining one, morning star, Lucifer.

The wound bit deep and Lucifer, cut down to the ground. I had only wounded the monster but he was unable to complete the sacrifice and he writhed in agony. The sun was now blazing and it was passing the appropriate time. There was still Parsifal X to deal with. The fire demon reached down with one red hot hand and grabbed me by the waist. I tried to cut him away with the sword but it had no immediate effect on the elemental demigod. My clothes were already singeing and I writhed with anguish due to the burning pain. In the distance I could hear a battle developing between the army and the surrounding solstice sun-seekers.

Lucifer stood up painfully and, using his vast demonic potency to ignore the wound in his heel, held a knife above my sons.

'The correct time has passed but still they shall die. Their sacrifice will give me some strength.'

'For God's sake this has gone on far too long, Lucifer. Put the knife down and release my grandchildren and my foolish son-in-law.' It was my mother-in-law, Mary.

She was speaking without the use of a megaphone but her strong voice was clearly audible over the noise of the battle. Lucifer, inexplicably as far as I was concerned, stopped what he was doing and stood rigid.

'No, you cannot make me obey!' he cried, growing considerably larger and hammering his fists at the air as if bashing them on an invisible wall. 'I will not obey!'

He shouted this again but the strength had diminished and he sounded more like a spoilt child than a devilish creature of almost infinite power. The creature shrank in size and went through some very rapid changes in shape ....a dragon, a goat, a young lad, an eagle, a young woman, ginger cat, snarling lion, middle aged bank manager, old man with a beard, monstrous bullheaded man. The changes kept coming in bewildering array and with each change the creature threw itself at the invisible cage which was clearly becoming smaller as defined by the reducing excursion of his movements. Eventually he stopped and stood up straight staring with unconcealed hatred at my mother-in-law.

Parsifal X had observed all this dropping me to the ground as he did so. I stood with my sword at the ready.

'Now separate the realities, stabilise them, leave us and don't come back,' Mary demanded in her best "consultant's wife" voice. The one that broached no argument.

'I have only one way of doing that,' replied Lucifer, eventually, reluctantly conceding that he must obey. 'I need the soul of the fire demon.'

Parsifal X laughed.

'Go ahead,' he said in his urbane manner, having shrunk back into his habitual suave human form. 'I have no soul so I am not worried about that.'

Lucifer laughed in reply.

'I know that you have no hidden soul. You are your soul. Fal Parsi. Pure fool.'

So saying the satanic monster clapped both his hands together. Parsifal X was whipped up into the black clouds that had gathered above the monument and then could be seen as if on a mountain top standing like Atlas, feet on the apex holding the realms apart. Beneath his feet was the faerie kingdom, around him was our own existence and above he held the heavens in place. He had a look of absolute anguish on his face, using all the enormous power he possessed, acting as a conduit for the greater cosmic energy required to accomplish the task and knowing that no Hercules would come to relieve him of his burden.

'I've put him there for an eternity,' laughed the Loki-like creature. 'Apart from the wound inflicted by the flea I have enjoyed this outing. But next time you sup with the devil, use a very long spoon..... Oh, by the way Mary, you have not aged well. You have let yourself go.'

So saying the monster and its black fiend followers faded from sight.

From behind the displaced throne a little gnomelike figure appeared.

'So it worked out as I predicted, did it?' asked the seer. 'We've got rid of that monster X and stabilised the realms. It could have been worse.'

I looked in amazement at the gnome.

'You knew this would happen?'

The gnome stared back.

'It would be incorrect to say I knew it,' the seer replied. 'But with a bit of steering through the difficult patches, yes, it is what I predicted.'

The gnome polished some glasses that it had extricated from its long white beard and then placed them on its nose.

'Parsifal X had been using too much power for too long,' the gnome peered at me as it said this. 'He started to combine the realms and I knew that the likelihood was that this would lead to the destruction of both the real and faerie realities. The only hope was to enlist the help of the eternal realm. Lucifer does not help mortals so I had to persuade Parsifal to request his assistance.'

'But how did Mary manage to stop Lucifer from sacrificing my children and make him stabilise the realms. Why did he listen to her?'

'Well, that's easy,' replied the gnome.

'Tell me, then!' I demanded.

'Your mother-in-law is a witch!'

- Chapter 35 -

I ran over and released the lads from their bonds and embraced them. Sienna and Mary also sprinted across the grass to us. I gave Mary a short hug and then wrapped my arms round Sienna and kissed her.

√ *Well, it's all over,* I thought. *The devil has dealt with Parsifal X and X has stabilised the worlds. All's well that ends well.*

'I'm not so sure that it is all over,' stated Mary, replying to my thoughts. 'Something strange is happening. Take a look.'

I followed Mary's pointing finger and saw the soldiers fighting the thousands of protesters. Surely they were going to stop fighting now they had seen the evil nature of their leaders?

But no, the fighting had continued and, as I watched, about one in a hundred of the soldiers burst into flames and doubled in size .... miniature versions of Parsifal X. They were driving the other soldiers on to fight even harder and they were clearly winning the unequal battle.

One of these flaming monstrosities came flying over towards me. This monster had the face of a burning skull. It landed in front of our family group and addressed me.

'You are foolish enough to think that you have won.'

'What are you? Tell me what you are?' I demanded.

'We are the other Parsifals,' answered the creature. 'We are all designated by letters.'

I suddenly realised what that meant. They were all fire elementals. Not individually as powerful as X but collectively even more dangerous.

'There are twenty-six of you?' I suggested.

'Many more, named for every conceivable different alphabet

and symbol, Arabic, Greek, Japanese,' the creature was proud of their number. 'And in addition there are smaller less powerful elementals... the Anibals, the Bekeals, Faisals, Isreals and Suneals.'

'So X ruled you as well?' I responded.

'He did and he named us. But he spent too long in his bodily form and hence was too lenient on the mortals. We will exterminate you. You are not needed since all we require is the power of your sun and the other stars in your universe. You stand in our way.'

The monster started to expand. Mary stood cursing the elemental to no avail and the creature threw a ball of lightning in her direction.

It did not hit her. A corruscating barrier of green light blocked the creature's assault. I instantly recognised that beautiful light .... I had seen it before in Faerie.

Simultaneously a sound of a hundred bagpipes hit my ears mingled with the breathy flute-like notes of panpipes and tinkling of bells. I looked up. Right above us were two enormous golden dragons breathing fire at the elemental and behind them I could see a rift in the sky through which the hordes of Faerie were pouring. Those that could not fly were being assisted by the others who could.... werewolves carried by flying horses, fairies carrying elves, dwarves and fauns on the backs of wyverns. I had half expected that the elves might turn up at the showdown but the really big guns, the dragons and the fairies, were there also. What had made them change their minds?

As the two largest dragons landed in a rush of hot air right next to us I could see on the back of the King of the Dragons a tiny figure waving a scrap of material. Then I had it. I understood what had happened. Parsifal X had sent his troops up to quell rebellion in the Highlands and Islands.

He had directly threatened the MacLeods along with everybody else in the world and the inhabitants of Dunvegan

Castle had correctly decided that the time had come. The MacLeods had waved the flag..... the famous fairy flag of Dunvegan Castle. This was a pact that predated any fairy or dragon agreement with Parsifal X making the treaties that bound them null and void. Once the flag had been waved the inhabitants of the Faerie Realm could ignore the now invalid covenant with Parsifal X and come to our aid and they certainly were doing so.

The magical cavalry landed and set to work. The giant dragons and the fairies made short work of the elementals despite their number. The high elves and the dwarves fought side by side against the cyclopean guard. The werewolves rounded up the human army like so many sheep. A few shots were fired at them but they shrugged them off. After all, nobody had thought that they might need silver bullets.

Lady Aradel, in fine silvery-gold dragon form, flew up to me and landed lightly on her feet, the incongruously small wings flapping as she did so.

'Good bye, Lord James,' she said, her beautiful voice sounding like tubular bells. 'I promised we would meet again. We shall meet at least once more. It was nice knowing you. Very nice knowing you!'

Then she and Clawfang, the Dragon King, both vanished.

'That was a female dragon wasn't it?' asked Sienna with a jealous note in her voice. 'How well did you know her?'

'I was her pet human,' I replied.

- Chapter 36 -

'The minister will see you now,' said the civil servant. Sienna, Mary and myself had arranged to see the reinstated Prime Minister, Darcy Macaroon but at the last moment we had been switched to meet the Secretary of State for Culture, Media and Sport. We had waited for one hour and a half and now it was to be a Minister of State, a chap from the House of Lords.

We were ushered into a room containing a very smart, long, wooden table and several chairs. On the table were a few printed sheets of paper and there was the ubiquitous jug of water and a few glasses. Sat on the other side of the table was an overweight, balding middle-aged man. Standing next to him, hovering would be more accurate, was a silver haired gentleman in a good quality sober suit.

'So good of you to come and see me. I expect you are very busy,' said the bored peer.

Which translated meant that he thought it was very good of him to see us and that he intended to make this as short as possible.

'Very pleased to be of assistance,' I replied. 'But let's cut to the chase. We are just recovering from a disastrous collision of metaphysical realities. We nearly lost the battle and we need to make alliances to ensure that it does not happen again.'

'I'm not so sure about that,' replied the peer and he looked round to his civil servant who was hovering next to his right elbow. 'Is that how you would put it, Sir Hubert?'

'No minister,' replied the civil servant. 'I would say that the administration acted swiftly to deal with and contain the emergency situation that arose from a natural disaster.'

'Ah, yes,' said the peer. 'There you have it. We acted swiftly to deal with a natural disaster. Providing support where it was needed in the worst hit areas. Would you add that last bit, Sir Hubert?'

'Very nicely put, minister.'

'Let me get straight to the point,' I said to the minister. 'We have come through a disastrous calamity and the world has just about survived. The population of the world has reduced to about a half that which it was before the disaster.'

'Yes,' said the bored minister. 'And your point is?'

'My point is that we were getting this world into a hellish mess before the disaster. With some help we may be able to have a fresh start but we will need to take some tough decisions. No more bankers taking excessive bonuses for gambling with other people's money, no more Members of Parliament taking liberties with their expenses, no more multi-conglomerate companies polluting the rivers, the seas and the atmosphere just to make a quick profit.'

'I'm sorry,' said the minister. 'I fail to see how any of this relates to the emergency.'

'The fairy kingdom is a reflection or shade of our own,' I explained. 'We have done bad things to our own world. Huge companies flouted the law and paid no taxes... and that resulted in a monster dominating their world. We destroyed rain forests and made species extinct .... they destroyed forests and killed the wood elves. Every time we do something evil here it reflects on the Faerie realm. It has to stop.'

'Ha, ha, ha!' laughed the minister. 'Fairies! Whatever next?'

'Are you saying that after everything that happened you still won't accept the existence of the Faerie reality?' I asked, incredulous.

'Everybody at Stonehenge saw the fairies, the elves, the dwarves, the dragons,' protested Sienna.

'We can put that down to mass hysteria, minister,' suggested Sir Hubert.

'Yes, mass hysteria,' concurred the Minister of State, looking down his nose at us in a condescending manner.

'So what stabilised the realities and what defeated Lucifer?' I asked. 'Because I saw the Devil himself put a fire elemental as a conduit to lock the realities in place. I saw it with my own eyes.'

'The eyes are easily deceived, aren't they minister?' remarked Sir Hubert.

'Yes, they certainly are,' smiled the peer.

'So what do you say stabilised the realities and stopped the tsunamis, earthquakes and hurricanes?' I asked.

'Oh, that's easy,' said the civil servant. 'It was Professor Breadstein's work that did that.'

'Yes,' agreed the peer, reading from a printed sheet. 'Breadstein was working on behalf of the United Nations at the Large Hadron Collider at CERN and managed to create a miniature black hole that removed the orphan planet that had strayed into our solar system.'

'That's right,' said Sir Hubert, chuckling at us. 'Removed the orphan planet. That's what he did. Not a single mention of fairies, goblins or gnomes. Or other similar ridiculous notions.'

'In fact we are going to give Breadstein a knighthood,' said the minister. 'That should convince the public. They'll soon forget the supernatural balderdash.'

'So we don't need your help and we will not make any of the agreements you suggest, will we minister?' said the civil servant.

'No we won't,' agreed the peer.

Suddenly Mary, who had kept quiet until now, waved her left hand. Both men went completely silent and she threw the jug of water over Sir Hubert. For a moment I thought she had finally cracked under the strain. Then I saw the figure of Sir Hubert sizzle and boil and fade away with an anguished squeal. A few drops of water had spilt onto the peer and he also evaporated with a sigh. No trace of their clothing or anything else was visible.

'So they were both elementals,' said Mary. 'I thought it was only Sir Hubert.'

Epilogue

'Why did Lucifer obey you?' I asked Mary as I sat with her and Sienna.

'And why did the devil say you had not aged well? You look very good,' added Sienna.

'Thank you dear. It's a long story. I'm descended from one of the witches of Salem, through my mother's line. We don't go on about it as it can be embarrassing and we have always thought it to be a bit of a joke.'

'But that can't be it all, mum,' replied Sienna. 'Because I'm also descended from them and so are the kids and he certainly didn't obey us.'

'You're right,' Mary agreed. 'There is more to it. When I was a young girl I lived in Croydon, as you know, Purley, to be exact. And I used to go to the local youth club. Every Saturday night we would go down to the church hall and listen to records, play table tennis and flirt with the boys. I was a good looking girl in those days.'

Mary tossed her head in memory of her lost looks. To be fair she was still a striking woman for her age. She continued.

'There was one boy who used to turn up who liked to play the field. He was a handsome devil. I think he only went in order to meet the girls. I don't ever remember him going to church, we mostly did, mind you. He had a foreign sounding surname which I can't recall but his first name then was Lucien. Anyway, I went out with him a couple of times and he was besotted with me. He used to write poetry, soppy stuff, love poems. Oh, he could write other poems as well if he wanted to. He produced a book of poems once, all modern with no rhymes and sold it to everybody in the club. I might have it somewhere or I did before the emergency.' She paused for just a moment to gather her thoughts. 'So he went out with all the girls but it was me that he most wanted. I was walking out with him quite seriously but I was not what you might call that free with my favours. We would go to the cinema and sit there in the back row. I saw one film three times....... all three consecutive showings and I can't remember a single word. One night, it was a beautiful moonlit night up on Croham Hurst, yes, one night right there on the Hurst he proposed to me. He said that he would love me and obey me for ever. I immediately said thank you, I'll accept that, before he had a chance to say another word. He looked momentarily shocked but went on to a full proposal. He said that he would give me all the jewels in the world, dominion over nations, make me a queen, loads and loads of guff like that.... if I agreed to marry him. Full vows, he said including the agreement to love, cherish and obey. I think it was the last bit that got my goat.'

'How did you reply?' I asked Mary.

'I said "Get thee behind me Satan". It was a mild amusement, a jest really but he took it badly. Stopped going out with me and disappeared off the scene. I didn't see him again but I heard about him occasionally. I thought he had ended up as an MP or in the House of Lords, or a banker or something.'

'Does this have a bearing on why Lucifer obeyed you?' I asked

'Oh, yes' Mary retorted. 'Don't you see. When Lucifer appeared I recognised him immediately. It was him! Lucien, I'd have recognised him anywhere.'

'What? Your boyfriend had cloven hoofs and a goat's head?' cried Sienna, astonished.

'Is that how you saw him dear? Oh no, a handsome man, very handsome man but the very devil. My boyfriend was Lucifer, the very devil. And he had sworn to obey me and I had accepted without swearing anything in return.'

When Mary finished telling us her story I sat back and had an amusing thought.

I'm not going to tell anybody this but my wife is an angel, my mistress was a dragon and my mother-in-law is a witch.

The End

You have just finished reading *Witch Way Home?*

by Paul R Goddard

The story continues in ***Witch Armageddon ?*** Why not read the second book in *The Witch, The Dragon and The Angel Trilogy?* It packs the same thrilling supernatural punch as the first.

Jimmy Scott is in bad trouble in New York and Joshua has joined a youth club that has some very strange and frightening members. Once again the family have to save the world from total destruction in this fast moving fantasy of witchcraft and supernatural phenomena.

The trilogy of multidimensional magical realism concludes in the third book: ***Witch Schism and Chaos?***